t w i n k

STORIES OF YOUNG GAY MEN

Edited by Jack Hart

alyson books
los angeles | new york

© 2001 BY ALYSON PUBLICATIONS. ALL RIGHTS RESERVED. CONTRIBUTORS
RETAIN RIGHTS TO THEIR INDIVIDUAL PIECES OF WORK.

MANUFACTURED IN THE UNITED STATES OF AMERICA.

THIS TRADE PAPERBACK ORIGINAL IS PUBLISHED BY ALYSON
PUBLICATIONS,
P.O. BOX 4371, LOS ANGELES, CA 90078-4371.
DISTRIBUTION IN THE UNITED KINGDOM BY
TURNAROUND PUBLISHER SERVICES LTD.,
UNIT 3, OLYMPIA TRADING ESTATE, COBURG ROAD, WOOD GREEN,
LONDON N22 6TZ ENGLAND.

FIRST EDITION: JULY 2001

01 02 03 04 05 [a] 10 9 8 7 6 5 4 3 2 1

ISBN 1-55583-629-1

COVER PHOTOGRAPHY BY BEL AMI.

LIBRARY OF CONGRESS CATALOGING-IN-PUBLICATION DATA
    TWINK : STORIES OF YOUNG GAY MEN / EDITED BY JACK HART.—1ST ED.
        ISBN I-55583-629-1
            1. GAY YOUTH—FICTION. 2. YOUNG MEN—FICTION. 3. EROTIC
    STORIES, AMERICAN. I. HART, JACK.
    PS648.H57 T87 2001
    813'.01083538'08664209051—DC21   2001023984

Contents

Introduction

Is there any more descriptive word in the gay lexicon than "twinkie"? I think not. It can only mean one thing: light, fluffy, tasty, filled to bursting with creamy goodness. In other words, delicious. Absolutely delicious. It doesn't matter if you're talking about snack cakes or young men.

The 24 stories in this book, ranging from the avant-garde work of literary icon Jack Fritscher to the straightforward storytelling of Dale Chase and Jesse Grant, are an homage to twinks everywhere. There are hitchhikers, laborers, and young men exploring their bodies. There are college boys, boys on the street, and boys next door. All of them lean, tautly muscled, sans body hair, and very pretty. Anything and everything an admirer of twinks could want.

So...read on. It's absolutely delicious.

And try not to gum up the pages with your cream filling.

—Jack Hart

The Boxer Rebellion
by Pierce Lloyd

When selecting a home, three things are crucial: location, location, and location. I was able to buy a roomy two-story house for a song, simply because it was located in a neighborhood populated by college students.

You see, I turned 35 last year. I broke up with my lover of three years and decided I needed a change of pace. So I took a new job in a college town. My salary was almost exactly the same in the new town as it had been in Los Angeles, but because of the dramatically decreased cost of living, I was suddenly flush with cash. I liked Los Angeles, but I didn't love it, and I was beginning to enjoy the life of a smaller town, even if I did live in the shadow of the university.

One thing my house did not lack was a view. My backyard diagonally bordered the backyard of a large fraternity house, and because the Midwestern summer was sunny and warm, as soon as school started in late August, I was treated to the sight of dozens of shirtless college boys. Doing yard work, playing ball, or simply out in the sun, the members of this athletic social fraternity had a knack for displaying their developing chests and stomachs.

Because I was frequently in my backyard cutting grass or working in my garden, I often exchanged pleasantries with the frat boys. They were a polite, sometimes rowdy bunch, and I overlooked their occasional loud parties as long as they took care not to step in my geraniums when they came over to retrieve their footballs.

When I was in college I never joined a fraternity. It just didn't seem like the place for a young gay man like me. Observing this testosterone-laden group of young men, I noticed that my "gaydar" had developed to the point where, even if a guy was masculine, talked tough, and had a girlfriend, I could still recognize some little spark in him. Of course, I didn't have much opportunity to test my theories.

One individual who touched off feelings of recognition in me was Brett, a six-foot blond blue-eyed jock who lived at the frat house. Maybe it was the way he carried himself. Maybe it was the care he took in his appearance. But most likely what I saw in him was myself 10 years younger, trying to do everything "right" so that no one would know my sexual orientation. I felt sorry for the boy. On the other hand, I envied him, sharing living space with sweaty, half-naked college guys as he did. Of course, my instincts could have been wrong. I wasn't perfect.

It wasn't until I saw Brett's smiling face looking up at me, along with the faces of some two dozen of his Greek brethren, that I decided to do a little exploration of the matter myself. I had purchased a school newspaper, and inside the front cover a full-page ad with photos screamed for attention. It appeared that my neighbors were undertaking a fund-raiser.

"The Boxer Rebellion!" the ad screamed. "Do you have housework to be done? Does your dorm room need cleaning? Need someone to weed the garden or type up a paper for you? Now is your chance to have your chores performed by an able-bodied college student—in his boxers! Ladies, let yourself be served by a scantily clad young man. Men, make your schoolmate your slave for a day!"

The ad went on to say that the service cost $15 per hour and that proceeds would benefit both the fraternity and a local children's hospital. Ever the philanthropist, I decided to call the number listed on the ad.

"Thank you for calling the home of The Boxer Rebellion," the voice at the other end of the line, probably an English major, said to me. "Do you have a worker preference, or would you like me to assign you one?"

I paused. "Brett, if he's available."

"And what kind of work do you need performed?"

"Housework."

"Can you be more specific?"

"I need someone to…clean out my basement."

We made an appointment for early evening the following Thursday.

Brett showed up promptly at my house, dressed in the traditional fraternity attire of a flannel shirt and jeans. I greeted him at the door.

"Hi, my name's Brett," he introduced himself needlessly. "Are you the one who hired me to do some chores in my underwear?"

At least he didn't beat around the bush. "Yes," I said, "I guess I did."

"All right. Well, I guess you know that this is for our annual fund-raiser. We expect cash upon completion of service. You cool with that?"

"Sure."

"Good," he said, finally entering the house.

"Would you like a drink?" I offered.

"Naw," Brett said, then, "Can I ask you a question?"

"Sure," I said.

"OK, dude," he said, leaning in conspiratorially. "This is just between you and me, dude. I mean, well, we're not supposed to ask this."

I agreed to keep it a secret.

"Well…are you gay? I mean, that's cool if you are. It's just…we get a lot of calls from guys. I wasn't sure if most of them were gay or what."

"Well, I can't speak for the others, but I know I'm definitely gay," I said. "Does that bother you?"

"Oh, no," he said. "Dude, I'm totally cool with that. I was just curious."

I bet you're curious, I thought. Or, more accurately, I *hoped*.

"So you don't have a problem walking around in your boxers then?" I asked. "I mean, I don't want you to be uncomfortable..."

"Oh, shit, no. Hell, that's when I'm most comfortable." Brett grinned, showing off his perfect straight teeth. *Straight,* I thought. *And for all I know, maybe this guy is too. I've been wrong before.*

Still, he seemed a little nervous, and I suspected it wasn't just at the thought of putting his chest and legs on display for a now known homosexual.

"Sure you don't want a drink?" I asked. "Gay men always stock the best beer."

He laughed. "OK."

One beer turned into two and then three. The alcohol seemed to help put Brett at ease, and we discussed his classes and his hometown. I wasn't surprised to find out he had once been homecoming king.

"So what's it like?" he asked me.

"What's what like?"

"Being a gay dude. If you don't mind my asking."

"Not at all. But what do you mean? It's fine. I fall for men, not women. Otherwise, I'm pretty much like anyone else."

"So...are you the man or the woman in the relationship?"

"Well, I'm not in a relationship right now," I said.

"Yeah, but I mean—"

"I know what you mean. And that's really just an old stereotype. There's always a give-and-take when two people love each other. But most gay men don't play out roles."

"Dude, I buy that," he said. It struck me that he said "dude" pretty nonchalantly. He didn't emphasize the word the way a surfer would. It just came out of him.

"I'd better get started," he said. "What's the job I'm supposed to do?"

"I need you to get some boxes out of the basement and bring them up to the attic. It's not too tough, but it's definitely a job."

I showed him the basement. There were about 30 boxes in odd sizes.

" 'Kay. I can do that." He untucked his shirt and started unbuttoning it.

"So," I joked, "did you bring along your own boxers, or do you need a pair of mine?"

He laughed and slid his pants off, revealing a pair of red-and-green plaid flannel boxers. He folded his jeans and set them on the floor, throwing his shirt on top of them.

He had a nice body. Not too much of a jock, just lean with a lot of definition. He had a great Apollo's belt—the indentations where the muscles of the stomach meet the legs. And, for a Midwesterner, he had a great tan. He smiled when he caught me looking at him.

"OK, dude, I've got to tell you—we're having a special offer. For 15 bucks an hour, you get this—me wearin' boxers. But we're also trying to raise money for a new pool table. So there's an unofficial deal—for an extra 10 bucks, one-time fee, you get me—wearin' a jockstrap."

He pulled at his waistband to reveal that he was wearing a jock underneath—and, in so doing, exposed a ribbon of the creamy flesh on the south side of his tan line.

I'm a sucker for a tan line.

"How much for you wearin' no jockstrap?" I joked.

"That's not one of the options, dude. Sorry," he said, smiling.

"I'll bite," I said. "I'll pay the extra 10 bucks."

"Awesome. The old pool table is getting really ratty. OK, check this out."

In a moment the boxers were folded up on the floor.

Although Brett's chest was smooth, I could see clearly that there was a lot of hair underneath the front of his jock and that his inner thighs were hairy. The jock itself was clean and white.

When he turned around, I watched his smooth, chiseled

butt as he bent over to pick up a box, revealing a thin, furry line. He lifted the box with little effort. "No problem, dude."

Then an idea occurred to me. "Brett," I said, "how would you like to make a bet?"

"What kind of bet?"

"I'll bet that you can't go the rest of the day without saying 'dude.' If you can work here for the next two hours and not say 'dude,' I'll give you 200 bucks."

"And what if I say d—what if I say it?"

"Then you take off your jockstrap for the rest of the night and work nude."

"Two hundred bucks?" He considered for a moment, then said, "I can do that." We shook hands.

I read a magazine in an armchair while he worked. Watching this young stud toil in practically nothing was an unparalleled erotic experience, and I placed a newspaper on my lap to hide my growing erection. I didn't speak, waiting for the right moment to verbally sabotage him.

It didn't take much.

"Want another beer?" I asked.

"No thanks, dude," he said.

"No thanks, what?" I asked.

He looked confused, then laughed nervously. "Shit, I said it." He paused. "I've really got to take it off now, don't I?" He laughed again. I nodded.

"OK," he said, grabbing his bulge through his jock as if to reassure himself. He peeled the white fabric pouch down and stepped out of it. His tan skin became pale just above his bush, and the pale skin enveloped his crotch in the outline of an abbreviated bathing suit. His pubic hair was light-brown and furry, looking like it was a little softer than most guys'. The shaft of his thin dick was darker than the surrounding skin, and even though he was completely soft, the head had a purplish tint to it. "There it is," he said, shifting his weight as he watched me check him out.

I realized he was blushing. I didn't want to torture the poor guy.

"Looks great. Now you can finish working." I sat back down, watching his pendulous cock swing as he finished transporting boxes.

About an hour and a half later, we were down to the last box. I had taken a mental picture of Brett's fantastic naked body from every possible angle.

Brett bent to pick up the final box, the largest one. He strained, then stood up.

"I can't lift this one. You want to lift it together?" I walked over and helped him lift the box, and we carried it up the two flights of stairs to the attic. It was hot in the attic. We were both sweating.

Back downstairs, I opened up a beer for each of us. I noticed Brett was rubbing his shoulder.

"Hurt yourself?" I said.

"Naw, just a little sore."

"Want a back rub?" I asked, adding, "I used to be a licensed masseur." (Which, incidentally, was true.)

"Serious? All right, dude."

He sat on the ottoman, his legs spread, his back to me. I took a firm hold of his shoulders and began kneading his muscles.

"O-o-oh..." Brett moaned, "that feels so good."

Pressing hard, I worked gentle circles toward the center of his back and then out again, gradually working my way lower. Brett closed his eyes and leaned his head back, letting me work in silence.

I had almost forgotten that he was naked when I caught a glimpse of his penis, gradually rising from its soft state into a partial erection. I didn't say anything, hoping not to embarrass him.

I have to admit, though, the intimacy of the situation was getting me a little hot too. I let my hands slide farther south until I was crouching behind him, rubbing the flesh where his hard back met his butt cheeks. He turned his head, and without opening his eyes he whispered, "Kiss me."

He didn't have to ask twice. I've never felt a man kiss so urgently before, as though years of frustration were being set free. Brett's eyes were still closed, and I couldn't resist the urge to surprise him. I grabbed the head of his now fully hard cock.

He gasped into my mouth. I felt the tiny hole at the top of his member, which was now dripping with precome. I rubbed it into his dick head, and he pressed his tongue against mine.

Brett pulled me around so that I was facing him. "You can jerk me off if you want to," he whispered. I started stroking him, then whispered back, "I'll go you one better."

I quickly leaned down and put his whole penis into my mouth. He gasped again at the feel of a warm, wet, male mouth on his cock. But he soon caught the hang of it, putting his hands on my head to ease me down onto him in rhythm.

His dick was a decent size, about six or seven inches. And it was extremely hard, sticking straight up out of his delightfully wild and fuzzy pubic hair.

After a few minutes of giving him head, I licked my way up his body to kiss him again. I took his wet dick in one hand, and I held his other hand in mine as I led him to the sofa, where I lay him on his back. Brett didn't say a word.

"I want to sixty-nine you," I said. Brett's eyes widened and he nodded.

I took off my clothes as Brett played with himself. Then I positioned myself astride him on the couch. Placing my cock just above his mouth, I licked and sucked his nuts. Finally I felt his lips around my tool. I looked down to see Brett's virgin mouth closing on my cock. After a while he got the hang of it, and we greedily slurped at each other's members. I parted his legs with my hands and played with his butt hole. At first Brett tried to shut his legs—without saying a word—but soon he relaxed, spreading his legs farther and even thrusting his ass toward my fingers.

Inspired, Brett started to stroke my anus, and I soon felt a cautious finger work its way inside. I had had enough of sucking him without seeing him, so I turned around on the sofa, kissing him passionately and pressing my dick against his.

"Ever fuck a guy?" I whispered into his ear.

Brett looked earnestly into my eyes, saying "No."

Without a word I stood up and fished a condom and lube out of a drawer. Brett lay there as I rolled it down onto his penis. I spread lube on his dick and also on my asshole. Lying down on the couch, leading him, I whispered, "Be gentle."

It took Brett a minute to find my asshole with his dick and another minute to work the head of his cock inside. Once in, however, he took off, slowly pumping into me as he stretched me out with his engorged cock.

"Does it feel good?" I asked. Brett's face was contorted, his eyes squinting tightly.

"Yeah," he breathed, "feels real good, dude."

With one hand I fingered Brett's ass. I jerked myself off with the other. Soon I was climaxing, gazing directly into Brett's contorted face.

It wasn't long before Brett was coming. He grunted loudly several times and hugged me close.

As we dressed I paid Brett for the housework. I resisted the urge to tip him exorbitantly, not wanting him to feel like a prostitute.

As he gathered his things and left, he seemed kind of distant, as though the reality of his first time with a man had just sunken in. I was worried that he was nervous or was having regrets, but right before he walked out the door, he grabbed me by the shoulders and kissed me again.

"Let's hang out again real soon," he said.

I'm game, I thought. My basement needs a lot of cleaning.

Alex
by Tim Chadwick

You can't imagine how amazed I was when I found out that Alex Carter is a cocksucker. Man! I had the locker next to him in every P.E. class since the seventh grade. My name's Joey Caldwell; that's why I was next to him. Caldwell, Carter…you get the idea. You'd think we'd have something in common. Hell, both our birthdays are even in the same month, but he's 19, I'm a year younger, and we're about as opposite as two guys can get.

It's not that I'm a wimp or anything, but I've been watching him wrestle and play football and baseball for years. The guy can kick some serious ass. No kidding, Alex is one of the toughest guys I know. He doesn't look like a cocksucker. He doesn't act like a cocksucker. He can't be a cocksucker. But he is—believe me, I know.

It was out by Wilker's pond. I wanted to get away from town and school and all the boring bullshit that we were going through just before graduation, so I skipped class and went hiking. It was real clear out that day, hot and quiet, no air moving anywhere. After walking in that heat for a while I decided I wanted to go swimming, so I headed up toward a big outcrop of rock that people liked to dive off.

As it worked out, I had been hiking the long way around the pond, so I had to climb up the back side of the rock instead of just walking up the other side the way most people do. As I was pulling myself up the last few feet to the top, I heard something up above me, a sort of low grunt, then a guy's voice saying, "Faster, I'm real close."

Well, I'm no dummy. I knew it was some guy getting a hand job or a blow from his girl. Maybe I should have just left, but I wanted to know who it was, especially who the girl was that was willing to put out like that. So, real quiet-like, I hoisted myself up the rest of the way while keeping my head down so I couldn't be seen. Then I sneaked up closer and peeked through a gap between two big boulders.

I could see one of them from the back, a tall redheaded guy in a white T-shirt. The guy's jeans were down around his ankles, and a pair of hands was squeezing at his buns. The first thing that clicked in my head was that the hands were way too big to be a girl's. Then I raised myself up a bit so I could see through a wider space in the gap between the boulders, and it became real clear that this was a guy sucking off a guy, a couple of fags. I couldn't believe it.

I also couldn't see who either of these guys was, and I wanted to know. The tall one looked like he could be young enough to still be in school. They could be students at Parker, the high school where I'm a senior. Hell, there was something familiar about the red hair on the tall guy. If there were a couple of faggots at Parker, I wanted to know who they were. I might be taking showers with these fruits.

I started looking around real quick for someplace I could move to so I could see more of what was going on. About 15 feet to my right the rocks ended. I moved real slow and quiet in that direction until I could peek around the edge.

When I got settled into my new vantage point, I heard the tall guy say something like "Shit, man! Don't stop! I'm so close my nuts hurt," so I figured they hadn't heard me moving. Now that I could see more of what was going on, my mouth fell open just like some dumb-ass cartoon character. I think I actually shook my head in disbelief. The tall guy was Rick Lathrop, "Big Rick," the fucking center on the fucking varsity basketball team.

Rick was one of the biggest jocks in school, one of the biggest guys in school. President of the class of '71. All the other guys were sure Rick was fucking any girl he wanted, and here he was getting his dick sucked by a guy. So maybe that was what was going on. Rick is such a big stud, maybe he was just really horny and letting some fag suck him off. I'd heard about guys letting fags suck them off. I just couldn't think of Big Rick as a fag, so that must be what the story was. Rick's just letting some cocksucker get him off. It's Rick, Rick's no fag. It must be cool.

So I'd figured out what was going on, but I still couldn't see who the guy blowing Rick was 'cause he had his right hand stuck up Rick's shirt like he was feeling around Rick's chest—so his arm and Rick's shirt blocked the guy's face. What I could see was that the guy wasn't sucking Rick's cock anymore 'cause the long shaft and dark-red head of it was sticking straight out in front of Rick.

I could also see that the guy on his knees had his pants down and was running his fist up and down his own cock. *Damn!* I thought. *This guy's got a big one.* For some reason I always figured fags would have pencil dicks, but this guy had a long, thick one that was more than twice the length of the fist he had wrapped around it. It was a big fist too. The whole guy looked pretty big—not as tall as Big Rick, but big and solid.

Then I saw Rick flinch like maybe the guy had pinched his tit or something, and I hear the fag say, "Just trying to make it good for you, man." And the voice sounded kind of familiar, but the guy had this real husky edge to his words like he was really horny, so it doesn't come to me who it is. Then Rick said, "It's OK, man. It's good, it's real fucking good." Then he reached out with his left hand, and I could tell he was putting it on the fag's head and I figured he was gonna force this guy to finish sucking him off, but instead it looked like he was stroking the guy's hair.

"You're the best, man," Rick said, "the best."

Then the cocksucker said, "Best you'll ever have," then slid his hand out from under Rick's shirt. He leaned back and stroked his big cock as he looked up at Rick, and Rick's shirt was no longer in the way, so I could see who the guy was. *Alex,* I thought, *it's Alex.* Then I said "Fuck!" Just like that, out loud, like no one else was there but me. I was that fucking stunned.

But I wasn't the only one there. Two of the biggest, baddest jock motherfuckers I've ever known were there too. Both their heads snapped in my direction at the same time. They looked shocked for about five seconds, then I could tell they had seen me and recognized me, and it occurred to me that maybe I was about to get killed.

I know, you're thinking that what I'd seen should have made me feel like I had something on these guys, but this was Big Rick and Alex the fucking Animal, Alex the best light-heavyweight wrestler in the whole fucking state. Alex! The guy I had been next to for every P.E. class since seventh grade and barely ever talked to because he was so fucking big and so fucking popular and I was...well...me.

For about a 10-count the three of us just stared at each other like it might all go away if nobody said anything. Then I lost my footing and had to take a big step forward, so I was standing out in the open, away from the rock I had been looking around.

I remember thinking that running might be a good idea. I was pretty sure that I was faster than either of these guys, but I was even more sure that they would eventually catch up with me, drag me off somewhere, and squish me like a bug, and no one would ever even notice but maybe my folks.

So I just stood there waiting to see what Rick and Alex were going to do, and finally Alex looked up at Rick and kind of smiled and said, "Well, ain't this real fucking inconvenient." Rick looked down at him and kind of shook his head and said, "Yep, real fucking inconvenient." And then I knew from the tone in their voices that for seeing Alex the Animal suck Big Rick's cock I was going to die.

Then Rick looked back over at me and said in a quiet, real controlled voice, "Caldwell, you want to come over here?" I knew this wasn't a question, but I decided to answer anyway.

"No, Rick," I said, "I don't think so." Then I took a step back, and for about a tenth of a second, running didn't seem like such a bad idea.

As soon as I moved, Alex stood up and looked at me like he looked at his opponents in a wrestling match just before he flipped them over and dropped them on their heads. I took a step forward, kind of hoping that putting myself back where I had been would keep Alex from reaching across the 15 or so feet between us and squeezing me till I popped.

OK, so they were both standing there with their pants down around their ankles, and I did just see Alex with Rick's cock in his mouth. Well, actually I didn't see Alex with Rick's cock in his mouth. I saw Alex on his knees, jacking off, while Rick told him how good he was at whatever it was that he was doing—but I didn't actually see Alex sucking cock.

"I didn't see anything," I said. And I wasn't looking at them both standing there with their pants down around their ankles, and I didn't come up here to go swimming. I stayed at home and studied. If I could believe it, maybe they could too.

Rick actually laughed. Not a great big laugh, just a real evil-sounding little chuckle. "You're not blind," he said, "and I'm not stupid."

"Rick, Alex," I said, "I didn't see anything, I won't say anything to anybody. I just came up here to go swimming and I ran into you guys."

"Ran into us?" Rick cocked his big head to the left a little bit and looked at me like I was an idiot 5-year-old. "If you didn't see anything, then how do you know you ran into us?"

"Ran into who?" I asked.

Rick didn't much care for that as an answer and took a step toward me. I stepped back, and Alex reached out and put his hand on Rick's shoulder. "Don't do it, man," he said, "the little shit runs like a fucking jackrabbit."

For the first time Rick sounded a bit uncertain. "Alex, if he talks..."

Alex bent over and tugged his pants up. Even with all that had happened, his big cock was still half hard. He gave Rick a quick punch in the arm and said, "Pull your pants up, man."

Rick gave me another evil look, then bent down and grabbed his pants, tugged them up, shoved his cock down into them, and yanked the zipper up.

"Caldwell," Alex said. "Joey..." He took a deep breath. "Come on over here. Rick won't lay a hand on you."

"You sure?" I asked him. Rick still looked like he wanted to slam-dunk me into some unseen basketball hoop.

"Rick," Alex said, "tell him you won't hurt him."

Rick gave Alex a dirty look and said nothing.

"Rick," Alex added, "trust me on this. Unless you're ready to kill the kid, you can't hurt him."

From what I could see, killing me was pretty much what Rick had in mind. But then he looked over at Alex, and I guess he just realized that they could both be in a world of shit and that he really wasn't gonna kill me. Then he kind of looked down at his feet, then back at me, but this time he didn't look like he was gonna kill me. He looked like he was almost afraid of me.

"I won't hurt you, kid," Rick said.

I think having Big Rick look like he was afraid scared me even more than the idea that he might break me in half. "Really, Rick," I said, "I won't talk."

"Joey," Alex said, "you've got to understand this from our position."

"I understand," I said. I didn't really; I didn't have a clue why the jock-superman-stud-senior of all times had been down on his knees sucking another guy's cock. I just wanted to agree with him so I could get the hell out of there and start forgetting what I had seen.

"What do you understand?" Alex asked in a voice so low that I had to step a few steps toward him to hear. "What do you understand?"

"I don't know," I answered him. "What difference does it make what I understand? I'm not gonna tell anybody what you did."

"What did I do, Joey?" He asked me, his voice even quieter.

"Nothing," I said. "You didn't do anything, so I couldn't see you do anything, and anyway, I wasn't here."

"Joey," he said, "that's bullshit. You're here, and you saw me sucking Rick's cock."

I just stared at him. I didn't know what he wanted me to say.

"That's what you saw, isn't it, Joey?" Alex asked me.

"Yes, OK, that's what I saw," I said.

"And now you probably think I'm a fag and maybe Rick is one too."

I guess that's what I should have been thinking, but I just couldn't look at Alex or Big Rick and see a fag. Fags are weird guys that talk funny and walk like girls. I thought Alex and Rick were the coolest guys in town, and now Alex was acting like he wanted me to call him a fag.

Alex just stared at me until finally I said, "I don't know what you want me to say."

"I just want you not to bullshit me," Alex answered.

From the way Alex's voice was starting to sound, I figured I must have been pissing him off. At the same time, way down inside, behind all my fear and confusion, I was starting to get a little pissed too. Hell! I hadn't done anything. I wasn't the one with Big Rick's cock in my mouth. I told Alex I wasn't going to tell anyone. What else did he want?

"OK, so I saw you sucking Rick's cock, but I don't think you're a fag and I don't think Rick is a fag. Fags are pussies, guys that act like girls. You and Rick aren't like that and…shit, Alex, I don't know why you were doing that to Rick, but I'm not gonna tell anybody, so it doesn't matter."

At this point Rick broke in. "Come on, Alex," He said, "I don't think the kid's going to say anything. Let's just get out of here."

Alex turned to Rick. "I got to make sure he's not going to talk."

"I told you, Alex," I said, "I'm not gonna say anything."

"See, Alex," Rick said, "he's not gonna talk, so let's go."

"I got to make sure he doesn't think I'm a fag," Alex said.

"I said I don't think you're a fag." I tried to look him right in the eye, but he didn't seem to want to look right at me, so I just repeated myself. "I don't think you're a fag, man."

"I need some proof," Alex said, more to Rick than to me.

"What kind of proof can you get?" Rick asked.

Then Alex did look right at me, and it was like some weird light went on in his head, and he said to Rick, "I want to suck his cock."

There for a few seconds the silence got really amazing. Rick broke it. "What the fuck?"

I knew what Alex had said, but it hadn't really penetrated very deep. Rick looked like he was going to crap his pants. Alex took a couple of steps toward me and repeated himself. "I want to suck your cock."

This time it sank in all the way. One of the biggest jocks on the planet wanted to take my cock in his mouth and suck on it till I fed him my load. I just stared at him. He grinned at me kind of like he grinned at his opponents just after he dropped them on their heads.

Rick took a couple of quick steps toward Alex, got up real close to him, and said, "Come on, man. You don't have to do this. He's not gonna talk."

Alex looked at Rick and in this real soothing voice said, "It's OK, babe."

"Babe." I heard it all right. Alex just called Rick "babe." Like Rick was his girlfriend and I was some other girl that Alex was about to kiss and he wanted Rick to know that it was no big deal. But I'm not a girl, and Alex wanted to do more than kiss me. And if Alex sucked my dick, it sure as hell would be a big deal.

I decided to follow Rick's lead and blurted, "He's right, Alex. You don't have to do this."

"But I want to," Alex countered.

Rick got right to the point. "But why?"

"If he likes it," Alex answered, "then he won't think I'm a fag and he won't tell."

"That's bullshit, Alex," Rick snapped back at him. "I heard Jerry Walsh talking about how he let some fag suck him off in the men's room in Frasier Park and how this fag wanted to touch Jerry's chest and Jerry told the fag to keep his hand to himself or he was gonna kick the guy's ass." Rick paused for a second, then asked Alex, "You want him to talk shit like that about you?"

"Jerry Walsh is an asshole," Alex answered. "And I don't think there's much chance of Joey kicking my ass."

"You know what I mean," Rick snapped.

"I know, Rick, but Joey's not like that." He looked over at me. "You're not like that, are you, Joey?"

If by "like that" he meant like Jerry Walsh, then I had to admit that I would rather be like a tall pile of dog shit than like that fuckhead Jerry. "No."

"See," Alex said to Rick, "Joey's cool. If he liked something, he wouldn't talk shit about it."

Rick shook his head like he didn't quite believe that this conversation was happening. I could fully understand how he felt—I didn't believe any of this was happening. Then Rick gave Alex this long kind of hard look and said, "OK, man, you do whatever you want, but what happens if he doesn't like it?"

"Yeah," I agreed, just because agreeing with Rick made more sense than agreeing with Alex. "What if I don't like it?"

Alex grinned at me. Not a big shit-eating grin, just a little grin accompanied by a slight raise of his eyebrows. Then it occurred to me that Alex had just won the match 'cause I had just agreed, in a roundabout way, to letting him suck my cock. That realization had an effect that I definitely did not expect.

My cock is about to get sucked. I thought. *My cock is about to get sucked by Alex Carter. Alex Carter, stud. Alex Carter, god of high school wrestling. Alex Carter, who barely ever talked to me in school, is now going to get on his knees and take my cock into his mouth and lick it and suck on it until I get my nut. And no one in the fucking universe has ever even touched my cock but me, and maybe it's about time that someone did and why shouldn't it be him if he wants to do it.*

This kind of stuff just started to take over my brain.

Yet! For some reason I should not want him to do this. So, what is this reason? *I'm not a fag. I know I'm not a fag. I don't talk funny and I don't walk like a girl and even if I do look at the other guys in the showers once in a while, so what? The sex ed teacher says it's normal for guys my age to notice other guys. It doesn't mean anything and, besides, Big Rick lets Alex suck him and there is no way that Big Rick is a fag. And! Even if all this shit that's happening is starting to give me a boner, I ain't no fag.*

Then I came back to earth and Alex and Rick were both staring at my crotch and at the bulge that was clearly forming there and Alex said to Rick, "I think he'll probably like it." Then his grin got bigger and he started walking toward me.

I just stood there. Alex stopped about two feet from me. "You ready for it?" he asked me.

"Yeah, OK, if you really want to."

"I really want to," he said.

Alex knelt down so his face was only about a foot from my crotch, then he reached out and ran his hands up the back of my legs until they were on my ass and pulling me toward him. His mouth opened slightly. His lips pressed against my crotch. My cock throbbed and tried to grow, but it was aimed down my leg and didn't have anywhere to go.

Then Alex was all over the front of my jeans with his mouth

and teeth like he wanted to eat his way through to my cock. God, it felt good. God, my cock was starting to ache. Then, just about the time I thought my dick was gonna snap in half, Alex leaned back a bit and looked up grinning. "Like that, Joey?"

Shit, yes, I liked it. But I didn't seem able to say much, so I just shook my head up and down a couple of times and watched to see what he was going to do next. Alex slid his hands along the back of my legs a couple of times real slow then around my hips, until he was covering the bulge in my crotch.

"Packed kind of tight there, Joey?"

I nodded.

"Bet it would feel a lot better if it was out in the open."

I nodded again.

Alex slid his hands toward the top button of my jeans. Instead of pulling it open he kept on going up under my T-shirt. The palms of his hands felt slick and warm against my belly, the touch of his fingertips so light it almost tickled. He stopped just long enough for me to let out a breath, then he slid his hands back down again until he could reach that top button and slide it through the button hole.

I was hoping this was it, he was going to suck my cock. At the same time I was hoping he wouldn't ever stop rubbing my belly. But most of all, I was hoping he would get my cock the hell out of my pants. What he did was slide his hands back up until the tips of his fingers met with my nipples. Then he gave them a little twist.

I guess I must have let out a gasp or something, 'cause Alex looked up at me and smiled, then he twisted a little harder. It felt hot, it felt great, it felt like my cock was going to break out of my jeans on its own.

I moaned. No shit! I actually moaned.

Alex grinned. With his right hand he kept working my nipple. With the other he tugged at my jeans until one by one the buttons popped open. When the last one finally came loose, all he had to do was let go and my jeans were down around my knees. My cock pushed out hard against the pouch of my Jockeys. I wanted to pull the damned things down and let it out, but I was afraid that if I did anything Alex might stop.

He did stop twisting my nipple...I didn't like it. Without even thinking what I was doing, I shoved my hand up my shirt and brushed them across the nipple that he had just let go of.

Alex hooked his fingers in the top of my waistband and pulled it out and over my cock. Finally, relief—my cock slapped up hard against my belly. Alex jerked my shorts down over my ass and pulled them to my knees.

His big hands slid back up my legs and cupped my ass cheeks. He glanced over at Rick. "Big dick for a little dude," he said, then let go of my ass with one hand and slid it up under my sac. "Low-hangers, I like that." He gave my nuts a gentle squeeze and tugged down on them. "Kind of nuts that carry a big load."

I watched his hand. Precome started to ooze from the head of my cock. Alex looked up at me.

"Ever had your dick sucked before, Joey?"

I shook my head. He rolled my nuts around in their sac.

"What do you want me to do, Joey?"

My nuts were starting to ache. Alex waited.

"Suck me," I managed to say.

The hand that was on my ass pulled me closer to him. My precome and his spit lubed our skin as his lips slid apart and over the swollen head of my cock.

"Oh, shit," I groaned.

He sucked me farther into him. His mouth was warm and wet and soft and every good feeling in the universe was crowding to get into that one split second of contact. Then it got better.

He started to slide his lips up and down my cock. The farther down my shaft he got, the more of him I could feel surrounding me. Finally, I was buried in him, my whole cock deep in his throat, every square inch of it surrounded by another person.

He held me in his throat like that for what seemed like forever. I swallowed hard. I wanted to pull back; it felt so good it hurt. I wanted to fuck his face hard and fast and shoot my load down his willing throat, but it was too soon. I knew it was too soon.

I swallowed hard, I tried to inhale, the breath caught in my throat. Alex slowly pulled his head back. I sucked air into my lungs and moaned like a puppy when you won't pick it up. Alex rotated his head so that his lips and tongue swirled around the head of my cock. My nuts pulled up tight in their sac.

I felt a hand on my shoulder. It was Big Rick. His other hand was wrapped around the shaft of his cock. I grinned at him. He grinned back. His hand ran down along my back until it was resting on the bare skin of my hip, then he knelt. As he did, he let go of his cock and ran his hand through Alex's hair. Alex pulled his mouth away from me and pressed his lips hard against Rick's.

My cock throbbed for attention. I was so fucking close. I reached out and brushed my fingers through Rick's deep-red hair. He slid his hand around from where it rested on my hip to where he could get a firm grip on my ass, then he turned me toward him. My cock slapped against the side of his face, leaving a wet trail across his cheek as he moved his head to take my cock into his mouth. Then he went down on me.

Where Alex had been gentle, Rick was rough and fast—no teasing, just rapid-fire, high-suction cock sucking. It was more than I could take. I managed to grunt out "I'm gonna come" just before I shot out a wad that felt like it had slammed up from the bottom of my feet. Rick didn't pull back. I felt his throat contract as he swallowed. I pumped out another load. He swallowed again. He had to swallow five times to get it all, then he pulled back.

I looked down and watched my cock slide out from between his lips. Alex was bent way over, doing for Rick what Rick had just done for me. In a few seconds Rick grunted, then a second later a shudder went through him and he grunted again. When Alex raised up I could see Rick's come running down Alex's chin. Rick leaned forward, licked the white goo from Alex's chin, kissed him, then bent down and took Alex's cock into his mouth. After a few seconds of Rick bobbing up and down, Alex reached down, held Rick's head, and let out a series of quick gasps. Thoughts of Alex's load mixing with my load flashed through my head.

I lowered myself to the rough ground; it scratched against my bare ass. I didn't care—I felt better than scrawny little 18-year-olds are ever supposed to feel. Rick stroked Alex's hair. I watched. My dick was getting hard again. When Rick raised up out of Alex's lap, they just knelt there breathing kind of heavy and staring at each other. I thought they were beautiful. God, what a fag thing to think. Finally Alex reached out, brushed a stray piece of grass off Rick's T-shirt, and said, "It was my fucked-up idea. You didn't have to do it too."

Rick grinned. "Sure I did."

They stared at each other for a few more seconds.

"You know," Alex said to Rick, "I'm pretty sure I love you."

Rick reached forward and rested the tips of his fingers on Alex's lips. "What a fag thing to say."

Alex lowered his head. "I'm not a fag," he whispered.

Rick pushed Alex's chin up so they were eye to eye. "Yes, you are, man. You're a fag and you love me, and I'm a fag and I love you." Then they leaned into each other and kissed, and I'm pretty sure a rainbow formed in the sky even though it hadn't been raining. Well, actually, there was no rainbow, but that's what it looked like and felt like, and then I started thinking what an asshole I was for sitting there and watching, so I cleared my throat.

They let go of their lip lock and turned toward me. Alex

blushed. "Guys," I said, "It's time for me to get going." I stood up and tried to shove my stiff dick back in my pants. They seemed to think this was kind of funny.

I looked at Rick and said "Thanks, man." It seemed like the right thing to say to the guy after he got me off like that.

Rick grinned. "No problem."

"You too, Alex," I added.

Alex looked at me and smiled, not a big smile, just enough that I knew he was going to be all right. I smiled back at him, then I turned and walked off down the path that led back to town. Nothing else has ever happened between them and me. They're kind of special to each other, and I don't want to get in the way of that. Maybe someday I'll have that same thing with someone. I'm pretty sure it's gonna be with a girl, but who knows—I'm no fag, but I'm no fool either.

Times Square Pickup
by Michael Luongo

The thing I remember most about him was his eyes. They were large and brown, and they squinted subtly when he smiled. The lashes surrounding them were long, and they curled back at the tip, bringing even more attention to his face. Those eyes told me immediately that this shy young thing walking beside me had to be Italian. And by the way he kept using those eyes to look back at me, I knew he had to be gay.

I walked close to him for several blocks down Broadway and made sure to smile his way when we came together at the corners. No matter how many windows he looked into, he seemed to have no other purpose than to see how long he could keep my attention. There was no use pretending he might be shopping in Times Square at 2 in the morning.

My job had brought me to the area, and I had just come from the Gaiety Theatre. I was in the AIDS field at the time and was trying to work with some of the sex places that had miraculously survived in spite of the puritans running the city. I was heading to my car to go home, 45 minutes away in the suburbs, but I decided to linger in the neighborhood instead. It was filled with brighter lights now and dangerously over-populated by big-butted tourists. If one looked hard enough, one could still find the sleaze the place was famous for. And I hoped I had found it in the image of this young thing.

By the fourth block it was obvious that I would have to do the talking. He was very young and well-dressed, too well-dressed for the area and the time. I doubted that he was the type to have gone to a Broadway show and stayed out late afterward. He had unbuttoned his dress shirt and loosened his tie. His dress pants were made of an inexpensive material and, by the cut, obviously bought in a young men's store.

They clung delicately to his buttocks. I was torn between watching them and watching his eyes, so I moved back and forth between them.

"Hi," I said when we had reached another corner. I think I even winked.

He looked at me silently for a moment and then squinted his large brown eyes again, just as he had been doing for the few blocks before. "Hello," he said very softly.

"Did you just come from work?" I asked, basing my question on the way he was dressed.

"Yeah," he hesitated for a moment before continuing, "I work at a hotel near here." He looked back and pointed down Broadway in the direction of a dozen different hotels. We stopped walking and stood against a building as other people, oblivious to our desire, strolled by.

"So you're the reason this place is overrun by tourists," I said.

He smiled bashfully, and I asked him his name. It was Michael, just like mine. It was the name of most of the people I met—no need to say "John" for anonymity anymore. He said he was from Brooklyn, and not surprisingly, from some part off the Belt Parkway, the same neighborhood where *Saturday Night Fever* was set. He was just on his way to the subway when I met him.

"So, you're gay?" I asked, not really thinking the question needed to be put forth.

"I have a girlfriend." The response came in a slightly butcher tone than any of his others.

I looked him over and analyzed him as he stood in front of me, bathed in the soft light coming from the store window we stood next to. We conversed briefly about what a hard day he'd had staffing the counter at the hotel. I mentioned trying to do some work at the Gaiety, a place with which he didn't quite seem familiar. The outer borough rolled from his tongue, coating each word he said with a Belt Parkway toughness. But it seemed overplayed, as if it were all to hide the fact that he really was gay in spite of his claim to a girlfriend. There was a certain softness to him too. If his mother had had only two sons, he would have been the one who grew up to be the priest, not the gangster.

"How old are you?" I finally asked, feeling like I was conducting an interview instead of a pickup.

"Nineteen."

I laughed. I was 10 years older than him. I let him know, and he said, "You don't look it."

"Thanks," I said, looking down. I liked the compliment, and I hoped the unexpected age difference didn't mean anything to him. I remember when I thought someone my age was old.

We kept walking; I led, my pace slightly faster than his. I wanted us to head in the direction of my car, as if by chance. But on the corners where our path zigzagged, he still looked up the street, as if wanting to continue on.

When we came to my car, I leaned against it, keys in hand, my arms wrapped around my body. It wasn't a message to communicate that I had to leave, but that if we were going to do something, we'd better do it soon. I fumbled with my watch as I spoke and then cut into our conversation, "What are you doing now?"

"Nothing," he answered in a low voice.

"Do you want to drive around for a while"—I paused, looked him up and down—then added, "and talk?"

We drove around the city, first heading uptown, then downtown. The progressive change of lights on the avenues kept us moving, hiding the distances we were passing. I thought it made sense to head to one of the bridges bound for Brooklyn because that was where he was from. I put my hand on his knee as I drove, unsure if I should probe further. He was young and he seemed inexperienced. *Should I make a move now?* I wondered. My worries were unfounded. He turned to me and smiled, then placed his hand directly on my crotch. My dick had already stiffened into a hard-on, oozing precome into my underwear. He stroked the head through my pants just as Varick hit Canal, making my penis twitch under my busting zipper.

I thought I could fuck him right there in the car, but where could we pull over? Wouldn't someone see from the sidewalk and maybe call or stand over and gawk? With things in the city the way they were, I didn't dare.

"You want me to drive to your place?" I asked, turning my head in his direction. There was virtually no traffic on Canal as I made my way to the Manhattan Bridge, Chinese signs flashing over the windshield.

"My house is not an option," he insisted flatly.

"Is anybody home?"

"My house is not an option," he said again, and then he repeated it several times like a broken record, though he was probably too young to remember what records actually were.

I thought I would still continue on despite his protests. Maybe we could pull over somewhere off the Belt Parkway and fool around. I had heard that men cruise just off the road, hiding behind the tall wild grass that grew along its swampy edges. I had often imagined seeing men doing things on my way to Kennedy or to Fire Island, but at this time of night I wasn't sure how safe it was.

As we got close to the end of Canal, the streets tightened under the strain of bridge-and-tunnel traffic heading home from the clubs. The car slowed to a crawl and gave me more time to concentrate on looking at little Michael.

We talked about going to my house, and I promised I would take him home in the morning or whenever he wanted. Neither of us had to work the next day. Still, he was reluctant. At his age, he'd probably have to explain his whereabouts to his family, and his girlfriend's place might not be a ready excuse.

When we hit Mott Street I turned the corner. I had thought of something. "I know a place," I suddenly said. But it was completely a last resort.

I had been carrying the keys to a friend's apartment while he was away all week. Knowing my job often meant I was in town till very late, he said I could use it for emergencies if I was too tired to drive home. He liked the idea of someone keeping an eye on his place, but I wasn't the only one with the key. Another one of our friends had one, and so did every member of his family. Still, he did say I could use it for emergencies. With no other place for me and Michael to consummate our relationship, this qualified as an emergency in my mind.

It was a trendy TriBeCa apartment. Everything had obviously been renovated, but the management kept the paint on the doorway's ironworks flaky and peeling so that the residents would still feel like they were living on the edge, even at $2,000 a month.

"This is the place," I said, looking up at the camera in the lobby, wondering if my friend ever reviewed the tapes. The whole ride up the elevator, Michael and I looked back and forth at each other and then to the numbers lighting up above our heads. The door clacked open on 4 and we spilled into the hallway. I put my finger to my mouth and whispered "Shh, the neighbors," but Michael had been silent the whole time.

I entered the apartment cautiously and looked around the living room as the lights flickered on. We moved through the stale odor of an empty apartment into my friend's white-tiled, immaculate kitchen.

"Want something to drink?" I asked, dumping my shoulder bag onto the floor.

Michael was looking around the apartment, and he could sense my own apprehension in being here. "Is this your boyfriend's place?"

I laughed, but I understood why he asked the question. "I don't have a boyfriend."

"That's right, you told me." He seemed a little embarrassed, but he smiled anyway and walked closer to me. He suddenly kissed me and grabbed my ass tightly, a total change from his timid behavior outside.

Damn, I thought, hoping he didn't think he was a top.

He pulled my shirt off as I leaned against the counter with the edge of the Formica pressing against my buttocks. He stroked his fingertips over my stomach and smiled out the word "Hairy." I felt like I was on display or being clinically observed. He was so quiet while he touched me. He tugged at my belt, and I loosened it for him. He did the rest, and my pants fell to the floor with the metal buckle clacking against it.

I stroked my hard penis as he watched. He just stood back for a few moments, staring in wonder with a playful, child-like smile on his face.

I looked into his eyes and asked, "You like to get fucked?" I said it for the hell of it, thinking this Brooklyn boy would never crack his ass open for me. What would his girlfriend think? He simply looked at me in silence and batted his eyes wistfully. Then I was amazed at the speed with which he turned around, pulled his pants down, and bent over against the other kitchen counter.

For an Italian he was amazingly hairless, but it served all the more to show off how perfectly round and muscular his butt was. He stooped over and spread his legs as far as the pants wrapped around his ankles would allow, with his feet moving up and down with nervous anticipation.

I kept stroking my penis as I stared at his butt—so hairless I could even see a few pimples, the only blemishes on this otherwise smooth rear end. The skin was tan but with no lines, as if he lay nude at the beach, in the salon, or, God forbid, in the backyard of his Belt Parkway home. I imagined myself stalking him in the future for a better view.

I spat into my hand and rubbed the saliva into the crack of his ass to play with his nubby anus. I felt him open against my touch, and he stuck his head up, his mouth open, as if moaning silently. Every so often he turned around and looked at me with the eyes that had caught my attention on Broadway, and then he would offer the subtle smile that coordinated so well with it.

I spat again on my hand and stroked up and down the length of my shaft. My finger slipped in and out of his ass. I bent down to spit into the crack, moistening it for entry. It was there, kneeling on the ground, that I suddenly panicked. I was in the AIDS field, for chrissake, and I wasn't even sure if I had a condom on me to be doing what I was doing.

Michael sensed that I had become flustered. He stopped moving his head back and forth with the silent moaning and turned around to look at me with a slightly baffled expression that replaced his smile. I looked up at him and, with one hand still on the crack of his ass, I turned to my side and fumbled with my free hand through my bag until I finally found something deep inside of one of the zippered pockets.

It was some odd Australian package with a big yellow banana on it, left over from when I had given a "safer sex around the world" discussion to a college class. My boss had given it to me after a trip to Sydney's Mardi Gras, telling me to make sure to use it. Now seemed like the perfect time.

I stood up, quickly ripped open the package, and shoved the rubber over my dick head and down my penis. Michael's smile returned instantly when he saw my latex-coated shaft. I spit on my hand again, wetting the already lubricated condom, and bumped the moist tip against his pink puckered hole.

"Ready?" I asked, watching him nod silently in response. I pushed my head in. He was ready, willing, and able—but, best of all, he was tight.

He didn't moan at all with each thrust. Instead he rocked his head back and forth, enjoying the feeling. "Does that feel OK?" I asked in the gentle, almost psychiatric tone I had grown used to affecting when I picked up very young men who claimed to have little experience. I loved fucking them, and the fact that so much seemed new to them was part of the experience. I never wanted to make them do anything they didn't want to.

I pushed in deeper, thrusting quickly, every nerve from my head to my balls enjoying the intense sensation of such a tight, young ass. It proved to be a little too much for me, and every truck rattling on the street below and every noise in the hallway outside the door made me panic. I kept thinking it was my friend's relatives coming to the apartment. I didn't expect his mother to be popping in at 4 in the morning, but his club-kiddie sister home from college for the summer was always a strong possibility. This would not be a good way to meet her for the first time.

The gripping sensation of Michael's ass and my own nervousness combined until I suddenly felt myself come, my splooge hitting the wall of the condom. I felt the milky liquid squeezing inside of the rubber as I pushed in and out more quickly, catching the last of the best sensations just as I finished coming. I stopped thrusting and pulled out, the condom ripping off my dick, caught inside of Michael's tight ass. I gently tugged to release it, wadding it up into a sticky ball in my hand.

"We'd better go," I said to him, kissing him behind the ears.

At first little Michael didn't say anything. But then in a very flat, tough tone, the Brooklyn seeping back into him now that he had his ass closed, he said, "Where's my pleasure?"

"We don't have time, we've got to go," I said, wiping my dick down with a paper towel. I offered him a fresh one as I pulled my pants back up.

"Where's my pleasure?" he said again insistently. "You come, and I don't get to come. Can't you give me a blow job?" He had turned around, refusing to pull up his pants. I looked down at his hard penis, thick and bulbous at the head, and touched the back of my hand against its warm flesh. I smiled at him, but then I pulled away. "We've really got to go."

I could tell he was angry. "We can get together another time," I said. I must admit that I was being selfish, but I was intensely worried about someone popping unexpectedly through the doors.

I gathered the used condom and come-slimed paper towels into a little plastic bag and looked through the kitchen. I wet a towel and wiped away the lubricant streaks on the counter with their incriminating fingerprints. Even if my friend had a suspicion that someone was fucked in his kitchen, he could never prove it was me that did it.

Michael pulled up his pants reluctantly, still seeming more than just a little miffed. He left his shirt half untucked, and the buttons were open farther down his chest than when he had entered.

I kissed him again but got only a timid response. I then pressed him on toward the door, as if it were a duty that had to be fulfilled. I took a final check of the apartment, but it still smelled of sex to my nose. I hoped it would dissipate by the time anyone else came into the apartment.

We drove quickly through the Battery Tunnel into Brooklyn. Michael was pensive and silent, staring out the window most of the time. Sometimes we did look back and forth at each other, even holding hands when I didn't have to have both of mine on the wheel. He played with my thighs now and then, but I could tell he just wanted to get home.

As we got deeper into Brooklyn, Michael edged forward in his seat, pointing with each delivery of the words "Here, turn here," until at last we reached his neighborhood. I dropped him off a block from his house. He insisted that I not drive up his street, though I doubted anyone inside would be up at this hour. It was nearing 5 in the morning, and the summer sun was beginning to peek out over the horizon. I bent over to kiss him as he opened the door, but he pulled his face away. We were in his neighborhood now, and not anonymous Manhattan.

At my request we exchanged numbers and made tentative plans for the next weekend. When I called a few days later it was a totally wrong number. I hung up the phone, crumpled the piece of paper in my hand, slumped back into my bed, and thought of what had happened. The night I had with him still comes to mind whenever I pass in front of a hotel in Times Square.

That Boy That Summer
by Jack Fritscher

In his 18th summer between senior high and college, Engine remembered, he had beat off exactly 358 times for an average of nearly four loads a day. Early mornings he woke with a piss-hard that wouldn't go away. He walked to the bathroom down the hall, which was flooded with the early-dawn light of summer, with his dick big and hard and bobbing in front of his young belly. The weight of it felt as good, extended out over his big balls, as the heat of it in the cool morning air did. In the john he stood sleepily over the toilet, holding his large meat in his hand, aiming his rod down at the bowl. His piss was slow in coming. His hand felt good on his cock. His mind darted, waking up, to the kind of stuff he had plotted to dedicate his summer vacation to: He intended to beat off as much as he could, everywhere he could—thinking about and spying on, well, not spying actually, more like watching, no, studying, yeah, that was it, studying the guys he couldn't wait to rub shoulders with in the locker room come the fall semester.

Engine had scoped his plan start to finish. He knew what he wanted. He knew what he liked. He had, that summer, not yet let any man touch his dick. At the Y and in a couple of gas station rest rooms, and in at least one highway rest stop, men had taken a gander at the meat Engine flipped out of his jeans. They had tried, some of them, to cop a feel of his sizable rod. He let them look. He even let one or two of them kind of kneel in front of him while they looked at his dick and rubbed their own cocks.

Engine liked that. He liked the way grown men knelt to worship dick. The couple times that he had stepped back from the porcelain urinal, he turned with his dick hanging out of his fly and stood with his booted feet slightly apart. He noticed that as soon as the other man knelt in front of him, his own cock started its launch from its long, low-slung hang, filling up with a tidal flood of hard, swelling meat stretching the rosy pink skin of his young dick tight around the thick shaft that curved ever so naturally off to his left.

He liked to watch his prick's no-hands rise to fullness that flushed the thick mushroom head.

He was surprised the first time that a man kneeling on the hard tile floor in the gas station john moaned at the sight of his big tool. He stepped back half a pace when the man bobbed toward his meat. A thin strand of prefuck juice, clear as crystal, started as a big drop forming at the slit of his dick. His step back caused the drop to fall in a slow stretch of juice that the kneeling man wanted. But Engine wasn't offering that. No touch. Not yet. Not until he was ready. He wasn't prick-teasing. He was totally focused on what he had to exchange at the moment. He was OK in his head with men looking at his dick close-up, but he wasn't ready, at least not yet, not until he had beaten off enough by himself to let another man touch him, lick him, tongue him, suck him.

Engine knew about all those things. No one told him. He just knew. He was born knowing. His secret knowledge he kept to himself. His plan was to act on what he liked when he got old enough. What he liked was older men. Older men, to him that summer, were the guys on freshman college varsity. His plan was never to be touched until he was touched by one of them. He was satisfied, all the way up to the fall semester, to hang out near where these guys played summer ball, to park his old car near their van at the drive-in movie, and to strip off his own T-shirt and jeans close by the lockers where they peeled down and horsed around snapping each other's butts with towels while their dicks and balls flopped in their wild grab-assing before they headed down to the beach.

He beat off in the bushes watching them sweating in a fast and furious hardball tournament that lasted all summer.

He beat off in his old car at the drive-in movie, staring into their van, where they guzzled beer and smoked dope and made dirty jokes about the stuff on-screen.

He beat off in the locker room sniffing their socks and smelling the sweat in the pits of their white cotton T-shirts; he searched their white Jockey shorts, dropped carelessly on the floor in their messing around, for that special bit of skid mark that only the crack of a ripe, sweaty butt can blot, from into a trace of guys who are really hot shit.

He studied the way the college guys moved and found his own moves were already as sure as theirs. He studied the way they cut their hair and discovered his own natural bent in grooming matched theirs. He studied their cocks and balls. He inventoried the variety of their upperclassmen bodies. He liked what he saw. He liked the look, when he was alone in his room, naked in front of a mirror, of his own body and balls and cock. He knew he would fit in OK. He could hardly wait for the fall. The thought of walking into the senior locker room, stripping down, playing a little ball, and showering all together in a tiled room echoing with loud shouting gave him a bone-on. He could hardly wait to show off his dick, his sizable, big dick, to these guys.

He figured it might never happen, but he liked to think about standing with them all in a circle jerk. He knew they had done it. He had seen them late one night, half drunk and very stoned, standing stripped from a midnight swim around a small, warming fire kindled on the sandy shore of Twin Lakes. They started out laughing and taking bets on who could last the longest or shoot the fastest or who had the biggest dick versus who had the smallest gun; but the longer they stood in the circle, the closer they moved. The laughing stopped. Their individual energies seemed to combine into one group energy. There was no touching. Only the movement of their arms stroking their hands up and down the shafts of their hard cocks. There was no embarrassment. No shame. They were buddies, all of them, together all the time, each one of them thinking in the quiet of the summer night, mesmerized by the firelight, their own private thoughts, jerking off together as naturally as every other sport and pleasure they shared.

Engine could hardly wait to be part of a group of men like that. Dick in hand, he beat off 30 or 40 times thinking about how they had looked, each and every one of them, standing around the fire, their faces and chests and bellies and cocks lit from beneath by the orange-and-shadow flickering in the soft summer night air. He knew all his life he would remember this summer of purposeful waiting. He even laughed at himself for holding out, acting almost virginal, until he could do it with the right upperclassman in the right group of men. Until then, that summer, he'd kept his dick to himself.

One thing Engine knew for fucking sure: He might be a "technical" virgin because he'd never done it with anybody else, but he was not gonna be any slouch. He knew when he finally hit the sack with the right man at the right time, he would know precisely what moves to give and take. A guy doesn't jerk off a couple thousand times, thinking about all the things two men can do, without getting pretty good at basic pleasure.

Engine figured it took a lot of nerve for a guy to go out and make love to somebody else unless he had made pretty good love to himself first.

He liked to cup his hand around his cock and balls and move it slowly to his face. He held his palm and fingers steady and lobbed a nice and nasty wad of spit into his hand. His big cock kind of rolled expectantly over on his left thigh. His dick liked stroking. His hand liked his dick. His head knew the right rhythms. His mind unreeled the right movies. Everything came together when his wet hand wrapped around the hot head of his dick and slid down the heavy shaft to his cock root at the top of his tight balls. He liked to feel the hose-thick vascularity of the big vein that ran up the underside of his dick from his nuts to his cock head. He was always rock-hard.

That summer he played with himself in constant anticipation of the first man he would have and of all the men he would have after the first. He was absolutely and totally clear about the downright righteous encounter of man-on-man pleasure. That summer, with 358 comings under his belt, he'd developed a taste for his own come, and through his own come a taste for the come of the college guys he would soon join. He licked his own hand. He wanted to know for sure what his load tasted like so he'd know exactly how he tasted to the guys when they came back in the fall from working on construction jobs and from playing ball, and from their own secret pleasures.

He had big hands. He had big cock. He had big plans.

He loved that summer, when he had teased himself with total anticipation. He remembered all those private young loads he had shot on his own belly. He recalled how perfectly that summer had set him up for all the man-to-man fucking and sucking to come.

Sometimes, later on, pile-driving his dick, face-fucking some guy in a roadside toilet, he knew he'd think back on that summer when he had heated himself up to a hot, fevered pitch that would spur him on for a fucking lifetime!

The City of the Dead
by C.J. Murray

He was thin as a shadow but muscular, with long legs and a hard stomach and ass. The first time I saw him I thought he was a shadow as he moved between the tombs in the City of the Dead in the New Orleans cemetery. I blinked and squinted hard to see if he was real. He seemed to belong there as he straightened the broken vases and picked up gum wrappers and broken flowers from the narrow alleys between the whitewashed tombs. I thought he must be a caretaker. I watched his long, thin, elegant fingers brush the tops of the crypts as he cleared away the dust and peeling white paint.

On my third visit, I asked if he worked there. He just stared at me with those deep-set black eyes, under the neat brows that made a slash across his face.

He was good to look at, so fine and noble, with his perfect straight nose and dark lashes. He stood there looking at me, his black hair falling straight on both sides of his face. Then he nodded yes to my question. Without a word he turned and walked away. I didn't follow. I added him to the growing number of strange characters I had encountered since I'd moved to New Orleans. I slipped him into the slot with the transvestites and prostitutes who worked the corner of Conti and Bourbon; with the man who had no legs but sat on a homemade square of wood with small wheels attached underneath so that he could push himself about with his hands; with the man who stood on a red plastic bucket at the corner of St. Peter Street with his penis and balls tucked back between his buttocks, dressed in a woman's red swimsuit, waiting for donations to be tossed into the little basket at his feet.

I thought that the research paper I was writing paled in contrast with these local characters. The paper was my editor's idea. He planned a series on old cemeteries in the Deep

South, and New Orleans was a hotbed of them. Or perhaps he thought that in my present state of mind I needed to be surrounded by the dead and the silent. Harold, my editor, was a good friend, and he was aware of how deeply David's death had overwhelmed me.

I took a few more pictures and a few notes then called it a day. When I developed the pictures in the little bathroom I used for a darkroom in my apartment, the boy's face peered back at me in one shot of the endless crypts. His lips were curved upward in the corners, and his shiny white teeth showed in his dark face. I studied his high cheekbones and wide shoulders. And I stared at his belly in the tight white T-shirt. My eyes moved to his crotch and the outline of his cock and balls beneath the faded jeans. I felt myself harden. I was attracted to him, as I always am to young, sexy boys, especially those with such an open vulnerability.

I missed David so suddenly and so completely that it was like a physical blow. He had been gone a year, and the pain had not lessened with the change of cities. There had been a few other men in that time, used only to provide release but with no emotional attachment, and I did not expect to find another like him. He was so young and beautiful that I had hesitated in approaching him when we'd met. But he had not turned me away, and we shared a year of happiness. He died alone at the hands of unknown assailants who had slashed his body with an ice pick. His loss left me stunned and numbed.

I tossed the picture onto the table and went out. I walked the cobbled streets, watching the evening crowds and listening to other people's conversations. I went into Patout's, gave my order to the waitress, and when it came I ate more from habit than hunger. Then I walked down to ZU'S, the gay bar on Rampart.

The music was loud enough to drown out my thoughts, and the man dancing on the small stage was hot enough to make the front of my jeans tight. I watched as several men paired off and left, then I watched those who snuggled in the dark corners, with their hands reaching under shirts and into jeans, their eyes glazed with desire. I chatted with those who approached me and watched as they gave up and moved on, as if sensing my inability to respond. I drank steadily, until I began to forget the fine features of David's face, the feeling of his body against mine, his hard cock demanding and pressing into me as his arms held me and his words filled my ear.

When I left the bar it was hard to remember the way back to the apartment. When I eventually found it, I walked past the doorway and up the five blocks to the entrance of the cemetery. It was locked, but I turned the corner and found the low place in the fence, hoisted myself up and over, and then strolled among the crypts.

It was darker than I had imagined, and I headed toward the lights nearer the center, looking at the huge winged angels as I went. The sounds of the streets dissipated as I went farther into the rows and rows of crypts. I turned a corner and was face-to-face with the boy. I started and stepped back. I knew I was very drunk and that he could possibility be dangerous, but I didn't really care. I was intrigued. We stood facing each other for a full minute. He was taller than I'd thought but just as beautiful, with his perfect features and graceful movements. He grinned shyly, which gave his face a beautiful expression.

"Come," he said, turning to lead me through the cemetery to a small, unkempt building in the very heart of it. The building was nearly covered with vines, and a slab of marble served as a doorstep. He held the French door open for me, and I stepped inside. The interior was sparsely furnished: a couple of chairs, a table, and a bed. The top of the table was covered with lit candles. Beyond that small room was another that seemed to be a small kitchen. The bathroom opened off the living room–bedroom. Over his bed hung a huge picture of two men wrapped together in lovemaking—both of

them slim and beautiful, their faces taut with passion. I recognized one of them as my host. He motioned toward a chair,
and I sat down. He sat on the floor in front of me. I was fascinated that he had offered me his small, sheltered place.

"Do you want wine?" he asked, and when I nodded he got
up and returned with two glasses.

"My name is Tallent," he said. "I have seen you here taking pictures and writing."

"I'm Adam. I'm doing a piece on cemeteries. This one is
as fascinating as any I've seen."

He nodded and smiled a little.

"We get a lot of tourists here, most all of them come to see
Marie Laveau's resting place. They stand and laugh and talk
and show her no respect. She, who is still filled with the magic
and who can share it." He pulled his long legs up with his
arms about them. "But you are lonely for your friend, not
interested in my history lessons, no?" His voice had a slight
French or Cajun accent.

"How do you know about him?" I asked, suddenly much
more aware of just how drunk I was.

"Perhaps you should move on and find someone else.
Maybe that is what he would want," Tallent said softly.

"I want no one else. David was my heart," I said, and the
tears burned my eyes. The boy nodded and was silent for a
while. Then he said, "I had someone too. Someone who loved
me and who is gone. Someone who is never far from me, or I
from him." I wondered if that explained why he was always
here with the dead. Then he went on.

"He died uselessly, protecting me, and it did no good, except
to kill him. Now he is still and quiet, and I am lost. He was my
heart and my life. We were together since we were children."

He raised his eyes to me, and I saw his tears, tearing him
to pieces. His eyes were brimming, and his mouth quivered.
The muscles in his face moved as he spoke. He was so fragile
and beautiful that I wanted to take him into my arms.

"You can, you know," he said, reading my thoughts, it seemed. Or had I spoken out loud? "I will allow you to love me. I will become anyone you want me to be. I will be your David."

I felt a slight chill run over me. And I was suddenly angry. Angry at him for tormenting me with his foolish games, his weirdness, and his beauty. My head felt heavy, and my arms and legs didn't want to work. "What the fuck is your problem? You are a ghoul! You know that? You hang out in a cemetery and talk this crazy shit. You are damn freaky!" I tried to stand and to leave him, but my body was very weak. Had he drugged me?

"Perhaps you are here because you too are closer to the dead than the living," he said.

I looked at him, and he was on his feet. My vision dimmed, and my head ached. His entire body seemed to burn with a faint luminescence. The light outside the cottage dimmed, and he glowed brighter as the stolen light moved to him. It seemed as if light sparked from his fingertips. I could hear his voice but not the words. Then he pulled his shirt off over his head and I saw his chest, with his hard-brown nipples and a light dusting of black hair and the fine line that ran down his stomach and into his jeans.

He slowly unzipped them and wiggled them down from his hips. He wore no underwear, and I was staring at his hard thighs and the black clipped pubes that surrounded his thick, long, dark, uncut dick and the heavy balls that hung behind them. He knelt before me and placed his fingertips to my temples. His fingers were soothing, and I was suddenly very tired and happy, like a small child after a day of playing. I wanted to be carried to my bed.

I stared into the strange boy's eyes. He leaned over and kissed me, and I reached out for him. I felt the stubble of his dark beard and smelled his skin. I saw his full lips, slightly parted and upturned at the corners. His hair felt slippery, and it gleamed. His touch was demanding. He pulled me to my feet and led me to his bed.

I stood beside it as he unbuttoned my shirt and took it off. He touched my nipples, gently at first and then with sharp pinches that ran to my dick and made it jump and twitch. He kissed me again, then licked up my neck to my face. He gave me light little kisses on my eyelids and nose, and then his tongue moved back down my neck, down to the center of my chest, and I felt his fingers at my zipper. His tongue slid lower as he pushed my pants down, and my cock sprang out, hard, engorged, and dripping. He dropped to his knees, licking and pulling my pubes with his teeth, taking one ball and then the other into his mouth. His thin fingers kneaded my ass cheeks, and I felt him spread them as his mouth took my dick. He slid me far back into his throat and sucked me slowly and deeply. I felt one finger at my hole, poking and feeling and slowly tracing the rim of my anus. Desire made me weak. I looked down, and he was gazing up at me with my cock deep in his throat. I twisted strands of his hair in my fingers. He slipped a finger into my hole and then another as his mouth moved faster and harder on my cock. I felt the come start to rise out of my balls, and then he stopped.

He stood and pushed me back onto the bed and lowered himself onto me. I felt the tip of my cock at his hole as he straddled me, and then he lowered himself farther and I entered his hot, velvety gut. He leaned over and kissed me, pushing his sweet-tasting tongue into my mouth and across my teeth. Then he sat up, reached behind him, and pulled on my balls with one hand, pinched my nipples with the other, all the time riding my pounding dick. His head was thrown back, and I could see the tender place at the base of his throat.

Tallent's eyes were glassy and his mouth open as he fucked himself on me. His skin felt like silk as I stroked his chest then reached for his cock. It was huge and hard, and he groaned when I took it and began to stroke him. I pinched his perfect little nipples and alternated between stroking him and rubbing my thumb over the head of his dick. Precome drizzled from it. I thrust my hips and he moved with me, riding me as I milked him closer to orgasm. Abruptly he stopped and pulled himself off me. The scent of us filled the room as he stepped off the side of the bed and stood up. He reached under the bed, removed a small whip, and handed it to me.

Then he crawled up onto the bed on his hands and knees. I looked at his perfect little ass, then I drew back and hit him across it with the whip. He made a small noise, and I hit him again. I moved behind him and looked down as I pushed my cock into his ass. I began to move, matching the touch of the whip across his back and shoulders with my thrusts. After a minute I felt my balls snap up, and then I filled him with my come. I rested a minute and then pulled out of him. His cock was swollen and purple, and he made small grunting sounds as he hunched the air. I whipped him again as I reached between his legs from the back and grabbed his nuts, pulling and releasing. When he came, his hot spurts perfectly matched the rhythm of the little whip across his beautiful ass.

I threw it down and pulled him into my arms. He fitted himself against me with his head against my chest, both of us sticky with come, and I pulled the sheet over us. Sometime later I awoke and looked at the boy, and it was David's face that I saw. But I was too exhausted to question it.

The sun woke me the next morning, and I sat bolt upright, expecting to see Tallent and the little cottage. But I was alone in my bed in the apartment. I threw my feet over the edge and rubbed my aching eyes. The sour taste of old liquor rose in my throat, and I barely made it to the toilet to throw up. I showered, washing away the dried come on my chest, and then dried off, staggered to the kitchen, and started some coffee.

I settled into a chair on the balcony. The warm, humid wind rustled the leaves of the banana tree in the courtyard below me. The empty ache was back stronger than ever. I had no memory of returning from the cemetery. Had I even gone there? Had I whipped and fucked the beautiful boy that lived there? I had never struck anyone in my life, and my face burned with shame at how much I had enjoyed whipping him. Or was I simply so drunk that I dreamed the whole thing, beating myself off and giving into my grief and longing? Did I see David there because I wanted to punish him for leaving?

My head began to clear with the second cup of coffee. It had to be the boy. That thin, strange, beautiful little sex toy had drugged me, let me fuck and whip him. My cock hardened as I thought of him. He was just another strange occupant of this strange city, another to whom I had given supernatural powers. I was attracted to him: to his long, graceful, silky limbs, his hard little ass in his tight faded jeans, to his flat stomach and chest beneath his white T. I liked his cold, black eyes, his sensitive mouth, and his fine nose. I wanted to touch his forearms, kiss his full, sensual lips, and fuck his little ass again.

Tallent was cleaning the alley beside Marie Laveau's tomb when I got to the cemetery. I watched him as he touched the tomb, tracing the groups of three Xs with his fingers. He did not touch the chicken bones, candles, and flowers that were placed before it. I watched him lean against it for a few seconds as his hand slipped down his stomach to his bunched basket.

He stroked himself through the faded cloth with his thumb for a few seconds. Then he pushed himself up, and I followed him back to the cottage. I stood outside for a long time thinking of David and me and of the boy inside. I was still standing there when he opened the door. I walked in and sat in the same chair as the night before. Tallent brought me a cup of coffee mixed with hot milk and placed it before me on the table. His long hair was caught back at the nape of his neck. I had not seen a man as beautiful as him in many years.

We sipped the coffee in silence for a few minutes. I drank in the sight of him as well as the coffee.

"I can be who you want. I don't have to be me," he said softly. "I need someone, and I—"

"Why do you think you have to be someone else? You are beautiful and smart and you have your own gifts to offer. Any man would want you, Tallent."

"Long ago I learned that I can do some things, and see and hear things differently from others. Things that I do not always want to hear or see or know. I want to be like others, not just some freak that deserves to be punished, some *thing* that is evil and unwanted. Even my family was frightened of me. They called me a son of Marie Laveau. So I came here. They are not afraid of me here, these dead. They are my friends. But sometimes I want to be with the living. I want a hand upon me, touching me, wanting me. Sometimes I want the light of another."

His eyes were glassy with memories of his self-imposed punishment and isolation, and when I stood, he drew back as if afraid, clutching his hands to his chest. He looked like a sulking child.

"I'm not afraid of you, Tallent. I see you as very beautiful and very desirable, and you are frightened of what is perhaps a unique gift. I would like to get to know you, to love you without having you try to be someone else. I want you to leave the dead here as I will have to leave my dead one behind."

He moved in front of me and knelt, leaned over, and rested his head against my chest. I stroked that shiny silk hair, then put my arms around him and pulled him to me.

"Come with me, Tallent. Come with me to my place. Stay there awhile and we can talk and love. Maybe we can find what we are looking for, what we both need."

I felt him nod. I pulled him to his feet, then picked him up and carried him to his bed. This time I undressed him, taking time to suck and nibble on his nipples. I passionately kissed his eyelids, his dark brows, and then I removed the rest of our clothing. I felt his cock grow thick and hard. His hands were touching my face. I ran my hands down his stomach, stroking his inner thighs, his sharp hipbones, and his stomach. The tip of his cock brushed my forearm. I lifted his long legs and looked between his cheeks at his tight little hole. It was pink and hairless and quivering. I leaned down and placed my face between his cheeks with my tongue at his hole. I hardened my tongue and pushed it into him. I felt him twitch and heard him moan. I worked his hole for a while and then pushed in two fingers. He was tossing his head and groaning. I twisted my fingers and then pushed in a third. The precome was oozing from his dick in a steady stream as I stroked his prostate. I grabbed his cock with my other hand and ran my tongue over the end as I pulled back the dark foreskin. When I looked at his face, I saw that his eyes were open and staring, his face twisted with passion. I alternated between his asshole, cock, and balls. I removed my fingers and pushed my cock into him all the way to my balls on the first stroke.

I felt him tighten, his body shuddering as he took my long cock. I fucked him slowly at first and then twisted and moved from side to side as I thrust faster and faster between his cheeks. I stroked his cock very slowly, holding off making him come. Tallent whimpered like a small kid, the veins standing out in his fine neck. I pounded his little ass in that position for a while and then pulled out and turned him over. I pushed my dick into him and reached around to his throbbing length. I stroked him hard, and I felt his balls pull up against his body, and he came all over his chest and the sheets. His ass ring began to spasm, and that yanked the come out of me. We lay in each other's arms on the damp sheets for a while until the sun was getting low and the shadows long. Then I kissed him and we dressed.

When we walked out to the cemetery he clutched his small

sack of belongings in one hand. I held his other hand in mine. I stopped for a second at Marie Laveau's crypt, and with my fingernail I carved three small Xs into it. My thanks to the Voodoo Queen for my beautiful, living gift from the City of the Dead.

A New Puppy
by Simon Sheppard

OK, I confess: I'd never seen anything as cute as Sean before.

When he first contacted me in the online chat room, when I first read his profile, I got more than a little nervous. He was just past 18, his profile said; this made him legal, but this also made him very young. Legal or no, he was more than young enough to be my son.

"hiya," he said, the word appearing in that little on-screen window that holds, on occasion, so much promise but more often than not is filled with bullshit.

"How you doing?" I typed back.

"kewl. how r u?"

Not a promising beginning. I spend half my life working with words. Correctly spelled words.

"Fine, thanks."

"watz up?"

"Just cruising." I was looking for an actual fuck–type meeting that night, not a semiliterate conversation with a boy who lived hundreds of miles away. I was in San Francisco. Sean, his profile said, was in Anaheim. Along with Disneyland.

"me 2"

I was beginning to feel like I was chatting up the Artist Formerly Known as Prince.

Sean continued, "im in2 older dewdz."

At which point my crotch and my brain parted ways. I was getting hard, rapidly.

"And?" I was playing it cagey, in case his parents were watching over his shoulder.

"i want u 2 fuk me"

There it was then. I was unzipping my pants.

I told him about my writing, my kinks, my open relationship.

He said I was "kewl."

He told me about living with his parents, his aiming for premed, his girlfriend.

"Want to swap pics?" I asked.

When I downloaded his picture, I gasped. I must have. I'd never seen anything as cute as Sean before. He was standing, shirtless, in front of an ocean and a sky, both as blue as a David Hockney pool. His head was cocked, hair jutting wildly from it, his face innocent, smiling, perfectly lovely, perfectly 18. His body was lean—thin, even—and hairless. The sunlight molded itself around tight pecs, prominent nipples, and impossibly low-fat abs. His pants were riding, as was the fashion, halfway down his hips, showing a strip of red plaid boxers, then baggy khakis. It looked like he had a nice basket, maybe.

I made myself breathe.

We chatted for a while. Sean was still in the closet and living at home while he finished college. He'd only had sex with a few guys, fellow students, mostly jerking off, and one or two of them had sucked his cock. Lucky boys.

He had a girlfriend. They had sex. But he knew he was queer. Queerer—he wanted to be an older man's sex slave. He wanted to be stripped down, collared, tied up, used, and fucked. He was so young. So innocent.

He sent me another photo, one of a skinny young guy like him being tied up by two burly men in leather.

"yeah i mean i kno itz not real and posed and all but it getz me off thinkin of bein like that"

"I would do that to you, Sean."

"yeah I kno u would u r so kewl"

I couldn't help it. I shot off, messily, all over myself.

In the weeks that followed Sean and I chatted often. I was always the one to send the first Instant Message when he came up on my Buddy List, but every time he seemed glad to see me, always had time for me, time to chat.

I was beginning to like him, for all the right reasons and some of the wrong ones. Because he was young and beautiful and still confused and sometimes unhappy. Because I seemed to help him, provide a sympathetic ear, speak from experience, and validate his desires. And because I couldn't help imagining him sitting at his computer while we chatted, upstairs in his parents' house, the door locked, his hard dick jutting from his baggy boxers, him spitting on his hand, jacking off. Was this last one a Right Reason or a Wrong Reason? Did I have to decide?

He seemed so sweet. But would he have seemed as sweet if his body weren't so perfect or his smile so bright? It didn't really matter anyway. I was his benevolent, more-than-a-little-twisted, online gay uncle. He was my teenage fantasy. It was safe. He would never get the permission, the leisure, the balls to fly up to San Francisco and make our imaginings real. We would never really meet. And that was probably for the best.

"I want you to know something, Sean…I mostly go online to actually meet guys and hardly ever maintain long-term cyber-only relationships. But knowing you gives me a great deal of pleasure…I know you don't think you're special, but you're special to me."

"kewl and do u meet a lot of guyz"

"More than I should. :-)"

"kewl so like how u do that i mean im askin 4 real how do u meet online that way"

"Depends on the man, Sean. It's usually not that tough, assuming the guy's not playing games."

"kewlness"

"And usually it gets pretty kinky, if that's what he wants."

"hmmm i like the idea of bein ur servant in ALL aspects"

"Yeah, but if we met, do you think you would go through with it, boy?"

"yes sir sir but cautiously"

"No problem." How could I be falling so hard for someone I'd never met, whose voice I'd never even heard, whom I'd only seen in one frozen oceanside moment?

"since trust is a part there would b a start that would b more like a new pup when u get one"

"Yes, but that's not going to happen, at least not for quite a while."

"o yes it iz"

"What?"

"I've decided," Sean typed, "to tell my parents some story and fly up to San Francisco. Is next weekend OK?"

I was brought up short. Too fast, too sudden, too scary. "And then what, Sean?"

"u r the writer. Mayk up the rest."

I'm in the arrivals lounge at SFO. Sean shows up, baggy clothes, carrying a backpack. Crooked smile on his face. He doesn't look exactly like his E-mailed image. Of course not. In person he's slighter, even thinner than his picture. His face is less perfect, which just makes him sexier.

"Hiya, Dad," he says.

I give him a great big hug. I don't care who sees it; for all anyone knows we might actually be father and son. Then I kiss him directly on his lips. He pulls back, blushing.

"Hey, Sean. Good to see you."

He looks in my eyes, smiles broadly, leans over, and kisses my lips. I'm getting a hard-on.

"Let's go back to your place and fuck," Sean says. Hearing him talk, you wouldn't know that "fuck" is spelled f-u-k.

Sean has never been on a motorcycle before. The ride up 280 goes well enough, but I can tell from his body that he's a little nervous. Still, his arms are wrapped tight around me, his crotch pressing into my butt. All this is new to him. I wonder what he's thinking. We get to my place.

"Dude," he says, "that ride was fun."

"Hella fun," I say.
"Hella fun."

"You hungry?" I ask when we reach my living room.
Looking in my eyes, Sean reaches for my crotch.
"Hey," I say, not believing I'm saying it, "slow down."
"Why? You've got a hard-on."
"Do you?"
"Yeah," says the adorable thin boy. "Want to see it?"
Without waiting for an answer, he unzips his saggy chinos and pulls out his dick. It is, like the rest of him, impressively cute.

Along about here I'm thinking, *What the fuck have I gotten myself into?* And then we're kissing. He kisses well for such a young kid. I hold onto his narrow body and fall in something like love. Everything is just so fucking spectacular. Like the stars.

"Can I suck your cock, Sir?" Sean asks.

The idea of this boy, this boy I've wanted so fiercely, whom I thought I'd never meet, the idea of watching my cock sliding into his mouth, it's almost more than I can bear. But he drops to his knees, unbuttons my jeans, and it's real—Sean from Anaheim is sucking my cock.

You can tell the ones who only think they're sub bottoms: They play with themselves without a second thought. Sean, though, has all his attention on me. His hands are on my thighs as he takes my dick down his throat with surprising expertise.

"Enough, boy. Strip," I say. "Then get on your knees. I'll be right back."

I go to the bedroom to fetch a few things; I like the idea that when I get back to the living room, I'll find young Sean there, stripped naked, kneeling on the carpet. My carpet. My boy. My fantasy.

When I walk back into the living room, there he is: his young, thin body stripped bare, his hands gripped behind his back, and his eyes cast down. He looks every inch the bottom boy; either he's been reading S/M porn or his instincts are impeccable.

His cock isn't huge, maybe about six inches, but it's standing straight up, and as I walk toward him I see a drop of precome glinting at its tip.

"Welcome to San Francisco, Sean," I say.

"Thanks, Daddy," Sean says, without looking up at me. "Thanks, Sir."

I'm standing inches from him; my prick, still out of my pants, just above his beautiful face. I take the broad leather collar I've brought from the bedroom, position it around his neck, pull the end through the buckle, tighten it, fasten it. Sean sighs and shivers. My cock is throbbing hard.

I walk behind him. His back is tapered, slender, just this side of bony. His thin wrists are crossed at the small of his back. I'm shaken by a wave of lust, maybe love. By the need to have power over this cute, cute boy.

I'm still carrying the handcuffs I brought from the bedroom. Leather restraints are better for long-term bondage, but metal cuffs make for great theater. I kneel behind Sean. At the first touch of cold metal he jumps slightly. I surround a wrist with a cuff then ratchet it down slowly, each metallic click making it all seem real, final. He's here. He's naked. He's mine. Click. Click. Click.

I ratchet the second cuff down. Click. Cold steel against delicate wrists. I touch his ass for the first time. I stroke the smooth, round flesh.

"Thank you, Sir," Sean says. He's still trembling.

I allow myself to wonder just what he's feeling and how much responsibility I bear.

"You doing OK, Sean?"

"Yes, Sir. May I suck your Daddy cock some more, Sir?"

I've got to hand it to the kid, he knows just what to say. I stand up and stick my cock in his face. He opens his mouth wide and gobbles it down. I grab the collar and guide my shaft in and out of his wet, hot mouth. Suddenly I want to fucking use him for real, just fuck the innocence out of him. Fuckin' boy. I shove deep into his throat. He starts to gag. I keep my cock in there for a second, just to show him who's boss. He tries his best to take it. I pull on the collar. He starts to squirm away. He's drooling. I slap his face. He groans.

What the hell am I doing? I pull out. He gasps for air. His dick is still standing straight up. I stroke his face.

Just then his beeper goes off. It's sitting on top of the pile of his clothes in the corner of the room.

"I'd better check that," Sean from Anaheim says. "Sir."

I go pick up the pager and show him the readout.

"It's my folks," he says. "I should call them back. They don't know where I am."

I unlock the cuffs; they're biting into his wrists anyway.

"Phone's over there."

He pick it up and dials. "Mom?" he says. "It's Sean. You called?" He's standing there naked, a collar around his neck, his cock still hard, and he's talking to his mother. I've got to give the kid credit—he has guts.

"Yeah, I'm fine," he's saying. "Listen, I think I'm going to be spending the night over here at Brian's, OK?" His naked body is impossibly lithe, his limbs thin but graceful, the angle of his hipbones catching the light. "Bye, Mom," he says, "I love you too."

"I bet she's younger than I am," I say. He tells me her age; she is.

"I'm sorry," Sean says, "I just didn't want her to worry. And I arranged an alibi with my friend Brian." A lopsided grin. "He's clueless why, though."

"Sean," I say, tucking my softening cock back in my pants, "maybe you should get dressed."

Sean looks puzzled. Maybe a little hurt, or is that my imagination?

"You're a really, really nice boy, and I like you a lot."

"So what's the problem?"

"I'm just worried that you're not, I don't know, ready for this." And am I?

Sean puts down the phone and walks over to me. He stands against me, looking into my eyes, and reaches for my belt. He unbuckles it, unbuttons my jeans, and pulls them down to mid thigh. My cock leaps up, intensely interested again.

"Fuck me, Daddy," 18-year-old Sean from Anaheim says. "Fuck me."

"And you've never been fucked before?"

He smiles. "I want you to be the first."

I strip down and sit on the sofa. "There's lube and rubbers over there," I say.

He unrolls a condom onto my cock. I usually find putting on a rubber to be distracting and irritating. Now, with this beautiful boy smoothing the tight latex down over my stiff flesh, it's bliss. He lubes me up.

"Let's grease up your ass as well, boy," I say. I hold out my hand and he squirts it full of lube. I reach around him and finger the crack of his ass, finding the tight, hot hole, loosening it gently with my slippery fingers. "Breathe, Sean," I say. "And want it." My finger is gliding in and out, but he's still tight, very tight. "Are you sure this is what you need?"

"Yes, Daddy."

"Then come sit on Daddy's lap." I think of him talking to his mother on the phone.

Sean climbs on my lap, straddles me, wraps his legs around my waist. We sit face-to-face, our hard dicks rubbing together, our faces inches apart.

"Can I kiss you, Daddy?" he asks.

His tongue enters my mouth, his breath fresh and sweet, a boy's breath. I reach around and grab his ass, lift him upward, positioning his hole just over the tip of my throbbing cock. His tongue still deep in my mouth, he lowers himself onto my dick, his hole tight and resistant. I stroke his face and push myself upward into his virgin ass. He wriggles around until my cock head is inside him. Our tongues do their wet dance. His mouth opens wide, and I shove my tongue into him, as far down his throat as I can. He slides down on Daddy's cock until it's all the way inside him. He pulls his face away and leans back slightly. I look at him, at Sean, my beautiful boy, a man young enough to be my son. In gratitude, astonishment, and fear, I stroke his face, his chest, play with his tits. I bend over and take a nipple in my mouth, lick it, flick the tip of my tongue against it, nibble at it, bite down gently, harder, stretch it out with my teeth, bite down until he gasps.

Then we're kissing again, and he's riding my cock—my cock buried deep inside his firm, young butt. And I reach around and slap his ass.

"Oh-h-h, yeah," he says.

I slap harder. I look down; his dick is spewing precome. Our bellies, mine hairy, his smooth, are soaking wet with it.

He's riding up and down on my dick now, his ass relaxing, accepting, hungry for a man's dick. I spank him with both hands, slapping his ass cheeks with resounding cracks.

"Oh Sir, oh Daddy Sir, I've needed this, I've wanted you Daddy, oh Daddy." Sean is speaking in tongues now, a holy roller with a dick up his butt. "Fuck my pussy my pussy my fucking pussy Sir oh Sir."

And I look at him and realize, with all my being, that here is this young, beautiful, hungry queer boy, the young man of my dreams, his half-formed boy's body shiny with sweat, and he's wearing my collar, and he's riding my dick, my man dick planted firmly inside him, his hunger, his innocence, need, and I can't help myself—much as I'd like to, I can't stop myself. "Oh, shit!" I scream. And I'm coming and coming, shooting off deep in his rich, warm darkness, and his young sperm is jetting upward, past eye level, landing on him, on me, on our faces, the sofa, everywhere.

A week later I was online. Sean's screen name came up on my Buddy List.

"Hi," I typed out in the Instant Message window.

"dewd!!! u r awesome watz up"

"Sean..." I typed out, and then I didn't know what else to say.

Fuckee
by Joel Valley

I usually venture out on the scene in search of love, but I have accepted that a fuck is usually the most I can expect. I can handle that. On a Thursday night in November 1992, however, the Curzon (Liverpool's one and only matte black bar) was dead, and even a fuck seemed unobtainable. It wasn't worth the effort of braving the November cold, but how was I to know that? It was depressing. Just 20 or so of us 30-somethings talking in small groups or standing alone against the wall. There wasn't a twinkie in sight.

In truth, we were all cruising each other, but we were all familiar faces. If I hadn't fucked any of those guys already, it was unlikely that I was ever going to, which was probably shortsighted of me, but, hell, that's what I felt. No one interested me and, although I knew the faces, I didn't really know anyone I could talk to. They were—like the matte black walls, the mirrors, the cigarette machine, the fruit machine, the bar counter, and the safer-sex posters—part of the fixtures and fittings. Regardless, I stuck it out in hopes that the man of my dreams might show up. By 1 A.M. it was obvious that he had better things to do on a Thursday evening. I accepted the fact and left to go home.

Outside it was cold, but I cheered myself with the thought that at least it wasn't raining. A cruel wind was blowing in from the Irish Sea, and the ground was icy. I buttoned my jacket, plunged my hands into its deep pockets, and walked toward the taxi stand 50 yards down Victoria Street. There was no queue, which was unusual, but then I realized there were no taxis, so why should there be a queue? It suddenly became evident that the only people who had made their way into the city center that night were the crotch-hungry, and as the attendance at the Curzon had proved, there were precious few of us. I found myself considering the idea of opening my own gay bar in the suburb where I live but then thought better.

I waited a few minutes, but still there was no sign of a taxi. In fact, there was no traffic at all. Bad weather has that effect in England, and I should have realized that. In the scheme of things, it isn't even relatively bad weather. What, for example, would the average Brit do when faced with a winter like those in Nova Scotia or Minnesota? Rather than stand in one spot and freeze, I thought it best to walk. Lime Street, the main drag, was a matter of minutes away. Surely there would be a better chance of finding a cab there.

I continued up Victoria Street toward Lime Street and came to the intersection with the entrance road to the Mersey tunnel. I crossed over and climbed the steps in to St. John's Gardens, which backs onto St. George's Hall. The Hall, some say, is the finest example of neoclassical architecture in Europe. The back of it, however, looked cold and foreboding.

As I progressed through the park, something suddenly caught my attention; an aberration in the light, perhaps. I stopped to make it out. I realized that what I saw was the frozen breath emanating from someone standing on the steps about 20 feet in front of me. My interest immediately perked; I felt my adrenaline rush, and my dick automatically stiffened. Do guys still cruise here despite the murders, the beatings, the video cameras, and the newly improved lighting system? I couldn't believe it. I ventured toward the steps, and there he stood facing the neoclassical facades of the Walker Art Gallery across from the Central Libraries. His back was toward me, so I couldn't make out his features. It was, however, obvious that he was a young guy: the purple jacket with NICHOLSON emblazoned across the back of it in yellow, the close-fitting Armani jeans, the chunky boots, the full head of short dark hair.

I approached as closely as possible without disturbing him and took a long, lingering look at the small, pert, beautifully formed globes of his ass. The back seam of his jeans traced his butt crack perfectly. As I took a few steps farther he realized my presence and turned immediately. He gasped and stared at me.

"Sorry, mate," I said.

"It's all right," he replied. His accent was deep and slightly husky, unlike the all-too-often high and campy accent I associate with many young Liverpudlian guys—gay or straight.

I smiled. He smiled back and nervously turned away.

"Mind if I join you?" I asked, and stood next to him.

"Sure, no problem, mate."

Our eyes met. He knew I was aware of his reason for being there. I winked at him, and he smiled back nervously before looking away.

He was taller than me. I'm 5 foot 7, so he must have been about 5 foot 9. He was slim without being skinny. His padded jacket made him seem broad, but his waist revealed the reality of his svelte torso. In the light I made out the features of his face: white, luminous, unblemished skin; brown eyes; a small but relatively wide nose; thin, dry lips. His slicked-back hair was short, dark-brown, and parted down the middle. He was maybe 19, 20, or maybe 21 even. He was gorgeous. He shivered and coughed.

"Been here long?" I asked.

"A little while," he said, turning to size me up again.

"Fucking freezing, eh?"

"You bet," he said, rubbing his hands together before cupping them to his face and breathing into them.

"Any luck?" I asked.

"Just you."

His reply initially deflated me, but then he smiled, and I knew that maybe the evening wouldn't be such a loss after all.

"Come here often?" A cliché, I know, but it's only a cliché because it works.

"Only me second time," he admitted.

"What brings you here tonight?"

"Been out with mates. It was naff, so made me excuses and got off. Felt horny so 'ere I am."

His frankness was a turn-on.

"You?" he inquired, staring into my eyes.

"Me? Well, I went to the Curzon. It was dead, so I left. Couldn't get a taxi on Victoria Street, so decided to walk to Lime Street. Cut through here and saw you."

"Right," he smiled.

"This has been the best part of my evening," I said.

He laughed.

"I'm not joking." His face reddened. "The Curzon was absolutely shite."

"Never been."

"Why's that? Good-looking guy like you'd bag off, no problem."

"Too risky. I don't wanna be seen going to gay bars."

He coughed again and rubbed his hands together.

"It's fucking freezing, ain't it, mate?" he said.

"Yeah, but we could always keep each other warm."

He flushed and looked down before laughing and smiling back at me. I moved closer to him and placed my hand on his right cheek of his ass. He leaned toward me and kissed me briefly on the lips.

"OK, but not here, eh? It's too cold."

"My place then?"

"It'll have to be. I live with me parents."

I turned to face him and pulled him into me. I kissed him properly, my tongue entering the warm moistness of his mouth. He tasted of beer (or maybe we both did). His lips were cold and dry, and I felt stubble on his chin. His arms pulled me close. I realized he was trembling; I wasn't sure if it was from the cold or nervousness. I slipped my hand down the back of his jeans, but the bushes behind us rustled and he pulled away.

"What was that?"

"Just the wind," I said.

His trembling was now visible.

"Can we go? I'm really cold."

"Sure. We'll have to walk to Lime Street to get a cab, though."

"I've got me car."

"Great. I'm Joe, by the way."

He offered his frozen hand. "I'm Dave."

We shook hands, which somehow seemed quaint.

"Me car's this way."

He quickly led me to his car, which was parked 20 or 30 yards away on William Brown Street. All of a sudden he turned and said, "Are you a fucker?"

I was momentarily taken aback. Did he mean Do you fuck or did he mean Are you gonna treat me like shit? After some hesitation I said, "Yeah, I'm a top. I fuck, if that's what you mean."

"Good," he said, and we climbed into his car.

I put my hand on his crotch and massaged the inside of his thigh as we drove toward the suburb where I live, but I realized he was unsure about it, so I stopped. He looked at me several times and smiled in between asking which way to go. Gradually his shivering ceased, and by the time we arrived at my house about 10 minutes later, he seemed warm and a little more at ease. He parked the car in the drive and we got out. He followed me to the front door.

"Nice place," he said.

"I'm not sure I agree."

Once inside he jumped on me, and we fell against the wall and he kissed me.

"You're eager," I said, coming up for air.

"Fuck me," he replied, and stuck his lips on me again.

"Don't you want some coffee or something first?" I managed to ask, as I pried him off me so I could stand up properly.

"No, just fuck me."

I turned the lights on and led him upstairs. Outside the bedroom he stopped and said, "You're definitely a fucker, right?"

"Yeah, why?"

" 'Cause I'm a fuckee."

"Right, best get you fucked then, eh?"

The moment we entered the bedroom, our clothes were literally ripped off and thrown to the floor. In a matter of what seemed seconds he was naked and all over me. It was too frantic.

"Fuck me now," he said.

"Hang on," I said as I reached over from the bed, onto which we had fallen, to the bedside cabinet. I removed some condoms and a tube of K-Y, which I placed on the bed next to us.

"Fuck me!" Dave demanded, grabbing my cock and licking my chest.

"In good time." I removed myself from his grasp, stood up, and looked at him lain on the bed. His body was slim but toned—definition without bulk. He was hairless except for his dark pubic hair. His skin was pale and unblemished. His cock was short, thick, uncut, and hard.

"Turn over," I said.

He obeyed. I climbed onto the bed and nibbled the nape of his neck before slowly running my tongue in swirling motions down his spine to the base of his back. He groaned. I parted his small, firm ass cheeks and ran my tongue down to his rosebud sphincter. I pulled my mouth away then spat, letting my saliva form a tiny pool before slowly working my tongue into him. He initially tensed, denying me access, but then relaxed and allowed my tongue full entry. I grabbed his hips and pulled his ass into my face. He groaned again as I worked my tongue in and out of him.

"Fuck me, Joe," he demanded.

"OK," I replied, standing up on my knees and reaching for the K-Y. I put the K-Y on my tongue and shot a squirt into the palm of my hand; the lube tasted oddly sweet. I threw the tube back onto the bed and applied the lube in my hand to my stiff cock before kneeling back down and placing my face into his ass. I parted his ass cheeks again and pushed my tongue into his delectable hole. He pushed his ass against my face, and his own hands pulled his cheeks apart as I reached under him to stroke his rigid cock and fuzzy balls. He groaned as my tongue applied the K-Y to his asshole. I raised myself again, grabbed a condom, and expertly removed it, ripping open the foil packet and sheathing my stiff cock.

Dave was now facedown on the bed with his body weight resting on his elbows. He had raised his ass, and his legs were slightly spread. Changing my mind, I reached down and pulled him up off the bed. He was reluctant.

"No, not like that. Stand up," I demanded. He obeyed.

I wrapped my arms around him and stroked his left nipple with one hand while grabbing his cock with the other. Dave shuddered and groaned as I worked his stiff prick. He slipped a hand behind and directed my cock to his asshole. He gasped as I entered him, then momentarily tensed before relaxing, allowing my cock to slip inside him. He was tight, very tight. I moved my cock deep inside and he bent forward, placing his arms onto the bed. I slowly withdrew my cock and entered him again. He writhed and pushed his butt into me. I repeated this several times, then I guided his body forward and to the side a little. He took the hint and climbed onto the bed. My legs were on either side of the corner of the bed. Dave was on his hands and knees on top of the bed. I began to pump my cock frantically in and out of his tight hole.

"Fuck me," he groaned. "Fuck me."

I watched my cock slip in and out of Dave as I fucked his ass. I saw his tensed, V-shaped back, leaned forward, and I kissed the nape of his flawless neck.

"Roll onto your back," I whispered.

We somehow managed the maneuver without becoming unhitched. I was then able to pull him toward me, resting his lower back over the corner of the bed, and fuck his ass harder and deeper. I pulled him into me and thrust rhythmically while he held onto my shoulders. He occasionally leaned into me and slipped his hand down the crack of my ass to tickle my balls from behind. My thrusts grew faster and deeper and harder until I could no longer control myself.

"I'm gonna come," I said.

"Go on. Go on, shoot your load."

A few deep, hard thrusts later, I exploded into him. Breathless, I collapsed on top of him. After a moment I raised myself up and was about to withdraw.

"No," Dave said, "not yet. I wanna come with you in me."

I kept my cock in him even though I wasn't able to keep it hard. He stroked his thick dick while I fondled his soft, hairy balls and caressed his thighs. He came after just a few strokes, his come squirting from his swollen cock in an arc and landing on his hairless chest.

Dave lay before me smiling, content and spent.

"That was great," he said. "It hurt at first, but then it was OK—not like I imagined, but great anyway."

"You mean you'd never been fucked?"

"This is me first time. The other guy I had wanted me to fuck him. He was a fuckee, he said. I did it, but it was naff 'cause I'm a fuckee too. I've always known that."

After disposing of the condom we lay in each other's arms, savoring the warmth of each other. He stroked my chest and played with the hair on my thighs. I assumed he would stay the night and we would have a repeat performance in the morning, but as I was nodding off he suddenly got up.

"I gotta go," he said.

I watched as he dressed, seeing his perfect little ass disappear into his white Calvin Klein briefs. After putting on his boots he said, "Thanks, I'll be seeing you."

"Hang on, take my number," I said, picking up my trousers and rummaging in the pockets for my wallet. "Give me a call. Maybe we can do this again sometime." I handed him a card.

"Sure," he said. "Sure. No need to get up. I'll let meself out."

"OK, see ya, Dave."

"See ya, Joe."

He was gone.

He never did call, but, being a realist, I never expected him to.

A Continental Summer
by Sean Wolfe

It's been a long summer, to say the least. Don't ask me why, but when I made the decision to audition for the U.S. tour of Continental Singers 11 months ago and ride around in a bus with 37 other high school and college kids—performing in a different city every night for three months—it seemed like just the thing to lift my spirits after my first year in college.

Getting to know all the other kids my age from all over the United States, playing pranks on our married "chaperone" directors, and seeing new cities are wonderful experiences. Our sponsors, who are members of the schools and churches where we sing, always treat us like we walk on water—and what 20-year-old doesn't get off on that?

But it's a lot more work than I'd ever imagined. We're trapped in a cramped bus—with no bathroom—that's on its last leg and has a temperamental air conditioning system that halfway works maybe two days a week. That might be all right if we were touring Alaska but makes it really rough when we've spent the majority of our time in the hot and humid Southern states in the middle of summer.

There are 19 girls on my particular tour, and, of course, they can't calibrate their menstrual cycles, so it seems someone is always having a bad case of PMS. The 19 guys on the tour (including myself) probably use more gel and hair spray than the girls and just can't be bothered with their petty female problems. Between the bitching and moaning of the PMS-ing girls and the whining and groaning of lovesick boys who left their girlfriends back home for the summer, our 10- to 14-hour bus rides every day are an unimaginable joy, let me tell you.

When we arrive at our performance site each night, the

girls bitch and cry about having to lug their suitcases into dressing rooms and the guys bitch and cry about having to set up the bleachers and heavy equipment. Then we put on our "Continental Smiles" as we eat the potluck dinner provided before performances and have about an hour to dress and get ready to sing and dance our little hearts out.

It was a lot of fun the first few weeks, but it's really gotten on my nerves lately. Except for our staying with host families. I like that a lot. It's interesting to meet people from other parts of the country, and they're always so nice to us. Each family volunteers to take two to four of us into their home after the shows, feed us the next morning, and get us back to the bus for ungodly-early departures. Once the larger group is broken down into smaller groups of the same sex, we are much more tolerable and usually have fun together.

I was almost one of the lovesick boys who'd left his girlfriend behind for the summer. My preacher's daughter, no less. But we split up six months ago, when I was sure I'd be gone for the whole summer, which disrupted her plans of getting engaged, apparently. It turned out to be a good thing, though, because about halfway through the tour I began experiencing those feelings most of us do in our teens and early adulthood and found myself daydreaming about a couple of the guys on my tour. I could lie and say I tried to suppress those thoughts, but the truth is they are probably the only thing that has kept me sane the last half of the tour.

Justin is 22 years old and graduated from UCLA with a degree in music performance a week before we started touring. Besides being a musical genius on keyboards (he learned our entire two-hour concert in just a couple of rehearsals), he is every girl's dream and about half the guys' wet dreams. He's the epitome of Mr. All-America: Tall, lean, and muscular, he has blond hair and blue eyes, long eyelashes, a golden tan, and a pearl-white perfect smile. Everyone on our tour loves him, and he seems to loves all of us too. He's one of those guys who can talk nonstop for hours but never irritate anyone.

Richard is just the opposite but somehow has managed to consume about as much of my daydreaming time as Justin. Rich is 19 years old, about 5 foot 7 inches of solid muscle (it's obvious he spends a lot of time at the gym), with jet-black hair and large, beautiful brown almond-shaped eyes that always seem a little sad. His father is Puerto Rican and his mother is Filipina, which accounts for his gorgeous, smooth, brown skin. He's pretty shy, for the most part, but when he opens his mouth to sing he blows us all away. He has a solo in our show that leaves not a dry eye in the house.

The last time I was host-paired with Justin was three weeks ago in Tulsa, Okla. Our hosts were the Kendalls, a fairly young couple whose only son was also on tour with the Continental Singers but in a different group than ours (there are 15 groups touring different parts of the world).

After our show we all went to the Kendalls' home and talked for about an hour before heading to bed shortly after 11.

I was nervous about stripping down to my underwear for bed in front of Justin that night. I'd been lusting after him since the first night we spent together and was sure he'd be able to tell and get me kicked off the tour. But he talked softly as he undressed in front of me and climbed into bed still chatting away as though he were none the wiser.

I pulled the covers up to my chin and tried to keep the small talk going for a little while, then said good night. I noticed Justin was tossing and turning restlessly for quite a while, but I figured he was just wound up from the performance and couldn't sleep. About an hour after we lay down, my eyelids grew heavy and I drifted off to sleep.

I'm not sure how long I'd been asleep when I woke up. I was a little disoriented, not knowing where I was at first. I blinked a few times and remembered we were in Tulsa as I turned onto my back. Justin was not in bed beside me, and I rubbed my eyes to adjust to the darkness and orient myself a little better.

That's when I noticed the light coming from the doorway to the bathroom that connected to our room. I thought Justin had probably gotten up to pee, but after a couple of minutes when I didn't hear any tinkling sound, I got out of bed and walked to the bathroom door. Sometimes the food provided at our potlucks isn't the best, and I was just about to knock on the door and ask Justin if he was sick when I heard a low moaning sound from inside the bathroom. The door was open just a couple of inches, so I peeked in.

Justin was sitting on the floor, naked, with his back against the bathtub. His long legs were spread wide, and one hand was wrapped around his cock, sliding up and down slowly. His head was tilted back and his eyes were closed. His top teeth lightly bit his bottom lip as he gently massaged his hard cock and moaned softly.

I'd dreamed about his dick many times over the past few weeks, and each time his cock looked almost exactly the same—long and thick with big, bulging veins. I guess that's what I expected to see on a guy who was in every way perfect. I was a little surprised to see that in the flesh it wasn't quite what I'd expected. It was very average, actually; probably the only part of Justin that was average. Maybe 6½ inches long fully hard, average thickness, cut.

Not that its averageness made it any less appealing to me. On the contrary, just seeing it pulse in his hand and hearing him moan in delight made my heart race wildly. As my own cock grew hard and pressed against my underwear, I felt a large drop of precome ooze out of my piss slit and cover my dick head. I sat on the floor and crossed my legs, making myself more comfortable so I could watch Justin get himself off.

He slid his hand up and down his hard cock slowly and lovingly, seemingly content to take his time, which was fine with me. A couple of times it looked like he was going to shoot, but then he stopped and moved his hand away from his dick and took a deep breath. I got a clear shot of his full cock when he did that and found it hard to swallow as I watched it pulse against his belly.

I reached down to touch my own dick a couple of times but realized I would cream almost instantly if I did, so I just left my dick inside my underwear and returned to watching Justin.

He was in his own little world, oblivious to the fact he was being watched. He repositioned himself a couple of times on the floor to make himself more comfortable, and a couple of times he reached down with his free hand and massaged his balls and the area around his ass as he stroked his cock. I don't know how he kept from shooting several times before he did.

But he obviously had other plans, and what he did next sent me over the edge. He lay flat on his back, lifted his ass off the floor, and threw his legs behind his head so that his dick was only a couple of inches from his mouth. He moaned a little louder, and grabbed his cock in one hand and the back of one of his legs in the other. He pulled down on his leg until the head of his dick just barely touched his lips. I swear I stopped breathing, and I'm sure the only thing that kept him from hearing me gasp was that his own moaning was even louder.

His tongue licked the head of his cock a couple of times, and then he slowly sucked the head all the way into his mouth. I'd never imagined this was even possible; I was mesmerized as I watched Justin lick and suck his own dick head. My heartbeat tripled in my chest and my cock pounded against my underwear as I watched secretly from behind the door.

Justin's face turned a little red as he moved both hands to press harder against his legs, and I watched more of his cock slide slowly inside his mouth. He was now quivering a little as he had a couple of inches of his own dick in his mouth, and I could hear him sucking on it pretty strongly.

He opened his eyes and moaned a little louder, and then I saw his entire body convulse for a moment. He stayed in that position for a few seconds and then let go of his legs, and his cock slowly pulled out of his mouth. With his dick head only an inch away from his mouth, he squeezed his cock with one hand, and a long final drop of white silky come trickled from his cock and onto his tongue.

Justin swallowed hard and took a deep sigh as his legs unfolded and his body slumped limply onto the floor. I realized I was still sitting there, entranced with Justin's show, and stood up to tiptoe as quietly as possible back to the bed. It wasn't until that moment that I realized the front of my shorts were soaked with hot, sticky come. I hadn't even touched my own cock and I'd shot a huge load all over myself!

I didn't have time to rummage through my suitcase for a new pair of underwear, since I heard Justin pulling his own on; and so I just ran and jumped into bed, sticky and wet, and pulled the covers over my shoulders, pretending to be asleep.

Justin was in bed and asleep in less than two minutes. I, on the other hand, spent the rest of the night sticky, confused, excited, and unable to sleep.

I've been trying hard not to stare at Justin too much the next few days. I couldn't believe how he kept right on talking and laughing and singing as if nothing out of the ordinary had happened, but I resolved not to be the one to let it slip. I could be just as good an actor as he. I did, however, make absolutely sure my roomies were 100% asleep before I found it necessary to slip away quietly into the bathrooms of kind hosts from that point on.

Next week is our last week of tour. We're back in sunny California now, and emotions are at an all-time high. We seem to have forgotten all about the bitching and moaning we've been doing the last half of the tour, and now we're all crying that we don't want it to end. Addresses are being exchanged, promises never to forget one another—all the same old crap.

Last night's concert was exceptional. Not only have we had three months to perfect it, but it was in Richard's home church, so everyone was that much more hyped. It's always exciting when you perform in a member's hometown, and everyone goes out of their way to make it special.

Richard was just as quiet and reserved yesterday as he always is, sitting alone near the back of the bus and writing in his journal. Everyone has a special place in their heart for him. He was all jittery about performing for his home crowd, but he kept cool the whole time. When we arrived, we unpacked and set up our equipment as usual, and then Roger, our assistant director, gave out our host assignments.

I was a little surprised when I learned I would be staying with Richard at his home. I figured he'd just get to stay by himself. I looked over at him when our names were called out, but he didn't even look up from his journal, so I didn't think anything else about it.

Like I said, the concert went great. Richard's solo drew a rousing standing ovation, and he blushed as he walked back to the bleachers and joined the rest of us. He was so cute. Several of us were teary-eyed as we watched him. We all know he'll be famous someday, but at the moment he was just one of us.

After the concert we tore down the equipment and loaded the bus, and then headed to our host homes. It was a little later than usual, since everyone in Richard's church wanted to chat a little longer than most after the concert, and we were exhausted.

Richard's parents, Mr. and Mrs. Gomez, were the perfect hosts. They could tell Richard and I were tired, and though I'm sure they'd have loved to stay up and talk for hours; they only kept us up for about a half hour before they went to bed.

Richard showed me his room and we looked through some of his high school yearbooks, laughing and joking around at how cool everyone thought they were. We had to board the bus early the next morning, though, so we decided to hit the sack fairly early.

I offered to sleep on the couch so Richard could have his bed to himself, but he refused and said it was more than big enough for the both of us. We undressed and lay in bed next to each other, making small talk for a few minutes and then growing quiet.

I was just about to fall asleep when I felt Richard roll onto his side and face me. I was on my side too, with my back to him, and could feel his soft breath on the back of my neck. I kept my eyes closed, not knowing whether he was awake or asleep, my heart doubling its pounding in my chest. I could smell the sweet fragrance of his cologne and his minty breath on my neck, and I struggled to keep my breathing normal. I wasn't sure what was happening, but I figured feigning sleep was the best course of action.

It seems Richard thought a little differently than me, because a moment later he moved his body even closer and draped his arm around my waist, until his front side was spooning my backside. I felt his semihard cock press against my ass through my underwear and couldn't suppress a sigh.

"Are you awake?" he whispered.

"Yeah," I swallowed hard, and stared straight ahead in the darkness of his room as my heart raced even faster. "I guess winding down from tonight's concert is a little harder than usual. I'm sure it's even worse for you," I whispered back.

"Maybe a little."

"You were great tonight, Richard. I hope you remember all of us when you're big and famous."

He scooted closer to me and hugged me tighter for a moment. His smooth, muscular chest rested against my shoulder, and his face was an inch from my ear. His hand moved slowly under the blanket and caressed my stomach. I tried hard not to gasp, but I don't think I was very successful.

"Look," Richard said, "I know I can get kicked off the tour for this, but I figure what the hell. There's only a week left, and I'm already home, right?"

His voice sounded a little shaky, but his arms were strong as he turned me onto my back and stared into my eyes from just above me.

"I'm not sure..."

"Sh-h-h," he said, and leaned down to kiss me. His lips were soft and sweet, with a touch of the mouthwash he'd used before bed. He cupped my chin in his hands and kissed me harder, letting his tongue trace my lips a couple of times before gently pushing its way into my mouth.

I don't know where the loud ringing in my ears came from, but my head spun as Richard's tongue worked its way slowly into and around my mouth. I felt my body go limp (all but one rebellious appendage of it, that is) as I sighed and sucked softly on his probing tongue.

He pulled out from my mouth as he kicked the blankets to the floor and moved his body so that it lay flat on top of mine. His body was hot and every muscle tight and hard and smooth. Even in the dark I could see his eyes never left mine as he stroked my face, neck, and chest.

"If this isn't cool with you, just let me know," he whispered. "I'm sure we could pretend it never happened and get through this last week."

I wrapped one arm around his thin waist and pulled him down for another kiss.

"This is definitely cool with me."

He smiled and reached to squeeze my cock gently. I shuddered as his hand caressed me. He moved from my dick to the top of my underwear, which he pulled off in one slow move. Fully hard, my dick throbbed against my stomach. Richard lowered his body back onto mine so that my cock was sandwiched between us.

"You feel so good," he said quietly.

"So do you," I answered, as I let my hands move slowly across his smooth, tight ass for a moment before pulling off his underwear. He lifted his body so that his underwear could slip down his legs, and his thick, heavy dick flopped onto my stomach, resting right next to my own cock. The skin was soft and silky, and I felt the heat from it even before it touched my belly.

I tried to show some restraint, I swear I did, but out of nowhere my hand reached down and wrapped around his cock. It was long and thick, and the silky foreskin moved freely across it as I moved my hand slowly up and down the length of his pole.

Richard took a deep breath and lay flat on his back next to me. He was still smiling, his eyes looking into mine, as I kissed him and massaged his cock in my hand.

His mouth was so sweet and his lips so soft, I could have stayed there forever and been happy. But I also wanted to know what the rest of him felt like, so I moved my kisses down his neck and across his tight, smooth chest. He took another deep breath as my tongue licked his tiny hairless nipples, and I felt his cock twitch wildly in my hand. It was now so thick I could barely wrap my fist around it, and by the time my tongue found its way to Richard's belly button, his cock head and an inch or so of his big shaft was brushing against my chin.

I loved the way his smooth, tight abs felt on my tongue, tightening as I trailed closer and closer to his dick. I kissed his stomach for a few seconds longer, and then stuck my tongue out to reach the tip of his cock. It was hot and wet, with a trail of precome sliding from the slit and across the head and onto my fingers.

I swallowed a little of it nervously. I wasn't quite sure what to expect, having never tasted it before, but I guess I liked it, because before I knew it, I sucked his entire cock head into my mouth and licked hungrily around the head for more of the salty, sticky fluid. I remembered Justin sucking himself off and swallowing his own come, wondering if this is what it tasted like as I eagerly licked until Richard's cock head was dry of his precome.

"Lie down with me," Richard said, and turned me around on the bed so that we were cock-to-mouth.

I was drunk with the taste of his dick and went right back to the task of licking and sucking it. I had his entire head and an inch or so of his thick shaft in my mouth when I felt his mouth wrap around my own dick head, and I almost choked. He seemed to enjoy my cock as much as I enjoyed his, and his hot, wet mouth sucked quietly, but with such heat and force that I had to pull out quickly before I shot my load.

Richard pulled me back down to his mouth by my waist, but this time he let my throbbing cock rest across his chin as his tongue licked and kissed its way along the underside of my balls and toward my ass.

I was dizzy with the delight of all that was happening. His tongue licked softly but hungrily across my balls and ass until I thought I'd faint with pleasure. When I stopped to think about it and realized I had half of Richard's thick, uncut dick down my throat, I choked and had to come up for air. I tried to sit up and change positions, but Richard held me tightly at the waist and kept licking around my ass.

"Do you like this?" he asked after a couple of minutes. I could only moan my response.

After a couple more licks, Richard pulled me up and off of him and kissed me on the mouth again, tenderly. I started to say something, but before I got a chance, he laid me on my stomach and spread my legs wide. I could no longer see him but felt his mouth and tongue as they tickled my ass and heard him open a drawer on the nightstand next to the bed. If I'd been thinking clearly, I could probably have figured out what was happening, but as his tongue slid slowly and steadily into my ass, I couldn't even have told you my name.

His tongue felt like wet fire as it slid in and out of my ass. Then he pulled it all the way out and kissed my ass cheeks gently before spreading them and sliding his tongue back inside me. Somewhere along the line Richard added a finger. I couldn't tell you when, because I was delirious with pleasure as I was being opened in ways I'd never imagined. Two probing fingers soon replaced his tongue in my ass, and I felt Richard's kisses move across the back of my neck.

"Just relax," I heard him whisper from a million miles away. I heard the ripping of plastic wrap as I wondered to myself how much more relaxed I could possibly get.

He slowly rolled me over onto my back and leaned down to kiss me again. His lips were softer and his tongue sweeter than anything I could remember. I felt the head of his cock press gently on my asshole, and a second later I realized why I was in the position I was in and that his kisses were meant to be a distraction.

Richard's cock head slipped inside me with what seemed like no resistance, but once it was inside I tightened up and cried out in pain. Richard kept his tongue inside my mouth and held me tightly against him as I tried to wriggle off his huge pole.

"Sh-h-h," he whispered, and kissed my lips softly. "My parents are right next door."

I hadn't realized I'd cried out so loudly the first time until he started sliding his dick deeper inside and I groaned out loudly again.

"It won't hurt so bad," he said. "Kiss me." He put his lips gently on top of mine.

I certainly didn't see how kissing him would make the pain in my ass hurt less, but he looked so sweet and I trusted him so completely that I did what he said. I kissed his lips for a second, and when he started moving even more of himself inside me, I slid my tongue into his mouth as I closed my eyes in pain. He wrapped his hot mouth around my tongue and sucked on it softly as he continued moving his hips forward for what seemed like hours. I felt each of his thick eight inches spread my ass open slowly, and when he was all the way inside me he rested there for a moment and just kept kissing me.

"You all right?" he whispered at the same moment I felt myself relax completely and the pain turn to pure pleasure.

I nodded, and a tear trickled down my cheeks. Richard wiped it away and kissed my nose.

"You sure?"

I tightened my ass muscles around his cock and lifted myself deeper onto him in response. He smiled, and even in the dark I saw his brown eyes sparkle as he began to move himself in and out of my ass with a slow, steady rhythm. It wasn't long before I was lifting myself up to meet his deep thrusts with a rhythm of my own, and both of us moaned in pleasure as our bodies became one.

Richard's eyes never left mine as he fucked me, and he blew me small kisses every time I raised my ass and squeezed it against his thick cock as it drove deeper inside me. We both struggled not to moan too loudly, extremely aware of his parents across the hall.

I had never felt anything like this in my life, and I wanted it to go on forever. A couple of times Richard grabbed my cock to stroke it, but I was so close I had to move his hand away. Every nerve in my body was on fire, and just the touch of his hand on my dick would make me shoot.

He was content to just keep fucking me, leaning down for a kiss every couple of minutes, and when he was getting close himself, he stopped thrusting and we both just lay still, his hard cock buried inside me, trying to calm itself down for another few minutes of bliss.

We went on like that for what seemed like hours. I thought I could have gone on forever, but was surprised when my cock shot out a huge jet of come that flew past my face and landed on Richard's headboard. A couple more followed, landing on my face and chest, even though I hadn't touched my cock since Richard had entered me.

With each shot of come from my cock, I felt my ass tighten even more against Richard's thick, uncut cock. He closed his eyes and moaned loudly, oblivious now to his parents' proximity, and shoved himself into me deeply with a couple of thrusts of his hips. Before I knew it he pulled out, leaving me with an empty feeling I'd never imagined. He quickly pulled off the condom from his cock and stood up straight, standing over my quivering body.

The come flew from his cock like someone had turned on a faucet at full force. Three shots hit the wall and headboard behind my head. Several more landed on my face and chest and stomach. I was amazed at how much come was pouring out of Richard's thick brown cock. Instinctively I stuck my tongue out and licked off some that landed on my lips, surprised at how hot and sweet it was.

When he was finished, Richard lay down on top of me for a moment trying to catch his breath. When I felt the heartbeat in his chest return to normal and his breathing slow down, he rolled off me and onto his side next to me.

"I'm so sorry," he said as he wiped his dripping come from my face. "I didn't mean to shoot all over you. I had no idea there'd be that much and it'd get on your face."

"Shh," I said, and licked my lips for any remaining trace. "It's OK. I liked it."

"You did?"

I nodded and smiled. "A lot."

"Me too," he said softly as he pulled me down and laid my head against his chest.

With Richard's arms around me I fell asleep almost immediately, and apparently neither of us moved an inch during the night. The next thing I knew, it was morning and Mrs. Gomez was knocking on the bedroom door to wake us up for breakfast.

When he first opened his eyes Richard had a panicked, guilty look on his face. But when I smiled and leaned over to kiss him on the mouth, he smiled back and hugged me.

Somehow we showered and got through breakfast with what seemed like perfect normality. When we arrived at the church and started loading the bus, no one seemed any different than they had the other 90-whatever days we'd been on the road, and we were soon off and running to our next city.

Richard sat near the back of the bus where he usually did and wrote in his journal, but I noticed several times he looked up and smiled at me.

About an hour ago, Scott, our director, came over and asked Cynthia if she would trade places with him for a moment. He needed to speak with me. My heart raced, since I just *knew* he'd found out about last night and was kicking me off the tour. But I couldn't have been further from the truth.

"I noticed last week, when we sent around the form asking everyone if they were going to tour again next year, you put down that you were undecided," Scott said.

"Yeah. I'm just not sure I can afford to take another summer off," I said hesitantly.

"Would you consider touring if I could make it a little more affordable for you?"

"What do you mean?"

"I've been asked to direct the Eastern European tour next year. It's been my personal goal for three years now, and I'm very excited about it."

"Congratulations, Scott," I said, and hugged him.

"Thanks. I'd like for you to be my assistant director next year."

"What?" I couldn't believe my ears.

"It's a lot of work, as you know. Coordinating communications with the churches and schools, disciplining other tour members, assigning members to host families, even directing the group a few times—well, you know all that Roger has done on this tour."

"Yeah, it's a lot of work."

"Yes, but it's fun and rewarding too. And it pays really well, I might add."

"I don't know, Scott."

"Come on. I'd really like you to. Several members of this group are already confirmed to go with me next year because I specifically want them there. Karla, Veronica, Richard, Justin, Beth, and Leo have all said yes. That just leaves you. What do you say?"

I glanced back at Richard. He had both hands brought to his lips in a pleading pose, and he winked at me and smiled.

"Sure, I'd be happy to," I said as I turned back to Scott.

"Great! We'll iron out the details and sign the contract when we get back to L.A. I really appreciate it. I think we'll have a great time."

I laid my head back in the seat and closed my eyes, already thinking of all the great times I can expect next summer. Richard is going tour with me again, and so is Justin. I can't wait to start handing out host-family assignments—oh, and all the other responsibilities too, of course!

A Tale of Two Twinkies
by Trevor J. Callahan Jr.

I don't usually like twinks.

This is true for two reasons. First thing is, I just love a hairy guy. Nothing like burying your face into the broad, massive chest of some hairy bodybuilder. That's what really gets me hard.

The other reason I don't like twinks? I am one. Blond hair, blue eyes, 6 foot 1, 175 pounds, athletic, muscular body, smooth chest, round bubble butt—you name a twink quality, I've got it. And when it comes to sex, I like a little variety, something different than screwing the guy in the mirror.

But having said all that, I've got to tell you about the time I did screw the guy in the mirror—and not mine.

Hey, I know that's a cryptic line, but if I tell you exactly what I mean, then, well, I've ruined the story for you. Better to start at the beginning.

You see, when I first went to graduate school, I lived in this dormitory for "older students"—those of us over the age of 21. Some of the guys on my floor were grad students too, but most of them were just sixth-year seniors struggling to finally finish their degrees and get the hell out of there.

At first I didn't like living in a dorm again. After all, I'd just spent four years walking down the hall to take a piss and, frankly, I wasn't looking forward to it again. Still, I was broke, and this was pretty much the only place I could afford to live.

Soon after I moved in, though, I discovered an upside to sharing showers with 20 other guys. At my undergraduate school the showers were each in their own little enclave—I never saw anything more than the occasional body wrapped in a snug towel. But here the showers were only covered by a vinyl curtain, so I got good looks at all the guys going in and out of the shower. What a smorgasbord of hot man meat!

Every morning I might see Kip, the former blond soccer stud who had one of the hottest asses I'd ever noticed on a man; or Jeff, a bodybuilding nut with one of the most ripped bodies I'd ever seen; big, burly Brandon, a hung, hairy stud who always got me hard; or even Renaldo, the smoky Brazilian with his dark hair and skin and long, loping cock. What a great way to wake up, to head off to the shower and bathe, shave, and brush your teeth with one or two other hot, naked young guys. Certainly got my juices flowing!

And yet out of all the studs on that floor, no one caught my eye more than Aaron. He was what you might call a tall drink of water—and a total twink to boot. He was 6 foot 6, lean and lithe, with short-cropped brown hair, eyes the color of cola, and a smooth, hairless body that had neither a spare ounce of fat nor extra muscle. He was just perfect; his waist melted into his pants (when he wore them, of course)—and his long legs curved into this perfect round ass—the kind of ass that only tall basketball-playing guys have. I love those asses! And to top it all off, he had the biggest cock of any guy on the floor. Now, I had a seven-inch prick myself, certainly not small, but Aaron's prick dangled well between his legs, and even though I had never seen him hard, it was clear he was the most hung guy in the showers.

And I wanted to be the one to find out just how big that prick of his got.

There was just one problem with that: Aaron himself.

Not that he was straight. Nope, good ole gaydar told me he wasn't. It's just that he was so mopey, so quiet and withdrawn, that no one could get close to him at all. He'd been living in that dorm a year before I moved in, and no one there was really friends with him. Still, there was nothing I liked more than a challenge—and his cock was one Everest I was determined to climb.

At first our conversations were limited to hallway encounters, nothing more than a "Hi, how are you?" kind of thing. Or sometimes in the morning I'd see him in the bathroom and

87

we'd talk while we shaved. I always checked him out then (pretty blatantly, I might add), and I was pretty sure he was checking me out too.

I was plotting long and hard about how to really spend some time with him when I found out I didn't have to plot anything at all. Aaron came to me.

"Hey," he mumbled as I opened the door. We stared awkwardly at each other for a moment (I was shocked as hell to see him) before I finally mumbled back a "hello" and a "come on in."

He sat on the edge of my bed, and I thought, *If only our clothes could come off, we could really have some fun.* "Hey, Trevor," he finally said to me, "Renaldo said you used to live in France. Is that true?"

I nodded. "I studied there a semester," I said. "Why?"

Aaron was staring at the floor, nervously wringing his hands. "You must be really good at French, then," he said.

"*Oui*," I said lightly. "What's this all about, man?"

"I've already failed French twice, but I need it to fulfill my language requirement. Can you help me? Please?"

French lessons. How perfect!

"Sure, buddy," I said, sitting next to him on the bed and casually tossing my arm around his shoulder. I gave his neck a manly squeeze and felt my cock spring to life in my pants. "No problem. Glad to help out anytime."

"Great," Aaron said, wriggling from my grasp and bolting for the door.

Well, it may not have been a picture-perfect beginning, but it was a beginning nonetheless. I was hoping the French language lessons might lead to some other French lessons, but for the first month or so Aaron and I stuck strictly to business. Still, I felt I was getting to know him a lot better. Finally I decided to try a more forward approach.

"Aaron," I said to him one time as we went over *-ir* verbs, "we should go get some dinner sometime, you and I."

"You mean like at the cafeteria?" he said.

I smiled. "I was thinking someplace more—I don't know—romantic?"

He looked at me with the most curious expression. "You mean like a date?" he finally said.

I nodded. "Yeah, exactly like a date."

I lived and died about a hundred times in the 10 seconds it took him to respond. "OK," he finally said. "Why not?"

It took me two hours to get ready for the date.

Normally I was much more suave, more cool, more collected. I rarely got nervous before going out with a guy. Hey, I knew I had what he wanted, so why worry? But in this case the shoe was on the other foot. Aaron was in the driver's seat, even if he didn't know it, and I was the one working hard to impress.

I showered, shaved, combed, and cologned—hell, I'd even gone out and bought a new shirt. When I knocked on his door at 6 o'clock I looked perfect, smelled perfect—I was ready. Tonight was the night.

Aaron answered the door, and we immediately shuffled off to dinner. Too bad. I was hoping for a little predinner tonsil hockey, but I suppose I could wait until after we eat. We went to a fairly nice Italian joint on the outskirts of town. I'd brought a wad of cash with me, so we liberally ordered a bottle of wine and sat back, getting ready to polish it off. (This marked another first for me—buying the other guy dinner. I'd never done that on a first date before.)

The meal was great. For a change, Aaron was pretty talkative, telling me things mostly about his family and friends back home. I learned a lot: His cousin was a professional wrestler, his Dad and two uncles had been in Vietnam, and he even had a twin brother, Lance. I loved getting to know him, so instead of going to a movie or a club after dinner, I just ordered another bottle of wine and we kept right on talking.

Somewhere between bottle of wine number 1 and number 2, though, Aaron started talking about his ex-boyfriend. I use the singular because he apparently only had one: some guy he had known "since we were kids," the guy he'd "first done it with," the one and only "true love of his life." Great. For the next two hours I heard a lot of drunken rambling about this guy, about how they got together, how often they did it, and how they had finally decided after high school to split up "because we knew it just wasn't right." Aaron had spent the last five years trying to forget that guy, even though they still occasionally "got together to do it, you know, right, Trevor?"

Yeah, I knew one thing—he was still head over heels in love with this guy (I didn't even know his name, but I already hated him), and even though Aaron had ordered the surf and turf, it didn't seem like I was going to get any of that monstrous cock tonight.

I took Aaron home, then went back to my room to jerk off. On my way back, though, I ran into a couple of friends, so I went out with them instead. I got cruised a lot of times that night (I was still all dolled up after my date, you know), but horny as I was, I didn't go home with any of them. I couldn't stop thinking about Aaron. I guess I had it pretty bad for him after all.

Still, I was determined to get over him. I didn't want some guy still hung up on his last boyfriend. I found reasons to avoid Aaron, to cancel our tutoring sessions, and, actually, almost three weeks had passed before I saw him again, coming out of the shower one morning, looking resplendently clean and sexy as hell. He saw me standing in front of the mirror brushing my teeth in my boxers and smiled a hello. I took in an eyeful, as usual, but I tried not to look too interested. Instead of covering himself up, though, as he usually did, Aaron took a long time drying himself off, using his threadbare towel to wipe off his chest, then his face, his legs and ass, leaving that hung cock of his completely exposed. I couldn't take my eyes off it as he kept drying himself. I felt my own cock swell in my boxers, but who cared about that as I watched this hot guy toweling off in front of me? Finally he rubbed his cock dry, rolling that huge organ around in the towel before finally stopping, wrapping the towel around his spare waist, and heading back to his room.

Wow. What was that? I mean, it was a pretty clear signal—he seemed to want me bad. But why now? What happened to that other guy? And why the hell was I asking myself these questions when that hot stud wanted me now? I dashed to my room, stashed my toothbrush and paste in my medicine chest, and, adjusting my cock, I made my way to Aaron's room. About halfway down the hall, though, I noticed his door opening. *Well,* I thought, *looks like he decided not to wait after all.* Aaron came out fully dressed. No matter—think of the fun I was going to have peeling those clothes off him! I stopped, waiting for him, looking hot and cocky in my boxers as he headed toward me. I nodded a "hey" as he came closer, then closer—and then right past me as he walked straight out of the dorm and on his way to class.

Fuck! I thought, as I headed back to my room. *What was that all about?* Puzzled, I tossed my boxers off and rummaged through my underwear drawer, looking for a clean pair. I finally found some and had just put them on when I heard a knock at the door.

I opened it. There was Aaron. "Change your mind?" I said, somewhat annoyed, somewhat sarcastic, and yet still somewhat hopeful.

He looked at me. "About what?" he asked.

I shook my head. "Never mind," I said, turning my back while I continued dressing.

He walked into my room behind me. "Why do that?" he said. "You look much better without any clothes on." And without another word he crossed the room, grabbed my shoulders, and planted a wet one right on my lips.

For a moment I was too stunned to respond. Then I finally met his kiss with one of my own before parting my lips to his probing tongue. His hands were busy too—one sliding down my boxers to squeeze the firm globes of my ass, the other cupping my stiffening cock and hot balls roughly. I did the same, grabbing at his denim-covered dick, hoping to see how stiff it was getting, when suddenly it hit me.

"Lance," I said. "You're Lance."

Lance was grinning from ear to ear. "And you must be Trevor," he whispered hotly in my ear. "Nice to meet you."

"Wow," I said, taking a step back to survey the stud before me. "I guess you guys really are identical twins," I said.

Lance wagged his head at me. "In almost every way," he said. "But Aaron's a bottom."

"And you're not?"

Lance smiled. "Not when I have an ass like that to fuck."

Oh, man, was I in heaven or what! Maybe I couldn't have Aaron, but Lance was surely the next best thing! "You can do anything you like with my ass," I told him.

Lance shook his head. "Oh, I will. But we can't right now. Later."

"When?" I asked eagerly.

Lance pulled away from me and made for the door. "Come to Aaron's room around 7. I'll leave the door open. Just come on in, crawl into the bed with me, and start sucking on my cock."

"Sure," I said, "no problem. But come on, man, let me have a little preview now."

"I wish I could, stud. But I can't. Tonight. Seven sharp."

"At least tell me how big that monster cock gets!" I begged.

Lance smiled. "Nothing doing," he said, stealing one last kiss. "Seven."

Seven o'clock couldn't arrive fast enough. Sure, I kept telling myself, Lance wasn't Aaron, wasn't the guy I had this crush on, but, fuck, he was close enough! And man, I was so hot for his cock, I didn't care at that point. I just knew I had to have that monster piece of meat in my mouth and up my ass!

When 6:59 hit I took my shirt, shoes, and socks off, and clad only in jeans (I'd been going commando all day. I love walking around letting my meat hang free, especially when I know I'm going to see some action later that day), I headed to Aaron's room. I knocked softly; "Come in," I heard Lance say, and I opened the door a crack and closed it behind me.

Aaron had a corner room, big and airy, lots of windows. It was Indian summer—his windows were open—and the lights from the university stadium gave a dim, almost ethereal glow to everything in the room. That everything included Lance.

He was on his stomach, spread-eagle on the bed, his skin creamy-white in the glow of the lights, those long, lean legs leading higher and higher to his broad, flawless back and that sweet, sweet ass of his. "What are you waiting for?" I heard him say. I slipped my jeans off (not an easy task with the boner I sprang) and slid onto the edge of the bed. I went right between Lance's legs, placing one hand on each of his ankles slowly, meticulously; squeezing my way up those lean, strong limbs, feeling the cool of his skin in the night breeze, before my hands went up and over the smooth round globes of his firm, young ass. I lowered my body between his legs, my hands now massaging his cheeks.

"Mmm," he moaned lightly, as I brought my face toward that perfect piece of boy pussy. I bent down and smelled him—musky, earthy, slightly sweaty, just like a man should smell. I kissed his left cheek, then his right, and then gently I bit into the milky flesh. "Ah," he whispered, as I moved my warm, sensuous lips to the crack of his ass. I leaned my face against his ass, pressing my mouth to his crack. Out came my tongue, gently lapping at that sweet rump. "Oh, fuck," I heard him say, and I smiled; I knew he was having as much fun as I was.

I used my hands to gently and meticulously pry his round cheeks apart, letting him savor the moment, knowing full well what would come next. Out flicked my tongue to gently tease his hole. Once, twice, three times I flicked my tongue over his hole, pausing each time to breathe in the beautiful flesh around me. Finally Lance couldn't take it anymore. "Just do it, man," he whispered, and grinning, I buried my face into the sweet folds of his beautiful boy pussy.

"Fuck," Lance hissed, a long and slow hiss as I probed his hole with my tongue. God, he tasted good! Just like I had hoped—clean yet musky. I was getting into it now and so was Lance. Furiously I dug my mouth onto that ass, licking and probing that puckered hole with my tongue and lips, tasting and sucking Lance's ass, and Lance responded by bucking wildly underneath my face, his hips thrusting with movement, his long, lean arm reaching back to grab my face, to shove it farther and farther into his sweet, eager ass. "Oh, Trevor!" he moaned over and over as I devoured his round, firm butt.

I reached between Lance's legs and felt his nuts—a tight package, smooth and almost boyish, but big, huge nuts ready to shoot wad after wad of sweet, sticky come. I fondled his sack delicately and then more roughly, and Lance responded by squirming excitedly beneath me. I released my mouth from his ass and dug even lower between his legs, lightly grabbing one of his nuts with my teeth before sucking it into my eager mouth. "Shit, shit!" Lance moaned, as I sucked first the one nut, then the other, before I finally tried to cram both of his already pulsing balls into my hot, wet mouth.

"Fuck, Trevor, you have one hot mouth, man!" Lance moaned, as I sucked his nuts. My hands squeezed his ass and thighs, one finger sometimes delicately probing and pushing against that tight hole of his. I moved my hands between his cheeks, sliding them over and over his crack, all the while moving them inch by inch toward that ultimate prize. His prick had to be as stiff as mine now, and I knew that huge cock was perched up against that smooth, flat belly of his. I couldn't wait any longer; I had to have it in my hands, to see it, know it, taste it.

I slipped his balls out of my mouth, placed them in my palm, and was only a second away from grabbing the ultimate prize when I heard a noise behind me. Before I could even whirl around, a large pair of hands grabbed my firm, round bubble butt. "This is so hot," a voice whispered in my ear, and I whirled around to find Aaron playing with my ass and nibbling my ear. He must have been watching all along! Or was he? Which guy was which?

"What the fuck is going on?" I demanded, breathless and hard, trying to sound upset but mostly sounding confused.

"Don't you get it yet?" the guy behind me said. His probing hands found my seven-inch poker and wrapped around it. "God, you have a nice one," he said. The guy underneath me whirled his head around to watch what his brother was doing.

"I mean it," I said, shrugging the guy behind me off my back. He stood up, a loose pair of gray shorts the only clothes he had on. I sat on one corner of the bed as the twin underneath me sat next to me. Each placed a hand on one of my shoulders. "What kind of game is this?" I asked.

"It's no game," the twin with the shorts on said. "I want you. We both want you. We didn't think you'd mind."

My mind was reeling. "OK, let's start at the beginning—which one are you?"

The twin in the shorts grinned. "Does it matter?" he said. I glowered at him. "I'm Lance," he said finally.

"So why all this secrecy shit? Why lie to me to get me here?"

"Look," Aaron said to me, "remember that guy I told you about, the one I was hung up on?"

"Yeah," I said, "your ex. The guy you're still in love with…oh," I said, suddenly understanding.

Lance moved behind Aaron and wrapped his lean arms around his twin's shoulders. "We're perfect for each other," he said. "We *are* each other. But, well—it's difficult. No one would ever understand."

Aaron nodded. "So we've tried to deny it all, pretend we don't feel this way. But we can't."

"What does this have to do with me?" I asked.

Lance shrugged. "Sometimes it's easier for us to be together if we're with another guy. I know it doesn't make a lot of sense, but, honestly, you're the first guy who ever seemed to care."

"So let me get this straight," I said, not believing a word I was hearing. "You two are in love, right? But to avoid acting out your urges on each other, you get involved in three-ways?"

Lance nodded. "Usually we just watch each other," he said. "But what you were doing was so hot, well, I just wanted to get involved."

"So you're using me?" I asked.

"Technically," Lance said, standing up in front of me. Aaron joined him. "But look at what you're getting in return," he said, lowering his shorts to the floor.

I looked into their faces. What I saw—it's indescribable. I once had a boyfriend who used to love to stare at his naked body in a full-length mirror. I used to love it too; it was like having two of them. But here, damn—I really did have two of them. Two very hot, smooth, good-looking twinks, one the exact image of the other, standing naked before me. Suddenly it struck me—I'm resisting this?

Smiling, I let my eyes ravish their bodies. Those broad shoulders; those smooth, barely developed boyish chests and pecs; the long, lean torsos, utterly hairless; the slim waists, their arms now encircling each other.

And then I came to their cocks.

God, I knew they were going to have big ones. I mean, I could tell from seeing Aaron in the shower every day. But holy shit, I tell you, I wasn't prepared for what I saw dangling stiffly from those boys' crotches. Each twin had nine inches of cock—

nine full, lean, hard, throbbing inches of prick—that's a foot and a half of dick combined! Their cocks weren't thick, but just like the rest of them they were long and lean, and right now they were pushed right up against the other, the heads coming together to form one monstrous cock, each of their piss slits oozing a single drop of shimmering white precome.

I looked down at my own cock, and I tell you, I have never had a stiffer prick in my life. I leaned forward, keeping my hands utterly by my side, opening my mouth wide as I went. The twins knew what I was going to do, and they moved their dicks even closer together, the two rods matching up perfectly as my stretched-out mouth barely covered both of their dripping cock heads.

Man, there's nothing like having a cock in your mouth, but two cocks, these two cocks—I tell you, I was almost ready to shoot a wad right there. I grabbed each of their cocks at its base and tried to cram as much cock as I could in my eager drooling mouth.

The twins smiled, and each one placed a hand on my head to guide me along. "Nice," Lance said, while Aaron just leaned his head back, relieved that his throbbing prick was finally getting some attention. For several minutes I moved my tongue all over the heads of their dicks, licking off any precome that oozed from their piss holes. Finally, out of breath, I leaned my face away from their cocks. "You know what I want?" I said, standing up off the bed. "I want to watch you guys go at it."

Lance and Aaron needed no further prodding. Aaron promptly flopped down on the bed, and his twin brother slid right on top of him. It amazed me how perfectly their bodies lined up. They began to kissed each other passionately, their mouths opening wide to accept each other's tongues. I could tell they'd done this many times before.

They became more and more urgent in their lovemaking, rolling around on the bed, their hands all over each other's asses and cocks. My own cock was spurting precome, but I didn't touch it, knowing only a few quick strokes would make me blow my load. The twins were moaning loudly now, and, fascinated, I watch as Lance pushed Aaron's head toward his own pulsing cock.

Aaron pushed his mouth eagerly into Lance's crotch. He nuzzled and licked his pubes, pausing languidly on his nuts, sucking and licking those balls roughly until they turned bright-red. Lance seemed to love this, moaning and thrashing on the bed. "Suck me, bro," he said, and Aaron responded immediately, easily sliding half of Lance's cock down his throat.

Lance motioned me over to the bed, and I took two steps toward him. He grabbed my cock and started jerking it. "Don't, man," I said, "or I'll blow my load now, I swear." Lance grinned and, sliding his long arm between my legs, he played with my ass instead, poking his long middle finger in, around, and finally up my hole.

I spread my legs to help him, but I couldn't take my eyes off Aaron as he swallowed more and more of his brother's nine-inch prick. I thought there was no way in hell he could swallow the whole thing. But Aaron seemed practiced in pleasuring his twin, and, sure enough, his efforts finally paid off when, taking a deep breath, he plunged the entire cock down his throat. His nose met Lance's pubes and he shook his head roughly. "Yeah, yeah, yeah!" Lance said, as I watched amazed. I'd never seen anyone take cock like that in my life.

It was about time I had some of that cock myself. I slid myself off Lance's finger and climbed onto the bed with the twins. They scooted over to give me more room. Soon I was staring Aaron square in the eyes as he continued thrusting Lance's wet dick in and out of his mouth. Aaron noticed me and stopped sucking on Lance, offering his twin's gleaming cock for my hungry mouth. Instead I went for Aaron's lips, and with Lance's prick directly between us, I started tonguing and frenching the twin in front of me.

Lance's prick got licked and tongued from both sides as Aaron and I played tonsil hockey. "Fuck, that's awesome," Lance moaned as I grabbed his nuts and gave them a manly squeeze. "Yeah, that feels great, guys," Lance said, as the two of us licked up and down each side of the monstrous dick.

Suddenly, though, I wanted Aaron's cock in my mouth more than anything. It had all started with his cock, after all. "Come here," I said, and he stood up right on the bed, his long prick slapping me in the face a few times in the process. Aaron grinned, and he grabbed that nine-inch poker and smacked me across the cheeks a few times more. "You want it bad, don't you, Trevor?" he said to me.

I nodded. "You don't even know," I said, as he whacked me in the face with his dick again.

Aaron grinned. "Then take it," he said. "As much as you can."

I popped the head of his dick in my mouth, paused for a second to swallow the big load of precome he gave me, and slid five inches of that prick down my throat easily. Normally, you get that much cock in and there isn't much to go, but the rest of Aaron's dick looked impossible for me to swallow. Still, I was determined to get it down. I bobbed my head up and down on his shaft, loosening my throat and taking a bit more of his long rod each time.

Lance didn't like being left out of the fun. He sat up on the bed, positioned himself behind his brother, and ate out that sweet ass of his. "Fuck, you guys, this is so hot," Aaron moaned, as his brother buried his face in his crack and I worked on that cock of his. We did this for several minutes, and I managed to get all but two inches of Aaron's prick down my throat. Lance stopped eating out that boy pussy and came around to coach me. "Come on, Trevor, keep working it man, you can do it, a little more buddy, tilt your head down some man, yeah, that's it, good, suck some more in, all right," Lance directed, as his long, strong fingers probed my ass again. He slid one in just as I managed to get about eight inches of cock in my mouth. "Go for it!" Lance shouted, while Aaron stood over me, moaning loudly, completely enthralled, fighting the urge to fuck my already stretched-out mouth.

I didn't think I could do it, but, man, I wasn't about to let these guys down. I had to swallow that cock! Finally I took one really deep breath and just kept going, and going, and going—until my nose hit pubes. Fuck! I'd done it! I'd swallowed all of Aaron's cock! "Shit, man," Lance said. "That's fucking fantastic. It took us months to be able to do that."

I slid that long prick out of my mouth. "Maybe I can get a job as a sword swallower," I joked. I motioned to Lance. "Stand next to your brother."

As they stood on the bed their heads scraped the ceiling, but I only had eyes for their cocks. I went down on one, then the other, getting most of the shaft in before flicking it out and moving to the next one. God, it felt so good to be stretched out by these monster cocks! "Fuck, man, he's good, isn't he? I mean, he's really good!" Lance said to Aaron. Aaron nodded, and then I could tell by the slurping sounds that the two of them were tonguing and kissing again.

For a good 15 minutes I sucked those cocks. Sweat was pouring down my forehead even though a cool breeze was blowing through the open windows. Finally Aaron pulled me off. "Enough," he said, "or I'm gonna come."

"That's cool with me," I said. I was eager for his load.

Lance pushed my mouth off his dick too. "I think it's about time, bro," he said to Aaron, "to work this guy over some."

Grinning, I leaned back on the bed as the twins got between my legs. Man, looking down at those identical faces a mere inch from my cock—I tell you, I've never been more turned-on in my life!

Lance popped the head of my dick in his mouth. By now I had a ton of precome oozing from my piss slit, and he lapped it up, leaving one sticky glob on his tongue to share with his brother. He did this by shoving his tongue down Aaron's throat, whose eyes lit up at the taste of my precome. Then Aaron pushed his face deep in my crotch and wrapped his lips around the base of my shaft while Lance went back to work on the throbbing head of my aching, stiff cock.

Man, could those two guys suck! "Fuck, guys," I said, as they expertly moved their lips, tongues, and mouths over my straining dick. For about five minutes they kept it up, switching positions so that they would alternate sucking on my head. Finally Lance just swallowed my whole damn cock, and Aaron dove even lower to suck on my full, heavy nuts. "Shit, fuck, damn!" I swore in ecstasy. Cock sucking had never felt so good before.

Each twin was also playing with my ass, at first gently, then a little more roughly, until each had one finger deep inside me, trying to yank my ass wide apart. With those two hot fingers up my hole, Lance sucking my cock, and Aaron trying to devour my balls, I knew I wouldn't last long. "Guys!" I warned. "I'm gonna shoot if we keep this up!"

Grinning, the twins stopped. Lance grabbed my hand and pulled me off the bed while Aaron turned his back toward me and began rummaging around in his desk. "Let's make a sandwich," Lance said as Aaron turned back around, condoms and lube in his hand. "We're the bread."

"Let me guess," I said, grinning. "I'm the meat."

"We're all the meat," Lance said, as Aaron flopped back down on the bed. He stuck his legs in the air, and I got in position in front of him, his feet on my shoulders. Lance slid in behind me. We each lubed up our fingers good; I slid mine into Aaron as Lance slid his into me. "He likes to be fucked hard," Lance whispered hotly in my ear. "So just shove it in him and go for it, OK?"

I nodded. "No problem," I said, eager to get my cock up Aaron's hole.

I could hear Lance grinning in my ear. "Incidentally," he said, "that's how I like to fuck—hard, fast, and furious." Inwardly I moaned. With a monster cock like that, I knew it would hurt, but I also knew it was going to feel great.

I finally finished lubing up Aaron and slid the condom over my cock. Lance grabbed it and slicked me up good. I positioned myself in front of Aaron's hole. "You ready, buddy?" I asked, looking down into his eager face.

"Go for it," he said.

As Lance directed, I didn't bother loosening Aaron up a bit; I just shoved my entire cock up his hole. "Fuck!" Aaron screamed, and again, "Fuck! Ah, shit, man, fuck!" But soon he settled, and I let my cock sit up his tight hole, letting him adjust before I started pounding it into him.

"How's that cock feel, bro?" Lance asked Aaron.

"Big," Aaron replied. "Not as long as you, bro, but thicker. Starting to feel real good up there, though."

"Oh, yeah?" I said. I slid my hips back and thrust deeply into Aaron's ass. "Shit!" he screamed, then "Yeah!" Gritting my teeth, I fucked Aaron just as his twin had told me—hard, fast, and furious. Soon we'd built up a really quick pace, and I could already feel my cock tingling with orgasm. Sweat beaded off my forehead and dripped onto Aaron's creased stomach, his moans and my grunts intermingling with the still night air.

In my intense desire to pound Aaron's ass, I had momentarily forgotten about Lance. But the big-dicked guy behind me had slipped on his condom, lubed up, and watched me closely. He knew right where to place his cock so that when I thrust my hips back to plow Aaron, the head of his cock popped right into my ass. "Ow!" I yelled. "Fuck, man!" But Lance pushed ahead with me so that most of his cock speared my ass while I speared his brother's. "Goddamn!" I screamed. "Fuckin' A, man, that's the biggest fucking piece of meat. Shit!" I didn't keep fucking Aaron; instead I buried my cock as far up his ass as I could, trying to get away from Lance's stiff pole. I knew it wasn't in all the way, 'cause I couldn't feel Lance's pubes tickling my back or his balls slapping against my ass, but I knew it was pretty damned close. I craned my neck and saw only about two inches of cock outside of my ass. "Fuck, man! You just shoved seven inches of prick up my hole!"

"That's what you did to my brother," Lance whispered hotly in my ear. Beneath me, I stretched Aaron to the limit, pushing my cock in farther and farther to escape Lance's probing rod. "Relax, Trevor," Lance said. "Soon it'll start to feel good."

We stayed like that for a good five minutes, joined cock to ass, cock to ass, Aaron's own cock rigid as ever, until the pain in my hole subsided and was replaced with a nice, full feeling. "Yes," I hissed. Lance gently shoved the rest of his dick in, so slowly I hardly noticed it until his big balls slapped against my ass. After another two minutes I heard him whisper in my ear, "Ready?" I looked down at Aaron, who nodded, and, pausing only for a second, I nodded too.

We moved our hips in succession, Lance having the most control, slowly building up a rhythm. Having my ass full and plugging some other guy at the same time is great, but having it almost be the same guy, fuck, that was awesome! Soon we were fucking in earnest, Lance sometimes pausing to kiss me or to lean down and kiss his brother, and once even the three of us kissed, our tongues meeting in a frenzy of passion. Finally we began to really truly fuck; I felt Lance's cock pound into me again and again, sweat pouring off his forehead onto my back, while I kept plowing Aaron harder and harder. Finally I couldn't take it anymore. "Fuck, guys," I yelled. "I think I'm gonna come!"

"Do it!" Lance commanded, reaching to grab his brother's stiff pole, then jerking it. "Come, Trevor!"

I felt my cock tingle and turn; "Fuck, I'm coming!" I screamed, as my cock exploded in Aaron's ass. My own ass spasmed again and again against Lance's stiff cock. "I'm gonna shoot! I'm gonna shoot!" he suddenly yelled, and I felt that cock of his losing its wad up my tired, sore, but pulsing asshole.

For a second I stayed like this, panting. I had forgotten all about Aaron. Lance was jerking him wildly and he thrashed underneath me. "Ugh!" he suddenly moaned, as his cannon-like cock spurted load after load of come all over me. The first wad caught me right between the eyes, the second one shot straight into my mouth, and the rest dribbled all over my chest and abs before the last few spurts trickled down Aaron's pulsing nine-inch prick.

I felt Aaron's come roll around on my tongue, and I leaned over and shoved my tongue into his mouth. Eagerly he kissed his own come off of my tongue, and then, leaning forward, licked that first big glob right off my face.

Lance reached behind me, wiping the come off my chest, and gave Aaron his fingers to clean. "He likes come," Lance said.

"I noticed." I grinned and, leaning toward him, we kissed again.

Lance finally slid his long cock out of my ass. It seemed to take forever, but, man, it felt great on the way out! I took my cock out of Aaron's butt as well, and then the three of us collapsed on the bed. Lance took off my condom and his, tossed them into the trash, got a washcloth, and wiped our cocks clean.

The three of us clambered back onto the bed so that I was between the two twins. "So," I finally said as we drifted toward sleep, "you guys do this all the time, huh?"

Aaron shrugged. "Not that often."

Lance reached over and kissed both his brother and me. "But with you, Trevor, anytime," he said.

"Am I an honorary twin now?" I smiled.

Lance and Aaron laughed. "I guess we're triplets, then,"

Lance said, reaching his arm around me to grab his brother's cock. "But remember, I'm the older twin, so that makes me the older triplet too. And I say we should all go to sleep."

"Yes, bro," I said, kissing Lance quickly, then Aaron, and then watching them kiss before we all fell fast asleep.

All I Want for Christmas
by Dale Chase

The holidays are often a challenge because I haven't my family's expectations. Each year I travel from San Francisco to Los Angeles and endure a welcome that ultimately deteriorates into disappointment—theirs, not mine.

This year will be no different: Christmas Eve with my sister Ann, her husband Bob, and about half the extended family, then Christmas Day with our parents, their friends, and the rest of the relatives. I will be clucked at and fussed over and discussed behind my back. At least one aunt or cousin will offer up a friend or niece in hopes of bringing me around.

Bob greets me at the door. He's a big, amiable sort, perfect for the hyperdomestic Ann. He's dressed casually and wearing a Santa hat. I offer a hand but get a bear hug instead, and then Ann comes in, wiping her hands on her apron. She smells of cinnamon and chides me for my lateness.

From there I wade into the family and soak up the wave of greetings and affection the calendar dictates. I listen to the latest family news and ask questions I don't want answers to; I laugh at the same things I did last year; I sip eggnog when I'd rather have scotch. After what seems hours, I manage a look at my watch. Forty-five minutes have passed.

It is in Ann's kitchen that everything changes. In with the cluster of women is a beautiful boy of maybe 20, stirring gravy as the others usher food toward the dining room. "Oh, this is Johnny Ingram from next door," Ann says when she catches me staring at him. "His folks have gone to Hawaii for the holidays, and I couldn't bear the thought of him alone, so he's agreed to join us. Johnny, this is my brother, Ben."

"Hi," he says as he keeps stirring.

"My pleasure," I reply. "I see my sister is making you earn your meal."

"Nah, I volunteered. I like to cook."

Having little domestic instinct, I simply nod, off-stride for the moment, which both unsettles and intrigues me as my cock stirs.

Johnny watches the gravy while I watch him. He has a fresh, almost angelic look that seems appropriate for the season. Fair-skinned with curly black hair, striking blue eyes, high forehead, delicate nose, and small rosebud mouth, he adds up to pure innocence. He is relatively small in height and build—so boyish, I have to ask, "Are you home from school?"

"Yeah. I'm a junior at UCLA."

"What are you studying?"

"English. I plan to be a writer."

Ann sweeps in, takes the spoon from him, offers her thanks for the help, and shoos us away. When Johnny starts toward the living room, I suggest we avoid the crowd and go out back. "Sure," he says. "I could use some air. It's really hot in here." Beads of sweat dot his upper lip, and I think how wonderful it would be to lick them away.

Once outside, I find myself at a loss. I want to fuck him— that's a given—but there is more, a familiar mix I really want no part of. I sit on a redwood table and he sits beside me, which gets things churning in my gut, a silent onslaught that includes a nearly overwhelming need to touch him. I finally manage a question. "So why didn't you go to Hawaii with your folks?"

"They didn't ask. Once I started college, that was pretty much it. They figured they'd done their bit and it was time for them to have some fun. Can't blame 'em, and I like having the place to myself."

"Are you taking advantage of it, partying to all hours?"

"Nah, I'm not much of a party animal. I like a quieter scene, more one-on-one, you know?"

It's not meant as an invitation, but I take it that way.

Sweet little piggy opening the door to the big, bad wolf. "Yes," I say. "I do know. Kicking back, a little music, wine, conversation."

"I read a lot," he offers, and I almost say I do too. It wouldn't be a lie, but it's far from what he meant. Business journals, stroke magazines, daily newspaper. Instead I ask him his favorite authors and half listen as he goes on about Vonnegut and a couple of others I've never heard of. I wonder if he's experienced in physical matters, if he's discovered the infinite joys of cock. He has such an innocent look that it's difficult to imagine him in the throes, and yet I put him there, pink rump thrust up at me.

"Dinner," Ann calls, out the kitchen window, and Johnny hops up as if nothing has gone on between us. I, on the other hand, take a second, cock rigid, balls aching. "Go ahead," I tell him. "I'll be right in." He doesn't question this, hasn't a clue. It makes me want him all the more.

I can't wait for dinner to end, but when it does, I'm lost. Ordinarily, when I have a boy in my sights, things progress rapidly. I get what I want and am done with it, but this time I don't want to be done with it, I want it to continue, this thing not even begun. I want to possess this creature, take him home, keep him forever. Lost, I join the men in the living room and stare at a football game, mouth gone dry no matter how much water I take. I don't know where Johnny is. Sitting with the women in the dining room, maybe—or has he gone home? The thought of him alone next door is more than I can bear. I rise, knowing the bulge at my crotch will go unnoticed by eyes glued to a TV screen. I go to the dining room. No Johnny.

"What do you need?" Ann asks.

I shake my head, unable to respond. She smiles, so sweet, and I move past, through the kitchen, out the back door. I look across the low hedge that divides the properties and see lights next door. I step across, knowing I shouldn't. These are my sister's neighbors, I tell myself, but I keep going and find the back door open. I hear a TV, follow the sound not to the living room but down the hall to a bedroom. The door is open, and I am treated to the sight of Johnny lying naked in his bed, cock up, hand working. He's staring at a small TV that's playing a men-on-men video. He knows I'm there—I fill the doorway—but he doesn't acknowledge my presence. I slide onto the bed.

When I take his prick into my mouth, I taste his dribble and smear it around his crown with my tongue, then close onto his little shaft and start to suck. He whimpers and thrusts up at me, so I pull back, grab hold, and watch him come. His distance is remarkable. He bucks in my hand as he unleashes long streams, then falls back, closes his eyes. I play with his spent cock, squeezing and petting as it softens. He swims in pleasure, and I can see that he's experienced. I stand up, fish a condom out of my pocket, then undress. Naked, I crawl back onto the bed, and he opens his eyes and grins.

"I'm gonna fuck the hell out of you," I tell him, and he giggles, pulls up his legs, and presents me with a pink little pucker. He's very smooth, very little hair. I play with his tight little sac and he wiggles, flexes his ass muscle. I know he wants it then, so I suit up, lube myself with his come, then guide my prick to his hole. Just before I do him, I look at his face and decide he is possibly the most beautiful creature I've ever seen. My cock hovers at his rim. I look from his face to his crack, then shove in. He lets out a long moan, rocks back to get me in to the max, and I watch him get totally blissed as I begin a steady stroke.

Long before I come, I experience that other kind of stir. I am in free fall, naked skydiver taking the plunge, dick waving, heart plummeting. Everything in me shudders as an implosion thunders through my chest, churns my gut, fires my cock. I hear myself moan as I pump—I'm usually silent in my encounters—and I look into Johnny's eyes, find them sparkling, and press myself to him, press my mouth to his.

I want to devour him. Fucking isn't enough. My tongue finds his, prods him, tastes him, sucks him. And as I bury myself in him I unload, slamming into him with a climax that gains instead of subsiding, that goes on so long I think I'll pass out, pulse driving from cock and balls back into my spine and my ass and down my legs. I feel it in my calves, in my goddamned *calves*. I rear back and let out a howl, and when I'm done, tears are all down my cheeks.

I cannot speak. I'm on top of Johnny, cock far from soft. I've got my arms around him and swim in the feel of his lithe little body. I am where I want to be. Nothing else exists; nothing else matters.

Johnny's hands roam over my back, and his touch allows me to finally slide out of him. I discard the condom, then take him into my arms. He nuzzles against my chest. "Merry Christmas," he murmurs.

I chuckle, and he continues: "When you came into the kitchen, I about lost it. There I am in a room full of women, stirring gravy, and I'm getting a major boner."

"As soon as I saw you..." My voice chokes. I run my hand down onto his ass. "You're beautiful," I tell him.

"You too."

For a while we say nothing, and I start hoping we're on equal ground. I know I'm probably dreaming but can't stop myself. There's no panic this time, no fear. I kiss him. Innocent, sweet. I don't want to move from his side, but I must. Gifts will be opened soon, and I have to be there to receive my shirts and ties and aftershave. "I have to go," I tell him, then quickly add, "You know I don't want to."

"I know."

"Can I see you tomorrow?"

"Don't you have a Christmas thing? Ann keeps talking about the big celebration at your folks' place."

"I don't want to go."

"Don't you have to?"

"Yes."

"Maybe you can come by later."

"You'll be here, then?"

"Doin' my thing."

The following day I tell Ann I want to take my own car to the celebration. She objects but doesn't fight it. "Mr. Independent," she says, but that's the last of it. I leave before she does, driving along the beach instead of taking the freeway, thinking of Johnny the whole time. I wonder if his parents left gifts for him to unwrap, if they'll call and wish him a happy holiday. I hate the idea that he's alone, partly because I think it's wrong, partly because I want him, and this gets me to thinking about what lies ahead in the house at Playa del Rey, the big beachfront already crowded with friends and family. My parents do it up royal, always have. I'll walk in and receive a welcome, but it won't be like at Ann's. Mom and Dad don't ask about my life, and I know not to offer. It's their turf; we play by their rules. In their context I am the successful businessman from San Francisco, and that is their sole measure.

I am on the Pacific Coast Highway, almost there, when I decide once and for all what I want. I have to pull over because the ache inside me is so overwhelming I feel nearly sick. I look at others hurrying toward holiday celebrations and wonder if any of them can possibly feel what I am feeling. Do they have something genuine, or are they just playing their appointed parts, as I've been doing all these years? I take a few deep breaths, then pull a very illegal U-turn and head south. Traffic is light. In 20 minutes I pull into Johnny's driveway.

The living room drapes are open, and I glance over as I get out of the car, and there's Johnny, looking to see who's come to call. He's still wearing the robe; he grins and unties it, fondles his cock. I start to laugh.

The second the door closes behind me, I take him into my

arms. "Aren't you supposed to be somewhere else?" he asks.

"No," I tell him as I press myself to him. He pulls at my zipper, gets a hand inside. I'm already hard, already wet. "Jeez," he says, smearing juice down my shaft.

I pull away and close the drapes; he sheds his robe. Standing naked before me, he is everything I want. Part of me would like to tell him this, and maybe later I will, but for now I need to be inside him. He understands and lets me ease him to the floor. I quickly strip, then turn him onto his stomach. He thrusts his ass up at me, and I pull open his cheeks, run a finger down his crack. He wriggles, then gets a hand on his cock and works himself. I scramble for a condom, lube him with spit, then park my cock head at his rim, taking in the sight for a long second before I push in. He squeals with delight as I slide up his chute, and I lower myself onto him until we are one writhing, humping creature. I lock my arms around his chest as I thrust into him, and even though I'm desperate, I manage an incredible staying power, as if this is the ultimate fuck, the one and only grand finale. I feel his ass against me, his sweet little ass, feel my cock sliding into his spongy rectum. I hear him coming, breathy little gasps as he bucks beneath me. I savor his feel and the knowledge that I'm going to keep on fucking him until he comes again, that I can do it because he is all I want. For Christmas.

The Gift That Kept on Giving
by Trixi

It was my 33rd birthday, and I wasn't feeling old. Well, not *really*. I was feeling, let's say, "not young." Or, more to the point, I wasn't feeling attractive *to* the young. By young I mean the "boys"—the frisky, fresh men in their early 20s. Clean-cut, smooth-skinned, sheer-shirted boys with dilated pupils and tight asses. Not as young as the ravers or as used as the circuit twinks. They aim to please as a matter of pride. Sometimes their *only* pride.

My thoughts were interrupted by the honking horn of Patrick's old pickup truck out front, which he uses to collect the antique furniture he refinishes for a living. "Come on," he yelled in between honks, "one, two, thirty-three!" He honked again, hanging his silk-sleeved arm out the window. Bald head. Plucked eyebrows. *Honk!*

"Stop with the goddamn horn!" my neighbor hollered from a window upstairs. "Oh, yes," I muttered as I stepped out and waved an apology, "this night's going to be just wonderful." I hate the celebration of aging. But what I didn't realize was that Patrick had a thing or two (or three) planned for the evening...

A horde of my friends had rented an industrial space downtown for my birthday bash. The east side of the warehouse was divided into five unfinished rooms. The west side stood wide open—the perfect dance floor. Everyone had pitched in and decorated the place with dark-green balloons, candles, streamers, and, apparently, every man they'd ever met or made. The place was jammed with a Whitman's Sampler of men: leather and lace, bears and twinkies, businessmen and club kids, and a few in-betweens like myself.

Patrick grabbed my hand, planted a BIRTHDAY NO. 33 baseball cap on my head, and towed me through the throng, introducing me to a few people here and there but never giving me the chance to get to talk to anyone. "Let's dance!" he shouted above the mingling masses.

The speakers shook with house music. I could see the balloons suspended above us, vibrating with the beat. Lights spun from disco balls and lasers. To my left I watched a lean boy sway gracefully back and forth, his tight powder-blue shirt outlining taut, streaming back muscles and a tiny waist. When he turned around I lost my breath. What a beautiful young man. Maybe 23 or 24 years old, with a full mouth and gentle hazel eyes. Eyebrow ring and—

And Patrick shimmied up beside me, tooting his noise-maker and swinging his arms high above his head like a queer windmill panicking at the sight of Don Quixote. He tangoed around me, making enough of a scene to frighten away my pierced beauty. Realizing I was probably too old to interest that fine fresh face anyway, I resigned myself to dancing with my flamboyant friend.

There is a man I love with all my heart—and all my bank account, since he lives 1,000 miles away and won't be able to transfer here for another year. Daniel Douglas. Personnel supervisor by day, Judy Garland impersonator by night. Tall, compassionate, uncut, intelligent, and funny, with a fog of graying, thick red hair. He's sexy as hell—especially in a tux, and...1,000 miles away. So our relationship remains open. Neither of us do much about it. We just give ourselves permission in case anything, ah, pops up.

Last time we were together, Daniel blushed as he told me about his biggest fantasy: a scruffy daddy with a huge cock held tight in black leather pants, commanding his bitch to kneel and suck. *Turn over and let me see your ass. Nice...nice...* Spanking Daniel lightly at first, then harder, grabbing his huge dick and jerking it like he's shaking a can of shaving cream. Daddy uses his sticky precome to lube up Daniel's ass and probe around inside, with three thick oil-stained fingers stretching the way, before shoving his nine-incher inside.

Daddy enters slowly at first, then pounds harder and deeper inside Daniel's smacked red ass. He doesn't let Daniel touch his own dick, which is stretched beyond anything he's felt before. "Tell me to fuck you harder," he growls. "Tell me to shove my dick in as far as it'll go…" Ramming him.

"Loosen up and get ready, because I'm going to fuck you so hard you'll taste me coming at the bottom of your throat," Daddy says. Sweat drips from his chest down Daniel's ass crack. His dick beats Daniel's prostate as his balls slap back and forth. Daniel moans. Daddy's mouth hangs open, his breathing intensifying until he shoots pounding loads into Daniel's aching ass.

"What's your fantasy?" Daniel asked me after he finished his story, his hand absently dipping and redipping his tea bag into the now lukewarm water. I have a thing for hands. It's the first part of a man I notice, really. I fell in love with Daniel's perfect hands long before the rest of him. They are magnificent—long, rounded fingers with a fine dusting of pale-red hair. Marble tone. Immaculate nails.

"My fantasy?" I smiled, looking up from his hands.

"Yeah, your favorite fantasy."

So I told him in a hushed voice, our eyes locking to block out the coffee shop clamor around us. I told him about a pretty boy on his knees, willing to perform any service once the lights and glare of his sparkling crowd fades away. A scrawny 25-year-old in a dark room, sucking my cock like a starving fawn in the middle of winter. Begging to lick my asshole.

"Come on!" Patrick shouted in the middle of my visions. "Cake time!"

He grabbed me, and again we rushed through the sweaty mass of dancing men. Someone reached down and rubbed my erection through my jeans, whispering "Happy birthday," but Patrick gave me no time to see who was offering such a generous gift.

"Cake time! Cake time!" he shouted like a car alarm.

The music hushed and the cake came out, pulled by my good friends Doug and Ric. Ric winked—just a friendly habit, which took me a long time to understand. Friendly. *Got it.* Right. He winked again. *Tease.* My rod was already aching.

I blew out my bundle of candles with a little help from my friends while everyone around the warehouse sang "Happy Birthday." And then, as the candle smoke circled away, I looked up and saw my pierced Little Boy Blue again. He smiled at me. Deep dimples. A collar around his thin neck. Thin, muscular fingers clapping—

Clapping. Everyone was clapping and singing. I hardly noticed. I smiled back to Little Boy Blue, hoping I didn't seem like a hawk. No, I couldn't, I reassured myself. I was only 33, not 53, for fuck's sake. And I looked good: hairy chest, coal-black eyes, perfect goatee.

Patrick kissed my cheek and the singing died down. "Toast toast toast!!!" he sang. "Toast to my best friend on his birthday! A man with many amazing assets—oh, yes!"

"Patrick..." I stammered. But from the corner of my eye I saw Little Boy Blue smile. A ready smile. And I wouldn't disappoint him. Eight inches on a good day. And I think it just might be a good day after all.

Ric toasted me then abruptly disappeared with Doug. I turned toward my infatuation, watching the way his knees waved back and forth inside his wide-leg pants. One of his friends sauntered up beside him, noticed the locked stare between us, and quietly sailed away. Patrick, however, seemed hell-bent on disrupting my evening.

"Oh, my. He's barely out of the cradle!" he chirped as he pulled me away.

Now I was getting pissed. He shushed me, whirling us past the dancing to the dark eastern side of the warehouse, where the music was still loud but in a distant way. The makeshift walls ricocheted the beat. There were no balloons here, only a few candles some partygoers had dragged over to intensify the mood.

Patrick's paced slowed as we walked through a series of open alleys. No doors. I smelled some cigarette smoke from one of the corners.

We passed the first room. I peeked in and saw in the shadows a tattooed man topping a bear of a man. Bear was squeezing his own dick, his mouth open and waiting for the tattooed top to fill it with his more-than-ready rod. I felt my cock stiffen again as I watched Tattoo slowly slide up Bear's body. *Oh, my God, he has a Prince Albert. Fuck, that's hot!*

He knelt with his thighs straddling either side of Bear's head, rubbing his knob slowly—stopping to lower his ball sac just above Bear's mouth. Bear flicked his tongue out, licking the musky hairs with a groan. Tattoo grabbed his meat and planted it hastily into Bear's bearded mouth. Bear took it like a man—in one swallow. He dropped his own meat and focused solely on the dick in his mouth.

Bear used his hands to jack him up and down while playing with the ring shining through the engorged pink head of Tattoo's dick. He tugged it gently with his teeth. Tattoo moaned. Bear took the cue and sucked him down again like he was born to do it. Tattoo's muscular arms tensed up.

I reached down to grab my own rock-hard dick, feeling almost dizzy with excitement when Patrick intercepted and pulled me away. "Tut-tut!" *Goddamn him!*

Then for some reason Patrick shouted in the silence, "OK, let's go upstairs!" and he banged three times on the gray wall beside him. *What was that about?* We rounded a few wooden stairs, creaking as we climbed. My unassisted cock throbbed insistently as I still thought of Little Boy Blue—of fucking him the way Bear was getting it just a few yards away.

The upstairs was made up of three rooms—two smaller rooms to our left and right, and a larger room stretching along the entire distance of the back wall. We headed straight for the larger space and through its wide doorway.

The space was even larger than it appeared from the outside. White candles flickered along the edges of the brick-faced, graffitied back wall. It smelled like peppermint and sweat. Then I saw them—three young men sitting near the candles on the cold concrete floor, sharing a cigarette. They looked at my "33" baseball cap, then to Patrick, who nodded as he dabbed some perspiration from his scalp.

"This is the birthday boy," Patrick cooed to the diverse three. The tallest one, lanky in his black gothic wear, was flanked by a muscular gym boy in tight Levi's and a closely shorn young man with green eyes and thick eyebrows who flicked his tongue ring in and out anxiously. His T-shirt read QUEER in baseball-logo-style writing. His dick strained against his pea-soup army pants. Cocky Stud. I imagined him on his knees with his back against the wall, straining as I shoved my cock down his throat.

"What are you thinking?" he asked, flicking his tongue piercing again. I could smell his cK One. Tribal earring circles stretched his earlobes. A small eagle tattoo poked out of the neckline of his T-shirt.

Patrick nodded to me, then left with a self-satisfied sashay out of the room. As well he should.

"I'm thinking of you on your knees waiting to suck my dick," I said. And with that he took a final drag of their cigarette and knelt before me. I pushed him roughly back against the brick and undid my fly to reveal my rock-hard wonder. His eyes never left my dick, even as I took off my belt and tied his hands behind his back.

The other two in my own little sampler pack watched us. Goth Boy was daring enough to start massaging himself through his vinyl pants. Eyes coyly peeking out from under slick black bangs. Black painted nails. Gym Boy reached over assertively to help him. The passive Goth Boy sat back, allowing anything to happen. That got me even hotter.

I slapped my stiff prick across Cocky Stud's face, teasing him by placing the soft head against his lips but now allowing him to play. "Please," he pleaded. I slapped him harder. The candles flickered.

"Please, sir," he begged again, with the hint of a smile telling me he enjoyed this game. I yanked his short hair back and forced him to look me in the eye so I could see the surprised look when I shoved my dick in his mouth. I rammed it in quickly then slowed down, letting myself feel the wet heat of his mouth. I gently tapped my prick against the roof of his mouth then dropped his head and pushed farther inside. My balls tightened, feeling the pressure build.

By now the other two had shifted closer to us but remained on the floor. Gym Boy pulled at Goth's nipple ring and whispered something in his ear. Goth Boy closed his eyes and sighed. I hissed at them to shut up and wait their turn. I blocked them out for a few minutes, feeling only Cocky Stud's piercing against the underside of my dick.

Then I turned to Goth Boy. "Come here. Kneel behind me," I said without losing a beat of my face fucking. I pulled out and took off my pants. All eyes were focused on either my ass, my jutting cock, or my black-haired uneven sac.

I turned around and bent over slightly in front of the still-bound Cocky Stud, who immediately burrowed his face into my ass, licking slowly around my man hole. *Oh, fuck yeah.* Goth Boy moved timidly forward until he was inches away from what he wanted, looking up at me with eyeliner emphasizing brown eyes. I nodded affirmatively, letting him grab onto my fuck stick gently. "Suck it," I commanded. And he did.

I felt Cocky Stud's hot tongue probe deeper into my asshole, moving in and out hungrily while Goth Boy took more than half my considerable meat down his throat. He gagged a little but started again without missing a beat.

"Lick my balls." I spread my legs for access, knowing I'd shoot my load everywhere if he throated me again. Goth Boy crouched underneath me for position. I felt him take each ball into his mouth one at a time, moving his tongue between them and down, nearly meeting Cocky Stud's face as he continued rimming me, with his piercing hitting the sides of my hole each time.

"Gym Boy," I groaned, "come and fuck your friend so I can see you."

Gym Boy hauled himself up and tore off his jeans to reveal a small but anxious prick with shaved balls. He rolled on a condom as Goth Boy lowered his pants, swatted his dyed black hair away, then bent over and took my cock in his mouth again. Gym Boy eagerly lubed up his hole with a vial he had taken from his pocket. Then, without much preparation, he plunged into Goth Boy fiercely, causing him to recoil but not leave my dick. *He's a lot tougher than he looks,* I thought.

Gym Boy's eyes fixed onto the blow job before him as he plugged roughly over and over, each time driving Goth Boy deeper onto my rod and Cocky Stud's tongue deeper into my ass. Gym Boy's muscular arms bulged as his grip tightened on Goth Boy's frail waist. I felt Goth Boy wince with each pounding, and it intensified what I felt. I could barely hold it in any longer.

"Move back," I told Goth Boy, who promptly removed his painted mouth. Gym Boy watched with anticipation, still thrusting into the pale ass before him as I jerked myself faster and faster, meeting his pounding movements. "Oh, fuck...Oh, fuck..." he said over and over until he came with a gurgled moan up Goth Boy's ass while I simultaneously shot on his face. Streams of come dripped from his smeared black lips. He licked it up, smiling at me—a demonic pig-clown.

Gym Boy drew up his pants and pulled some smokes from the back pocket. Sweat glistened on his forehead. I could see patterns of red on his well-defined chest where his shirt was unbuttoned.

"Take off your shirt. Good. Now take off your belt," I

commanded. "And tie him up beside the other one." Gym Boy did as instructed, the unlit cigarette still hanging from his mouth.

Cocky Stud and Goth Boy knelt there wondering what I was planning next. Cocky Stud's eyes pierced the darkness as Goth Boy swam in it. Just as I turned to Gym Boy, ready to give him a pounding twice as fierce as he had just done, I saw Little Boy Blue standing in the entrance of the room. My cock flinched.

Little Boy Blue approached. "Tie Gym Boy here up with your belt like the others," I commanded. He did—but with a playful smile. "Now unzip all of them and let their dicks hang out." He did—touching them more than I thought he'd dare.

Then he turned to me and said, "What would you like for your birthday?"

"Lay down on the floor," I told him.

"No," he said with surprising confidence, "why don't you lay down? I want to ride you." Everything stopped. Utter silence. Then, to my amazement, I lay down just as instructed in front of the three others. His nipples poked through the thin fabric. He rubbed them with his delicate fingertips.

My dick pounded, engorging again as he slowly removed his powder-blue shirt to reveal a muscled but small chest with a patch of fine brown hair in the center. He leaned down and mischievously sucked the base of my cock all the way to the tip, where it rose to greet him. He teased the tip and the slit with a knowing tongue before standing up and removing his pants.

I looked at his cock. Not as big as mine, but nice. Hard and darker than the rest of his ghostly body. Trimmed but not shaved. The three along the wall had uncomfortable hard-ons, but they were so focused on the action they didn't seem bothered. Wax from the candles spilled all over the floor.

Little Boy Blue took out a tube of petroleum lip balm and squeezed a swirling mound of it into his hand. He lubed up his ass and moved over to me. Then he topped me as a bottom.

He sat on my dick, forcing it in a bit more each time he slid up and down. The pressure squeezed me inside. His body dropped lower and lower with each measured breath. His eyes closed as he concentrated.

I was amazed, feeling like I had never felt before. Dominant yet submissive to this young man. I never knew I could feel such power from this position.

I felt myself being sucked deeper into his tight, slick ass. He pulled apart his cheeks to give greater access. Even though I'd just come, I wondered if I could hold back shooting again.

The fucking became easier. He bounced up and down, leaning his hands on my furry rigid abdomen for support. He tipped his head back in ecstasy as he pummeled his gland. Harder, harder, harder, each movement bringing me closer. His thumb and forefinger circled my left nipple and squeezed while twisting. The pain shot straight into my core. At the same time he tightened up his ass and increased the speed of his fucking me. I felt ready to explode. "More," I barked, as I pulled him tightly by the collar. He pinched again, saying, "I love your cock." Then his ass swallowed my entire shaft! *Fuck!* "Oh, yeah..." he moaned.

I pulled him down hard again with my hands on his hips. He rode me so fast and deep that the room started spinning, and I let out a cry as I shot wave after wave of come up his hole.

Then he casually slipped off, leaving me spent on the floor, and moved over to blue-balled crew along the wall. He took his dick in his hand and let each one take a turn sucking it as if he were playing slots in Vegas.

After a few warm-ups, Little Boy Blue turned around and jacked off for me. Long, fast beatings. His legs shook. "I loved feeling your huge cock inside me," he whispered, shining up his rock-hard dick. Within minutes he braced his legs farther apart and came in a jagged, jutting stream all over the concrete right in front of me. Then without saying a word he got dressed, smiled, and left.

I stood up, picked up the smoke that had fallen from Gym Boy's mouth 15 minutes ago, and lit it. I'd never been fucked like that before. It made me feel even stronger than when I'd been the top. Amazing. Thinking about it gave me stirrings even though I know my dick was too tired to respond.

Patrick came in as if on cue and put a $50 bill in the mouths of each of the three belted boys along the wall. "Happy birthday, old man," he said to me. "You know, it was your lovely Daniel who let me in on your little fantasy for twinkies."

"How did you get the one in blue to come in?" I asked, my nipple throbbing pleasantly.

Patrick shrugged. "He must have wandered in on his own."

I never saw Little Boy Blue again—but he left me with the gift that kept on giving. When Daniel came to visit later that month, he was met by an older but much wiser man who not only knew his tops from his bottoms, but knew a little more about the spaces in between.

My Best Friend's Brother
Sebastian Caine

"Wanna hear something cool?" Chris asked.

"What would that be?" I replied.

Chris leaned over, placed his hands on his thighs, and began rocking his pelvis rapidly. I could hear an odd *swack swack swack* sound.

"What the hell is that?"

"My balls."

Shocked, I found myself highly aroused at this revelation. Chris was 18 years old at the time, the little brother of my best friend. He also had a fine ass. He was a late bloomer, and I don't think he hit puberty until he was 16 or so. He stood at about 5 foot 5, maybe 120 pounds, and had a high, tight, round ass, narrow hips, and a waist that tapered up to his broadening shoulders. This boy had all the potential of being a bona fide hottie. With piercing blue eyes, a devastating smile with straight white teeth, and spiked blond hair, he set more than his fair share of girls' hearts aflutter. Not to mention those of a couple of males, I'm sure.

I'd known Chris for probably half his life. He came to me whenever he had a problem, and I often woke up with him lain against me when I stayed over. Interestingly enough, I spent more time with him when I was there than with his older brother. But I never really thought too much about it. His older brother, Andy, gorgeous in his own right, often played on his computer. I had little interest in it, and being a bit of a kid at heart, I would often talk to Chris. It also helped that Andy was terrible with anyone younger and couldn't really deal with Chris and his idiosyncrasies.

Chris was a great guy and a riot to be around, and I wound up playing the role of his big brother when Andy moved away. He confided everything to me. One day he accidentally zipped himself up in his fly. I helped him get free and even inspected him. He was 9 at the time, and I no more thought of him sexually than I did my own mom. That's why I was so shocked when he showed me his new trick.

I came out to Chris and Andy about five years prior, when Chris was about 13. It was awkward. I never really discussed it with Chris or came out directly to him, but I knew he was aware of it.

Chris had just turned 18 when he showed me how he could make his balls smack against his crotch. There was much more to come.

"What were you doing when you figured out that you could do that?" I said.

"I don't know. During gymnastics I noticed that if I practiced certain moves, they moved a bit. So-o-o..."

"Ah-h-h..."

"I can make myself fart too."

Ah, to be a teenager again and to experience life's little joys, I thought.

"And just how the hell do you do that?"

"I relax my butt and then kinda draw air in."

My mind reeled with the possibilities that existed when one had that much control over his body. I felt my pecker twitch in my shorts. I guess he felt he had to prove it because, next thing I knew, he farted.

"Oh, that's charming, Chris. I bet you get lots of dates doing that."

Chris smiled at me. When I saw the gleam in his eye I knew I was in trouble. Without any further warning he launched himself and tackled me. I went to the floor and easily flipped him on his back. I could swear I felt something rather rigid against my leg as I moved to straddle him. As I looked down at him with my knees on his arms and my crotch in his face, I realized how suggestive this position was. He looked up to me with a glimmer that seemed to say he was well-aware of the position. Becoming uncomfortable, I released him and rolled back onto the floor, then crawled over by the couch.

"I gotta take a shower," he said as he jumped up and ran to the bathroom. His erection tenting out his shorts did not go unnoticed.

Conflicting emotions ran through my mind. *What the hell am I doing? Jesus, am I really thinking about him like this?* I've always been attracted to younger guys, but they were usually within a year or so of my 23 years. Still, the erection in my own shorts gave, pardon the pun, hard evidence of my own arousal.

With Chris's mother and stepfather out of town and Andy having moved out a week prior, I was alone with Chris for the next few days. Since he still had a couple of months before graduation, Chris's mother had asked me to keep an eye on him. Could I betray her trust? Then again, if he wanted this, what was I betraying? God, it sucked. I figured I was just misreading things. I could remember getting aroused by the simple friction caused by wrestling. Then again, I was gay.

Fifteen minutes later Chris came out of the bathroom. I was on the bed I used when I stayed there. Andy's old room had become mine for the time being. It had been some time since I had stayed in Chris's room. I thought he might feel uncomfortable after finding out I was gay. He would often curl up with me at night, but I figured he just wanted some type of affection because his father was dead and his stepfather had no interest. I was his sole male influence, for the most part.

He poked his head into the room. I could see water droplets ran down between his developing pecs as he stepped into the room. I inadvertently watched them course down his slim body, some drops dipping in his belly button, then continuing down his flat, firm stomach, coming to rest on the towel around his waist. I forced my eyes back up to his face.

"You going to bed already?" Chris asked.

"Yeah, I'm kinda beat."

He looked disappointed but chose that moment to turn around and pull the towel up just above his firm ass and ask me, "Is there a bruise here?" He was pointing at his thigh, just below the curve of his right buttock. My cock twanged. I swallowed and said no, pulling my leg up to try to conceal my erection. He just smiled and dropped the towel, then headed into his room.

Again my mind raced. *What the hell is he doing?*

I heard him come out of his room, and I shut my eyes, halfheartedly hoping he would slip back into his room, thinking I was falling asleep. Chris wasn't fooled, though. He leaped on the bed and straddled my chest just like I had done to him earlier. He was wearing only boxer briefs and a grin from ear to ear.

I looked up at him and noticed that he was still slightly damp, his hair sticking up in spikes. He grabbed my wrists and held my arms above my head. I could see water stuck in the hair of his armpits. My only thought was that this boy had done some growing.

"What are you doing?"

"I've got you pinned."

"Yes, I guess you do."

My dick had started its dance again, and I shifted, worried he would notice. At the same time, I glanced at his crotch and noticed that he had a tube-shaped lump straining at the leg of his underwear.

Chris caught my look, and, releasing my hands, he sat up and grinned mischievously. His eyes twinkled and he licked his lips.

I looked up at him. "What is that?" I asked, pointing at the bulge.

"Me," he replied.

Yeah, whatever. I reached my arm up over his thigh and pressed my index finger on it. It gave slightly, and I jerked my hand back as if burned when I realized he wasn't joking.

I looked up at him and gained a new respect for him. Eighteen or not, this boy was stacked. I figured his cock would be at least six inches when fully hard, if not more. And from the sound of his balls...

Chris gazed down at me again, and I saw a look I've seen before: desire. Wanton desire.

He looked at his crotch, then back to my eyes, and his hand ran down the Y of his crotch and his other hand rubbed my chest.

"What are you doing?"

"What do you think?" he replied, his eyebrows arched.

Trying to make light of the situation, I said mockingly, "Come back when you have some hair."

Chris laughed a sweet boyish laugh and with his right hand pulled his shorts down to the base of his penis. He had a patch of hair slightly darker and finer than the hair on his head. He allowed the waistband to snap back up to his belly and again gave me the look with arched eyebrows.

I looked at the bulge in the leg of his shorts and watched it move slightly as he began to harden. My own penis had become a rail spike in my shorts. I licked my lips and looked back at his eyes.

He pulled the leg of his shorts up to expose the pink head of his penis. My tongue darted out of my mouth of its own accord and wetted my lips again. His penis jerked as he marked my movement. Before I realized it he had moved, and I felt his hand grasp my penis through my shorts.

"Are you sure you want to do this?"

"Duh, why do you think I'm sitting here?"

I couldn't believe that he was seducing me this way. He was moving so fast. He was still wet from the shower, for chrissake. I tried to rationalize what was going on, to talk myself out of it, but I had no luck. When he leaned over and kissed me, I was gone.

Chris pulled his knees off my biceps and stretched himself

out over me. I felt his penis against my lower stomach. I was almost a foot taller than him, but he was close to my size where it counted.

I ran my hands down the back of his shorts and cupped his tight, hairless ass, and he began to grind himself against me, his tongue darting into my mouth. I pulled his shorts farther down, running my hands down his ass and thighs. As I held his shorts for him, he pulled his legs up one by one and freed himself. I tossed them on the floor and felt his hard cock hit my leg. It was now fully erect, and he was easily between five and six inches. I could just imagine how much bigger he would get, being a late bloomer. Our lips never parted. Our tongues still danced. Our hearts were racing and our breathing sped up.

Chris pulled back from me and grasped the waistband of my shorts and boxers and pulled them down together. My 6½-inch cock smacked against my stomach. He wrapped his fingers around it and started to pull the skin up and down. I looked at his smooth young body. He was up on one arm and looking intently at my dick. His nipples were dark, and his cock head was starting to turn a light-purplish color. His hairless balls lay on his thigh, and I noticed a drop of precome nestled in the hole of his prick.

I reached down and rubbed his cock as well. He moaned and fell back onto the bed beside me. He ran his hand up my stomach through the sparse hair and played with my nipples, running his fingers around them.

I continued manipulating his cock. My own cock throbbed with anticipation.

"Suck it," he said.

He arched his pelvis toward me. I released him and put my hand on the back of his neck. I felt the wet hair on the nape of his neck, and I pulled his face toward mine. Our bodies pressed together, and I felt his damp skin on mine. We kissed for a moment, then I made a trail of kisses down his neck.

Licking and sucking lightly, I tongued his Adam's apple and moved down to his chest. I licked his nipples, going from one to the other. They were hard, prominent little buds. I sucked them and nipped them lightly.

Chris's hands were on the back of my head, and he pushed me down. I licked my way down his chest and stomach, pausing to stick my tongue into his navel. Then I followed the trail marked with fine hair down to his bush. I licked and probed with my tongue, ignoring his young cock for the time being. I could tell he was going crazy. But I didn't want it to end too soon. I licked around his bush. and, pulling his legs apart, I nibbled on the tendon that ran up his inner thigh to the hard ridge beneath his scrotum. He moaned and giggled. I kneaded his naked balls with my right hand, pausing now and then to run my hand up his shaft.

He begged me to suck his dick. I smiled up at him and rolled him onto his stomach. I felt him grind against the mattress, my own cock throbbing and pulsing. I licked and nibbled his butt cheeks. His ass was beautiful, not a mark on it, and the pale cheeks were a slightly lighter color than his back. They arched up like two perfect round loaves of freshly baked bread. I pulled them apart and licked down the crack, which made him wiggle and groan. I found his little hole and darted my tongue into it. As I moistened his asshole, I felt it flower open.

Knowing I was about to burst, I rolled him back over and gave him what he wanted. Holding his cock in my right hand and his balls in my left, I ran my tongue down the shaft and licked around the tip. I felt his balls pull up and stopped for a second to lightly pinch his cock just below the glans. I felt his balls settle back down, and I began licking the tip again. I pursed my lips against the tip, as if kissing it, and slowly opened my mouth, taking in a little at a time. His cock head popped into my mouth, and I ran my tongue around it. He tried to thrust his cock farther in, but I held him out.

He moaned some more and pleaded with me to deep-throat him. I obliged. Moving swiftly, I ducked my head down and pulled him all the way in. He gasped and his balls pulled up again. Twice more I slurped his cock, and then he screamed, "I'm coming!"

I pulled off to jack him off. He twisted and writhed as I ran my hand down to the base and back up to the tip. Come squirted out and struck my face as I was leaning over him to watch everything. I licked his cock again and swallowed as another squirt shot into my open mouth. I pulled and pushed his cock as he kept coming, shooting his young seed up and onto my face and his stomach. His come was clear and tasted like honey straight from the comb. I licked it off his stomach and swallowed every bit. As young as he was, he had an awesome dick and balls, and he shot an incredible load. I continued to lick his tight stomach and moved back up his body. He licked his own come off my face and kissed me deeply.

I was getting ready to jack my own load when he shocked me yet again.

"Wanna fuck me? I bet I can relax enough."

I almost came just from the thought.

I started to shake and questioned again what I was doing. But he just kissed me again and rolled over.

"Lick my ass some more, OK?"

I didn't have to be asked twice. He rolled over, and I munched on his ass like there was no tomorrow. I could taste soap and the slightly salty taste of his sweat mingled with some of the come that had run down his balls and into his crack. He shook and quivered with the attention I gave his luscious ass.

I got his Cheerio so wet that I could stick a finger in him with ease. With a little prodding I had two in him. But I didn't want to hurt him, so I wiggled them around a bit to test the waters. He seemed ready and willing to take everything I could give.

"I've got some lube in the drawer," I said. "You wanna hand it to me?"

Chris stretched forward and pulled open the drawer. "This it?"

"Yeah," I said, taking it from him.

I smeared the gel on the tip of my cock and on his asshole. Poised with my cock against his ass, I hesitated.

"Let me know if this hurts too much, OK? Anytime you want to stop, say so."

"I'm OK. Just do it. I want you in me."

Taking a moment, I steeled myself then pressed into him. He pressed himself back against me, and I felt my cock head pop inside him. I heard him hiss between his teeth. I paused for a minute to let him adjust. He pushed back against me again; his asshole relaxed and opened for me. Before I knew it I was in to the hilt, my pubic hair against his upturned ass.

I grabbed his hips and slid in and out of him, his rectum tight around my cock. I groaned and felt myself reaching toward the pinnacle. He grasped my right hand and slid it around his waist. I found his rigid cock and began to rub him again. I rubbed his cock, then I went down and fondled his balls. His own hand would sneak past and rub my balls as well. A couple of times I thrust forward and rubbed our balls together. He moaned, and I felt him tighten up around my cock as he spent his load on the bed.

I could contain myself no longer, so I pulled out. He flipped over onto his back and grabbed my cock.

"Come on me!"

He jerked my cock, aiming me over his body. Ropy wads of come shot from my cock. One struck him on the face. He never stopped pulling my pud. He just stuck his tongue out and licked the come running alongside his lips. I came and came. Spurts of white-hot jizz covered his stomach and chest. I didn't think I would ever stop. When I was finally spent, I leaned down and licked my come off him. Leaving some in my mouth, I kissed his full lips. He parted my lips with his tongue and licked the come from my mouth. We snuggled in an embrace and fell asleep.

The next morning I awoke with a start. Chris was still tight against my body with his hand on my crotch. I felt a wave of guilt and tried to extricate myself from him. He stirred and opened his eyes. As I looked into his eyes, all feelings of guilt left my mind. I knew it had been what he wanted.

He released my dick and kissed me. I returned his kiss and delicately danced my tongue across his. I felt my body start to respond as I ran my hands down his body. I rolled onto my back, taking him with me. His cock was stiffening against me. We kissed passionately and he lightly touched my cock, his fingers circling the base.

He pulled away from me and, mimicking the actions I'd performed the night before, he worked his way down my body. I shuddered as he took my penis into his mouth and pulled the length of it into his throat.

Withdrawing me from his mouth, he asked, "Can I fuck you this time?"

I nodded and pulled him back up to me, kissing his face again and feeling his ass with my hands.

"I think I love you, is that OK?" he said.

"What do you mean?"

"I don't know, I just want to always be with you." He looked down and blushed.

"Chris, there are five years between us. What about school? Isn't there some girl at school you like?"

"I don't like girls. Isn't that obvious?" he replied, his tone tense.

"Yeah, I guess. Well, what about boys? Hell, your friend Josh is hot, how do you feel about him?"

"I don't know. We screw around sometimes and beat off together. He wanted to blow me the other day, but I wanted you to be the first."

My cock twitched at the thought of this fine boy and his equally fine best friend messing around. I was absurdly touched at the thought of him wanting me to be his first, and I told him so.

"You're so young. I envy you. I miss P.E. and all those hot naked boys."

"Did you really like it? It just makes me scared someone will notice me staring."

"Good point." I had to concede that. It was exciting but dangerous in school.

All during this conversation we were rubbing each other, and Chris picked up the pace. I responded. We fell into an embrace again and kissed for a few minutes.

He asked me to roll onto my stomach, but I told him I wanted to face him. I drew my legs up and told him to get the lube and smear it on his cock and my ass. He did as I instructed.

"OK, now press yourself into me. A little more..." I tensed slightly as he started to penetrate me and forced myself to relax. His cock was definitely up to the task. Not quite as thick or as long as my own but most assuredly not a little cock. He stretched my anus as he pushed his slight body toward mine.

His cock head pushed through, and my rectum tightened around his shaft. He moaned and closed his eyes for a moment. Reopening them, he pierced me with their cobalt-blue and smiled. Slowly, slowly, he pushed himself farther into me until I felt his pubic hair tickle my ass. I reached over his back and grasped his ass, pulling him tightly to me. He leaned forward, and I leaned up to kiss him. He pulled back and started to thrust. I was so hot my cock was pulsating, and I hadn't even touched it. Keeping my hands on his ass, I locked my ankles behind him and rocked with his body.

I noticed that he was counting.

"Why are you counting?"

"What?" His eyes glistened, and sweat was beading on his

forehead and upper lip. "Oh, I was told you last longer if you count your strokes."

I laughed and held him close. "Don't worry about that. I'll take whatever you can give. God, you are too cute."

With barely a pause he resumed thrusting, and his strokes became longer. A couple of times his penis almost left my ass. As he fondled my cock, precome oozed out all over it, and he smeared it down the shaft and across the head. He brought his hand to his mouth and licked some off his fingers. I moaned and pulled him tight again. His breathing came in little gasps and his pace quickened. His butt cheeks tightened as he slammed against my body.

It was more than I could take. "Oh, God, Chris, I'm coming!"

When I grasped my dick and started jerking, come shot up and struck my face and chest. I thought I'd never stop. He leaned forward to lick some off my face, and then he pulled out of me and cried that he was coming too.

I dropped my legs, and he maneuvered up onto my stomach and jacked off onto my chest and face. His hot and pungent jism coated my face. I licked it off of the tip when he brought his cock to me, and my fingers dug into his ass.

He rolled off me, both of us spent, and took hold of my hand.

We didn't speak; we just held onto each other as our come mixed and dried on my skin.

I rolled onto my side and looked at him. He smiled and ran his hand down my face. How could I ever doubt or forget the love he showed at that moment?

We would have several more interludes before I ended up moving away. His tenderness and honesty is still fresh in my mind. He was and is a special young man, and I try to see him whenever I'm in town. He's involved with a guy a couple years older than him now; he was always attracted to older men. I'm in a long-term relationship now. Chris still holds a place in my heart and figures heavily in my fantasies. My boyfriend understands, but I'm sure it pains him sometimes when Chris calls; he needn't worry, though, since I would never betray him. Still, I think Chris deserves better. If anyone ever hurt him...well, they'd just better watch out.

Pop Quiz
by Jesse Grant

I walked the corridors of the Dinsmore County Mall—alone like always. Not that I was lonely. I had a house full of fraternity brothers back on campus who were perfectly willing to guzzle beer, talk sports, or chase sorority babes with me. I didn't want that. I wanted sex. The kind of sex that didn't involve sorority babes.

My frat brothers didn't know of my desire to suck cock any more than they knew I was a 19-year-old virgin. In fact, they believed exactly the opposite on both counts. Most of them called me D.J., my nickname, short for Don Juan.

Ours was the jock frat. Nearly everyone in the house played a varsity sport. Those who didn't, like me, had done so in high school. Thus, my frat brothers were familiar with the intricacies of locker room bragging, and like the good boy hetero misogynist athletes they were, they had long ago trained themselves to believe every word, every innuendo, every boast. Tales of who fucked what chick, how hard, and where dominated our talk and were never questioned.

My undeserved reputation as a ladykiller started during pledging. I had chosen this frat because the guys were so hot, all of them buffed and polished, with shiny teeth and dreamy eyes. Heaven.

The first rule of pledging was that all pledges had to move into the fraternity house. We ate there. We studied there. We showered there. We slept there. The attic had been converted into a barracks-style dormitory for pledges, with rows of cots flanked by upright metal closets and footlockers. The last thing I saw each night was an army of scantily clad, tightly muscled male bodies. The first thing I saw each morning was the exact same tightly muscled army—enhanced by an incredible, unashamed parade of morning hard-ons outlined in briefs (always white) or boxers (always plaid).

I'd been around hot guys before but never this many or for this much time. I soon reached a feverish state, waking each night at least once, and usually more than once, to the not unpleasant sensation of shooting a load into my sweat-soaked Jockeys.

I've always liked wet dreams. I even went through a phase in high school when I stopped masturbating in an attempt to force more and more of them. It worked. But I missed jacking off so much that I dropped the tactic in less than a month. My wet dreams had been infrequent ever since, and I was happy to be having them again. But two or three times a night was too much.

I needed to get away. Away from the pointed nipples topping rock-solid pecs. Away from the rippling snowboarders' abs. Away from the firm asses packed brutishly into tight Levi's or—even hotter—serving as delicate, teasing shelves for the waistbands of baggy Calvin Kleins. I needed to cool my jets. I needed to stop thinking about sex every waking and sleeping moment.

I started leaving the house in the evenings. While my densely muscled, densely brained fellow pledges buried their perfect noses in book after book in desperate attempts to keep their GPAs high enough to stay eligible for sports and fraternity initiation, I went to the least sexy place I could think of: The Dinsmore County Mall. I immersed myself in teeming masses of fat, middle-aged couples with snippy teenage daughters, sweatsuit-clad oldsters walking themselves to numb, mindless deaths, and obnoxious junior high schoolers with beeping video games and rap-infested boom boxes.

After a few hours of hormone-killing reality, I'd return to the frat house to the inevitable question "Where you been, Mikey?"

"Well," I would answer, "I went out for a coffee at that new place on Fourth, you know. It was kinda crowded, so there wasn't really anywhere to sit except next to this lady. I think she was probably about 30 or so but really hot. Like, fucking hot..." Or I would answer, "Just to the library. But you won't believe what happened. I was in one of those private study rooms in the basement doing my calculus problems when in walks this Asian chick..."

My frat brothers responded as expected: "Dude, I gotta start drinking coffee."

"Right there in the library? Fuck!"

This was an easy bunch to fool.

After a few weeks "Where you been, Mikey?" changed to "Where you been, Don Juan?" which eventually became "Where you been, D.J.?" "D.J." stuck. Easier on the tongue than "Don Juan."

Another pledge with a nickname was Bill "Hands" McMillan, shortstop on the baseball team, nicknamed Hands because he almost never made an error. He decided to nap one afternoon on his bunk, right next to mine, apparently exhausted from his weekly quiz in remedial basket weaving.

His nap is what sent me to the mall.

After about 10 minutes of snoring, Hands shifted position. His sheet rode up over his hip, and suddenly I could see his cock, rock-hard, slamming up through the fly of his boxers. His hands, good as they may have been, were very definitely not his best body part. One look at his meaty tool was all it took to get my cock throbbing.

There were several other pledges in the dorm, but Hands was positioned so that none of the others could see his dazzling dick. I sneaked a few glances, a few more glances, and then a few more.

Torture.

When I caught myself blatantly staring, I knew it was time to leave. I pulled on a long jacket to hide my hard-on and stumbled toward the door.

"Hey D.J., where you headed?" I heard someone ask.

"Shopping," I stammered in response, too flustered to think of a good lie.

And so now I trudged the corridors of Dinsmore County Mall on a Tuesday afternoon. I'd never been during the day. My previous excursions had always been in the evening, when my sexual urges frenzied their way to unbearable. I had thought the place depressing at night, but daytime was worse. Utterly dismal. Exactly the comedown I needed after observing the fury of Hands McMillan's cock.

I passed a woman with three small children, another with a baby carriage, and a group of well-heeled older women. I window-shopped. The candy store. The expensive department store. The record store. The food court. The women's shoe store.

I saw him.

He emerged from the back room of the shoe store. Tall and lean with dark hair. Like me, except not blond. He wore black pants with his white shirt and tie. I stood at least 30 feet away, but even from that distance the outline of his cock was clearly visible. I watched his dick move as he walked. I stared. This was somehow better than the show I'd taken in earlier. I realized I was hard again, but I'd left my jacket in the car. There was no way to cover up. All of these thoughts and I still stared at his cock. He kneeled—in just the perfect position for me to see the outline of his beautiful meat. He opened a box of shoes. Blue pumps. Did he know I was staring? I looked up. He smirked. He knew.

I fled to the store next door. Sporting goods. I forced myself to peruse the fishing rods and camping gear. I'd never been fishing and despised camping, but I read every price tag. I tested every rod and unzipped every tent. I read a brochure on the thermal qualities of down-lined sleeping bags, and finally my aching loins relaxed. Still, I was flushed and suddenly very thirsty.

Flushed I could handle. Thirsty was a problem. To get to the food court, I would have to pass the shoe store again. I could manage, I decided. I just wouldn't look.

I meandered past, blatantly ignoring the shoe store. As I walked, I felt my hard-on return. Apparently just being in the vicinity of this guy turned me on. I hustled to the taco hut and ordered a Coke, then strolled to a table a good distance from the entrance to the shoe store. I plunged my straw through the lid and sucked down as much of the cool, sweet liquid as possible. Then, just as I began to relax, I felt a presence. I looked up and there he was. Him. Holding a Coke from the taco hut. He must have been in line right behind me. How had I missed him?

"Mind if I sit down?" he asked, helping himself to a chair. "It's a little crowded today."

I glanced around. We were surrounded by empty tables.

He smiled blithely. "What brings you to the mall in the middle of the day?"

"Uhhh..." I searched for an answer.

"You're not looking for a job, are you? Because if you are, I might have an opening. I could interview you right now."

"A job?"

"Yeah," he said. "C'mon. Let's have that interview." He took my arm and led me to his office, talking all the while.

I sat and tried desperately to remember the things he'd told me on the way in. His name was Jeff. He managed the store. Nothing more had stuck. I remembered clearly, however, that his hand on my arm felt strong and warm. I also recalled that he smelled the way freshly showered men smell after 10 minutes in a sauna—musky sweat and cedar. Mostly, I remembered the gorgeous bulge snaking down the leg of his pants.

He wheeled his chair out from behind the desk and sat facing me. "Let's begin," he said. "I want you to take off my shoes for me. Talk about them. Tell me how nice they are."

141

I took a deep breath and exhaled the word "OK." I dropped to my knees and fumbled with his laces.

"Be sexy," he said. "Sexy sells shoes."

"Sure. Sexy." Another deep breath. I wrangled his shoes off. "These are wing tips. They're very nice because…because…" I couldn't do sexy. I didn't know how, and anyway, I was busy watching his cock fight with his pants. It was bigger now than when we'd walked in. Longer and fatter. A lot.

He placed a finger under my chin and tilted my gaze to meet his own. "Not bad," he said. "But you could use a few pointers. Let me show you." He guided me back into my chair as easily as he'd led me into this office.

"Hiking boots," he said. Suddenly I was no longer wearing them. "Rugged. Good for the calves." He tested my calves. "Very nice. Firm." He slid his hands to my thighs. "Solid here too. Do you work out?"

"A little."

"It shows." He ran his finger along the ridge in my jeans. I was so stunned, I barely noticed the cool air hitting my cock. The hot breathing caught my attention. I glanced down to see my button fly open and my Jockeys being pushed down. Then his mouth was on me, warm and wet and slick. Sucking. I started to come without warning. He pulled his mouth back and worked my spit-lubed tool with his hand, praising me as I shot streaming wads of come over his shoulder onto his desk.

I slouched back into my chair, my body limp but my teenage dick still rock-hard. Jeff tugged at my pants and underwear, expertly whisking them off. Then he stood, taking my pullover jersey with him. He leaned back against the desk, holding my shirt with one hand, stroking his tool through his pants with the other. "You wanna show me what you've learned?"

I'd always been a good student, but I'd never enjoyed pop quizzes until this one. I dropped to my knees, this time naked except for my socks. I unzipped his pants. He reached in and pulled out his meat for me. I took it in my fists and squeezed. A drop of precome oozed out, dripping onto the floor. I licked his tip, liking the salty residue, then ran my tongue around his crown.

"You like this, don't you?" he said.

I sucked the head of his mammoth cock in answer, tonguing the slit, aware but not caring that I moaned as I did it.

He ran his fingers through my hair gently, front to back. Then he grabbed not so gently—pulling me forward onto his dick hard until I started to gag. He eased my head back to where I'd started. Then paused. He breathed once. So did I. Then he slammed into me, using his handful of hair to hold me in place. Again and again and again. Deeper with each thrust. Down into my throat, fucking my face. I loved it.

He pulled out as suddenly as he'd entered, grabbing his cock with his free hand and pointing at my face. With a primal grunt he let fly with volley after volley of hot come, spraying my lips, my cheek, my cheek again, my neck, my chin, my lips. And then one final squirt that just caught my earlobe. A dangling pearl earring.

He fell backward onto the desk, hooking his knees under my armpits, encouraging me to stand.

I obeyed.

"You're still hard, aren't you?" he said.

I looked down. "Yes."

His come, still warm, ran slowly down my face and neck, onto my chest. The little bit on my ear dripped to my shoulder and slid down my arm. Comfortable. Reassuring.

He reached over his head and pulled a pack of condoms and lube from his desk drawer. "It's time for you to fuck me."

He unrolled the condom onto my dick then lubed my tool. He told me he really liked my throbbing meat and that he wanted it inside him. "Your cock is perfect," he said.

He wrapped his legs around my waist and used them to pull me toward him, guiding me to his asshole, moaning softly on contact. I pressed against him, let the tip of my cock slide forward. Warm. Tight. A thousand times better than just his mouth. He rocked away from me, then toward me. Slowly. Back and forth. I moved with him, finding a rhythm. Nice. Easy. His ass caressed my shaft as I slid in, then out, then in. "A little deeper," he said. "A little bit deeper now."

And suddenly I was past the resistance of the inner ring I hadn't even known existed. He slammed his fists on the desk and whisper-yelled "Fuck me." His ass gripped my cock like a vise. I slammed into him, fighting the resistance. "Do it." Brutal. "Harder." His stiff rod bobbed upward with each thrust. Precome leaked onto his stomach in great drippy globs. "Yes." He grabbed his meat with both hands and began jacking himself. "Fuck me." No more whispering. "Fuck me. Fuck me." His ass tightened to the point where I could barely move, and then he shot, Jackson Pollack–painting his hairless chest with thin ribbons of jism. He relaxed ever so slightly when his orgasm ended. I pulled out, ripped off the condom, stroked my dick twice, and blew thick shots of come onto his cock and stomach.

I rested, then looked into his eyes and smiled. He pulled me forward. We kissed for the first time. Tongues. Gentle aftermath. He still smelled of sweat and cedar. I wondered what I would tell my frat brothers when I got home.

The New Boy Takes a Bath
by Keith Pruitt

The week had been long and tiring. Making 100 sales calls a day can be brain-numbing work. But it was Friday, and I was ready to relax. After work I would go home and rest a bit before going to the gym to enjoy the pleasures of hot bodies.

Midtown Austin isn't just a gym where gorgeous men come to work off high testosterone levels—it's Austin's newest hot spot for gay cruising and doubles as a bathhouse. I had joined shortly after they opened, and I still enjoy its atmosphere of camaraderie, not to mention the other things.

I drove the short distance to the facility and was surprised to find the parking lot almost full. I went inside and saw that the building was swarming with a large number of towel-clad men of all ages, shapes, and looks.

As is my custom, I walked up the stairs to the top floor, found my room, which was located near the wet area, quickly changed to my towel, showered, and went into the steam room. On the tile-covered concrete bench sat a couple of older, hefty men exchanging preliminary pleasantries. It was obvious, even to my novice eyes, that they were slightly uncomfortable at my presence. So after beginning to sweat, I decided to adjourn to the dry sauna.

The small area outside the steam and sauna was crowded with younger, hot, eager studs. They were talking about someone. "Did you see him?" One young stud asked another.

"Yeah, and I'll suck his cock before the night's over." I recognized the second specimen of youth and virility as a weekend regular. He was tall and sinewy, with a gorgeous tan and a smile that would melt an ice cap. He was also an arrogant asshole. His modus operandi was to go after every drop-dead gorgeous man in the house, even if the guy's dick was in someone else's mouth.

As I started to walk into the sauna, another young but slightly overweight stud walked out of the small room. I glanced down, saw that his towel was poking outward, his large dick signaling his excitement. I smiled, wishing he was glad to see me but knowing someone inside had caused his blood to rush into the head of his large, enticing cock.

I purposely brushed up against him, but he ignored me. Instead he walked into the shower, faced the opposite wall, and turned on the water. *He has a nice ass,* I thought. *Future pleasure.*

I proceeded into the sauna, a small room with dim light and wood benches running along the walls. The far wall was double tiered. I continued to peer out the window of the door, hoping to catch a glimpse of the yet-to-be tasted pleasure of the dude in the shower.

But soon I tired of waiting and turned my attention to the guys perspiring in the sauna. Most were older guys and didn't interest me. In the corner, however, I found a pair of coal nuggets peering deep into my baby blues. I swallowed hard and my knees became weak. It was his hair that first caught my attention: long, straight, and wet, dropping over his shoulders. My libido immediately went through the ceiling as it dawned on me whom the guys outside had been discussing. Now I understood why they were waiting. Why else would anyone wait in the drying-off area?

His eyes fastened on mine like lasers peering into my soul. My body went numb. I glanced up and down. He appeared thin but tightly packed. Every inch of his body seemed chiseled from stone. At first glance he looked to be a Native American, but in Austin it was more probable that he was Hispanic. Just my type, I thought. Thin, young, muscular, tanned, and ready!

The heat was beginning to zap my strength. I tried to dismiss any thought of laying claim to one so excellent in appearance, especially with all the wolves circling just outside the door. I decided to go to my room, leave the door open, and see what happened.

As I left the sauna, I noticed at least a half dozen guys, most young and hot. It was obvious they were all waiting for the same opportunity—the one stud everyone wanted. I walked the short distance to my room, leaving the door wide open, and toweled dry.

Within a minute, the young stallion who had captivated my attention emerged from the heated room and headed through the glass door into the hallway leading to my room. The guys who lined the hall reached down to their towels and groped their cocks, attempting to catch his attention. He came directly toward me, his eyes glued to mine as though mesmerized.

My sails collapsed as he passed by—with a parade of over-charged guys with hard-ons following in pursuit. "I haven't got a chance," I mumbled. I turned to get a cigarette off the wood table next to my bed, deciding to go downstairs for a smoke, since my desires probably wouldn't be realized. As I turned to the door, I saw someone standing in the doorway. It was him!

"Hi-h-hi," I stammered.

"Can I come in?" he said sheepishly, his black eyes softening with a smile.

"Please do," I responded, closing the door behind him. "How did you manage to lose your fan club?"

"What do you mean?"

"Surely you noticed all those gorgeous guys following you."

"I saw them, but I didn't know they were following me."

I was surprised by his sincerity. He obviously wasn't in the know concerning gay cruising. "Why, son, you're the hottest thing in this place."

He began to turn red.

"Those guys were tripping over each other trying to get to you. What I can't believe is out of all the young, handsome

147

hunks you could have had, you ended up in my room. Don't get me wrong, I'm thrilled, but I guess I'm a little astonished."

"When I saw you in the sauna, I couldn't get over your chin."

"You mean the Kirk Douglas dimple?"

"Yeah. And you have great blue eyes."

"Thanks," I smiled.

"I suppose you hear that a lot."

"I've heard it a couple of times," I chuckled.

"Well, I wanted to be with someone who had some experience and who could show me what it's like to be with a man."

"You've done this before, haven't you?"

"No. I've never been with a man."

I could tell by the way he was shaking that he was being honest. I invited him to lie back on the bed and relax, which he did, placing his back up into the corner of the room. As I touched his body, he shivered.

"Just relax, sweetie. What's your name?"

"Joe."

"Mine's Rob," I said, as I moved my mouth toward his firm brown chest. His nipples were taut, with a quarter-size area of soft, darker-brown tissue surrounding them. I gently sucked first one and then the other, swirling my tongue around the soft tissue.

Joe softly moaned then squirmed in the corner. I licked his chest and maneuvered down his smooth, hairless six-pack.

"That feels good," he said. "You definitely know what you're doing."

"I'm just getting started, Joe. Just relax and enjoy."

"OK." He smiled, then pulled the towel from around his 28-inch waist.

I was totally taken by the perfect beauty of his body. His powerful muscle tone, even though he was quite petite; his balanced development; his flawless smooth skin—they all added up to a heat building in my lower abdomen that threatened to prematurely erupt. I knew a mere touch from either Joe or myself would make my cock explode. I'm not quickly aroused now that I am middle-aged, so my raging hard-on amazed me. I was ready to go over the brink and unload a flood of come with such fierceness I could put an eye out. So I kept my hands away and concentrated on Joe.

As his towel slipped from his hands, my eyes riveted on his hard, throbbing cock. It was about seven inches, straight and thin, and nearly glued to his stomach. It bobbed with each heartbeat. I almost needed a crowbar to pry it from his chiseled abs. His rod felt like stone with a layer of thin stretched skin as I began to lick it. I felt myself losing control as I furiously sucked his golden rod. I'd suck on the mushroom head very slowly and then suddenly plunge it down my throat, sending Joe into fits of ecstasy.

I had rarely been in such heat. My dreams could have never concocted such a prize as Joe. Precome now oozed from my piss slit. I knew my automatic pilot would take over at any moment and I would jerk my meat to orgasm.

"Would you like to suck my cock?" I asked.

He hesitated, but then agreed and took my dick into his mouth. He only sucked me a short time before expressing a lack of desire to continue.

"I've never done that before, but now I know I don't like it."

"That's fine," I said. I once again took his throbbing cock into my mouth and throat. He moaned loudly as I swallowed his cock all the way to his balls. I chewed and swallowed those lightly hairy round nuggets and felt them drawing tight. He stopped me as I began licking his ass.

"I really don't think I get anything out of that. Suck on my cock some more."

I did, but I was beginning to want more.

"Would you be interested in fucking me?" I asked.

"I don't know. I've never thought about doing that. I'm not sure I'd know how."

"It's just like fucking a girl, but in the ass," I responded, assuming Joe would associate the experience.

"I've never done that either."

"You mean..."

"This is the first time I've had sex in my life."

"How old are you?"

"Nineteen."

I smiled. "Thanks for letting me be the first."

When he returned the smile, I melted. His smile was like the glistening dew of early morning on a newly blooming rose. I knew right then this was an experience I wouldn't soon forget.

I told Joe I would do all the work and that if he didn't enjoy fucking me, we could stop. He agreed to start with me riding his dick. My reassurance of his enjoyment seemed to calm his fears.

With a lubed condom in place, I gently sank my ass onto his rock-hard cock. His dick felt like a lightning bolt piercing my insides. It wasn't big, but it was so hard, and bent toward his stomach, that it felt like it was coming through the wall of my groin. After a few moments of pain, it felt incredible.

I rode his cock, first in slow motion, then picking up the pace. My hard dick was flopping up and down, plopping loudly against his stomach. At one point Joe grabbed my now wet cock and began pumping. I warned that I would soon explode, which Joe encouraged.

"I want to make you come all over my chest."

That was all it took. Suddenly I exploded a huge load all over his chest. He smiled as he wiped my hot spunk from his chest. He asked if we could change positions. He wasn't ready to stop, nor was I.

I stood beside the bed, bending over with my head against the side wall while he drove his stiffness in and out of my ass.

"I love it. I can't believe how good this feels. Your ass is so tight."

"Your cock is so-o-o hard," I responded.

"Are you OK?"

"You bet I am! I want you to shoot that load all over my face. I want to see you come."

He abruptly stopped, pulled off the condom, and threw it into the corner. I took his cock into my mouth and sucked it hard, trying to build him toward explosion, but he stopped me.

"I want to make you come. Please don't stop me," I begged.

"Yeah. I've got to. I've got a pass for 12 hours. I plan on having as much fun as I can. If I get off now, I won't stay. Like you said, there's a lot of hot guys out there."

"Well, I'm glad I can say I was the first. I'm honored that you chose me. Thank you." I bent forward and planted a gentle kiss on his lips. His dick was still so hard. My inclination was to go down on my knees and take him. But I knew he had made his decision, and I couldn't blame him.

We exchanged a final kiss, and he grabbed his towel and headed toward the showers. His entourage was waiting for his exit from my room.

Wow, I thought, that was perhaps the highlight of my life. I'll never forget Joe. In the three years since then, I've met a number of hot, young studs at the gym, but none will ever top First-time Joe.

Derrick
by Thom Wolf

Derrick knelt on the floor and pressed his face against the hard boards. He reached behind and planted both hands on the chunky cheeks of his ass, spreading his creamy buttocks apart. The flesh of his asshole was stretched and distorted by the tautness of his parted orbs. The skin of his ass was smooth and white, pale in contrast to the crisp, sunburned skin of his legs and torso. Shaved, the crack of his ass had the fresh, underdeveloped appearance of a prepubescent boy.

Derrick was 20. His well-toned flesh radiated with an energetic aura of youth and unspoiled innocence. The only hair on his body was the short blond crop on his head and a neatly clipped bush at the root of his cock. His hairless features gave his nude body the likeness of an angel. His face, now pressed uncomfortably into the rough floor, was soft and pretty.

Red was Derrick's master.

Red stood over the prone body of the young boy and stared down at his naked ass. Red was naked, apart from a leather harness strapped around his thick chest. The broad strips crossed over his shoulders and fastened beside his heart, defining his solid tits. Red's nipples were large and firm; they stood erect like hard pencil tops from the thick mat of dark-brown hair that covered his chest and stomach. His cock was also strapped up in leather and tied tight at the base.

Red squatted on the floor in front of Derrick's raised ass. On the boards at his feet lay a small bowl of warm water and a 100-milliliter syringe. Derrick waited, knowing what to expect. Red inserted the long nozzle of the syringe into the water and drew back on the plunger, filling the cylinder with fluid. He moved slowly, deliberately prolonging the excitement and anticipation.

"You know what this is for?" Red's voice was as moderate and drawn as his movements.

"Yes, Sir," said Derrick calmly.

"Well," said Red. "Tell me."

"It's to clean out my filthy ass, Sir. So that my hole will be clean for your cock."

"Too fucking right," growled Red. "I'm not going to stick my cock in a dirty asshole, am I?"

"No, Sir."

Red inserted the long nozzle into Derrick's splayed asshole. He depressed the plunger, expelling the soapy water into the boy. Derrick drew a sharp breath as the warm liquid entered his bowels, the sensation soothingly uncomfortable. As the cartridge emptied, Red withdrew the syringe quickly, witnessing the sharp contraction of the boy's ass ring.

"Don't you dare spill a drop until I tell you to."

"Yes, Sir," Derrick gasped.

Standing up straight, Red picked up a long, thin strap of leather. Derrick heard the sudden swish through the air an instant before the whip cracked against his ass. He gasped in pain and clenched his ass ring tight to avoid any spillage. Red struck his buttocks again. And again. The smooth white flesh began to redden and break in large, painful welts. Red displayed no emotion. He dealt the treatment without remorse.

Derrick struggled to control his sphincter. He couldn't hold back the tears that welled in his eyes and ran unhindered down his smooth face. His mind was closed to the pain of the whip. He focused all of his attention on his asshole, determined not to spill a drop.

Red stopped beating the boy and cast the whip aside. A heavy shroud of perspiration had broken across his broad forehead, his short fringe of red-brown hair stuck to his skin in damp strands. He licked the sweat that had gathered in his thick stubble.

"Stand up, kid," he commanded.

Derrick did as told without hesitation, tightening his ass as he stood. Red grabbed him and pulled his body tightly against his massive chest. His hands grasped and squeezed the kid's tender buttocks, and he forced his mouth down on the boy's lips. Derrick's hard cock pressed against Red's groin.

Red pushed the young man roughly away from him. They stared hard at each other for a moment; both pairs of eyes shone with excitement.

"Lower your eyes," Red snapped. "And turn around. Bend over."

Derrick obeyed him. He bent from the waist and raised his hips. Red's rough hands snatched at his sore buttocks and spread the cheeks apart. He squatted and inspected the boy's asshole.

"Well-done, kid. Not a drop spilled. Now go and clean yourself out."

Derrick moved hastily to the corner of the dungeon and sat on the cold, seatless toilet bowl. With hard-earned relief, he discharged the contents of his bowels into the pan and cleaned his body with the cold water in the basin prepared by his master. His ass was sore, but the pain only heightened the pleasure of servitude.

Derrick returned to the center of the stark room and stood before his expectant master. He held himself for presentation; arms straight and level at his side, stomach tight, chest raised, back straight. His clean cock stood as firm and erect as a stone pillar.

"Good," said Red. "Now get into position for me."

Derrick turned his back and leaned forward. He bent slightly at the knees and grasped hold of his calves. He presented his ass to Red. The hot and tender cheeks parted naturally from his prone posture and exposed the pink hole within.

Red pulled back the skin of his own cock and unrolled a condom over his fat meat. He snapped the rubber down tight at the base and squeezed lubricant into his palm. He fisted his cock until the swollen shaft was slick.

Pressing his bulbous head against the puckered asshole, he mounted his slave. He slowly savored each sensation as his throbbing organ was enveloped in tight, warm walls of ass. He filled the boy completely, until the leather strap around his dick scraped against the boy's ring.

Derrick strove to maintain his steady position as Red fucked his ass. His asshole, already so warm and tender from the enema he had received, accepted the big dick easily. Holding him by his hips, the older man fucked him, first with consideration and then with increasing force. The pace of his fast-plugging cock increased. He drilled Derrick with a demented fury, deep-dicking far into the moist passage. With a spasmodic convulsion, he discharged his load in long, heavy waves, filling the boy's ass with his milk.

The setup with Red was not a full-time arrangement. They had separate apartments and separate lives. Derrick shared a flat with a boy called Marc. Despite the occasional fuck, his relationship with Marc was platonic. There was no singular lover in Derrick's life. Only 20, he wanted to live his life carelessly while he was still young enough.

He was happy to enjoy a full sex life without the emotional complications of monogamy. The hot fuck sessions he had with Red were the nearest Derrick came to commitment. They had been seeing each other one or two nights a week for the best part of two years. He always looked forward to his evenings with Red, and he trusted him. He was happy to get into the whole master-slave scene. He played that way with Red only, ever. With any of the other guys it was simple fucking and sucking.

Marc did not approve of Red. He didn't understand, and Derrick had stopped trying to explain the unique traits of the association to his friend. It was difficult for him to describe anyway. Despite Marc's insistence, there was nothing dirty or kinky about what he and Red did.

Every Thursday night Marc and Derrick went out on the scene together. They would start off downing a bottle of wine at home before hitting the bars. If neither of them had any luck finding a new lover that night, Marc's cock would find its way up Derrick's asshole before they finally got to sleep.

That night the bars were packed. They had been forced off into a corner beside the D.J. booth. They were both pretty drunk and shouting to make themselves heard above the banging house music.

"No offense, man," said Marc, swigging his beer from the bottle. "But I'm not gonna spend another night humping that tired old rump of yours."

Derrick laughed. "No offense taken."

Marc was in form. "Just as well," he said, "because I've had enough of Red's sloppy seconds to last me a long time."

Derrick took a long swig of his beer. "You really know how to make your friends feel special."

"You know how I feel about Red. He's way too old for you. My God, how old is he anyway?"

"Thirty-eight. He's not old."

"Whatever," Marc scoffed, rolling his eyes. "I don't know what's wrong, but neither of us have had anyone new for weeks."

"I haven't been counting."

"Well, I fucking have. It's been three weeks. What's wrong with us? How come no one wants to fuck us?"

"Maybe it's the desperate vibes you're giving off."

"Fuck you. I'm telling you, neither of us are going home tonight until we get our hands on some fresh cock."

Thursday was always busy, and the crowds seemed larger than usual that night. The bar was packed from the counter to the doors. Marc's eyes were restless as he searched the crowd of faces; some new, some familiar.

"This place is packed," he said. "There's gotta be a couple of guys out there for us."

Derrick took another long swig from his bottle. He had almost finished it.

"Hey," exclaimed Marc, nudging Derrick's arm. "Look at that guy over there. The cute blond in the blue shirt. He keeps looking over here. He must be hot for one of us."

Derrick turned to look at the boy. As his head turned, so did the boy in question, and they met each other's gaze directly. Derrick was stunned; it was like staring at a younger, fresher-faced image of himself. The boy's hair was short, a softer, darker shade of blond than his own. His face was thin and boyish. He was just a boy, but he had the kind of fresh, well-proportioned features that even at 40 would maintain the appearance of youth. From the distance that divided them, Derrick could only interpret the glint in the boy's eyes as one of lust.

"The look says it all," remarked Marc. "It's your ass that he's hot for."

Derrick feigned disinterest. "I'm not into pretty boys. I like old men, remember?"

"The fuck you're not." Marc grabbed his arm. "Come on. We're going to introduce ourselves."

A faint smile touched the corners of the boys' full lips as they cut a path through the crowd toward the blond. Derrick realized as they drew nearer how tall and skinny the kid was. He looked about 15.

"Hi," said Marc, then introduced Derrick and himself. "Are you here by yourself? Are you going clubbing later? How old are you? You look about 12. What's your name?"

The boy answered the questions directly to Derrick. "My name's Jordan. And I'm 18, not 12. I'm here on my own, but I wasn't planning on staying much longer. I want to go to bed."

As Jordan spoke to Derrick it seemed as if the crowd around him had disappeared. There was no one there but the two of them. He moved closer. His pale-blue eyes looked deep into Jordan's intense green stare. The boy was wearing a very light, citrus-smelling aftershave. Without any need for conversation, they both knew in that moment that they were going to go to bed together.

Jordan was just like Derrick in many ways. There would be no master and no slave when they climbed into bed. No lessons or initiations. Just two young bodies, eager and fresh with a desire to share and explore each other. They would be equal.

Marc had vanished into the crowd; neither Derrick nor Jordan cared where. In the heavy atmosphere of the bar Derrick pressed close to the younger man and their lips met. They pressed their mouths together in hunger and held each other tightly. Jordan's full, fleshy lips tasted sweet. Derrick felt the hardness of his cock through the fabric of his clothes.

"Come home with me," Derrick whispered.

They left the bar in a hot, sexual daze.

In the back of the taxi it was an effort for them to keep their hands off each other. Their hunger was basic and impatient, a strong urge that yearned to be satisfied. Thankfully, the journey was a short one.

At the door of the apartment, Derrick fumbled with the lock. He struggled to insert the key. Jordan was behind him, touching him. His hands explored Derrick's back, squeezing and caressing the taut muscle. As the door swung open they tumbled inside. Their mouths were locked once more, and Derrick thrust his tongue into Jordan.

Jordan undid the buttons of Derrick's shirt and tore it from his body. Derrick had the larger build of the two boys; his chest was broad and well-developed. Jordan groped his hard tits. He broke free of Derrick's kiss and fastened his mouth over one of the hard nipples, then licked and chewed on the fleshy stub. His teeth were sharp.

Jordan's hands were now on the fly of his jeans. He loosened the belt and undid the buttons. Derrick's cock sprang free from his pants. Jordan dropped to his knees for a full appraisal of the organ. He held the thick shaft at the root and pressed his soft lips to the fleshy head. Derrick's fleshy jewel was wet with precome. Jordan flicked his tongue lightly over the glans with slow, adroitly executed strokes. Derrick groaned. He took hold of Jordan's head and guided his mouth over the thick head of his cock.

Jordan worked his lips over the heavy ridge and drew the shaft into his throat. The swollen dick was big, and he stretched his jaw wide to take its thickness.

Holding the boy's head in his hands, Derrick rocked his pelvis back and forth. The boy knew how to suck cock. He swallowed the full length of dick down to the chubby root, gently sucking and teasing.

"Oh, God," gasped Derrick. "Hold on a minute. Much more of that and I won't be able to stop myself."

They stumbled through the cramped apartment toward the bedroom, tearing at each other's clothing. Derrick was hungry, wanting to undress the boy and possess his fragile body. He tore open Jordan's shirt to expose his thin, underdeveloped torso; the definition of each rib was prominent and clear. Jordan had small, rosy nipples that gave the only hint of color to his pale-white skin. A little steel bar was pierced cleanly through his right tit. Derrick pulled down his jeans and underpants in one stroke and pushed the boy onto the double bed.

For a skinny kid the boy had a big, well-developed cock: It was long and thick, and it slapped against his stomach as he flopped back on the mattress. He had a tiny bush, just a sparse crop of red-blond hair at the root of his dick—the only hair on his body. His balls were small, compressed tightly within their compact sac like two exquisitely formed miniature eggs.

Jordan raised his long legs onto the bed and tilted his pelvis languidly to the ceiling, exposing his wide ass crack. Derrick knelt at the foot of the bed and pressed his face into the splayed, upturned buttocks. He breathed it in, inhaling the warm scent of the crack. He touched his lips to it, pressing softly against the smooth, hairless skin.

Jordan murmured. Derrick tongued his asshole, lapping greedily at the dusty-pink orifice. The sphincter melted effortlessly, and his tongue disappeared into the warm, silky passage. Tight walls enclosed him. Jordan squirmed and ground his hips into Derrick's face. Derrick fucked him with his mouth, soothing and spreading the tight hole.

He gorged himself gradually on the warm man hole before letting his attention drift higher, toward the tight balls. The tiny orbs rolled and shifted easily in their strong sac. Derrick opened his mouth and drew both of the little balls inside. He rolled them around his tongue.

As he feasted on the tasty sac, Derrick heard a noise outside and became instantly alert, listening with intent. He heard it again—a dull, metallic clank. He released the boy's testicles from his mouth and listened. Someone was at the front door.

"Shit!"

"What's the matter?" Jordan was disappointed by the interruption. "Why'd you stop? Go back down."

"Somebody's coming in," Derrick gasped.

"Who?"

"One of two people."

Red.

He had his own keys. He appeared at the bedroom door, filling the open structure with his tall frame. Derrick gazed between the wide ass of the young boy and the emotionless face of his master. He felt a sudden flush of guilt, followed by a tingling sensation of fear. It occurred to him, as if for the very first time, how dangerous Red was.

"You've betrayed me," Red spoke slowly, accentuating each syllable, his voice booming with power. "You've disobeyed me, little one."

Derrick trembled, both fearful and excited.

Jordan stared, red-faced, at the huge looming figure in the

doorway, unsure what to say or how to handle the ominous situation. He remained silent.

"So is this what you do every Thursday night?"

Derrick shook his head. His eyes were full.

"Answer me, you little bastard," Red bellowed, his face betraying none of the anger in his voice.

"No, Sir," Derrick said timidly, slipping easily into his submissive role. "Never. This is the first time."

"It's the first time, is it?" Red's accusing gaze fell upon Jordan.

The new boy refused to be humiliated. He cleared his dry throat and summoned the courage to speak. "Look, I don't know who you are or what's going on between the two of you, but calm down. Nothing has really happened here yet. I'll get dressed and leave the two of you alone." He moved toward the end of the bed.

"Stay where you are, kid, and keep your fucking mouth closed until I tell you otherwise. I'll deal with you when I'm ready." Red undid the chunky buckle of his belt and slipped the thick leather strap out through his jeans.

"Come here," he said to Derrick.

Derrick stood up, his gaze lowered, and walked toward his master. His naked body trembled. He turned his back to Red and bent over. He grasped hold of his calves, offering his scared and marked buttocks to the older man. He glanced fleetingly toward the bed and instantly recognized the glint of excitement lurking beneath the surface fear on Jordan's face.

The first heavy-handed stroke brought an involuntary gasp of pain from Derrick. He remained locked in his dutiful position as Red repeated the blow again and again. The crack of the leather was loud and frightening in the tense bedroom. Red was merciless in punishing his faithless slave; he beat the boy's buttocks into a raw rage.

Finally he relented, and the angry crack of his belt ceased. He dropped the instrument of discipline to the floor and wiped his brow with the back of his arm. His face and neck glowed warm and wet with perspiration.

He raised the thick sole of his boot to Derrick's buttocks and kicked him over. The boy collapsed in an untidy heap.

"Stay there and don't fucking move until I'm ready for you," the master barked. He turned his blazing gaze toward the bed. He saw straight through the emotion in the boy's face. The deep hint of uncertain excitement.

"And you," said Red. "You little fuck. What are you doing here?"

"I...I..." Jordan stammered.

"You came here to get fucked, didn't you?"

Jordan was silent.

"Answer me," Red snapped.

The boy nodded.

Red undressed. With steady fingers he unclothed his big, hairy body. His physical size was both impressive and intimidating. The sight of his thick, heavily veined cock caused the young boy's eyes to widen. Red stretched a condom over his swollen cock head and rolled it down to the base of his dick.

The man stepped toward the bed, grabbed Jordan, and lifted him effortlessly to the edge. Jordan's young ass hung over the mattress. Red grasped his legs and lifted them. He held the back of the boy's thighs and pushed his knees tight into his chest, tilting the angle of his ass upward. Red spit onto his cock, lubing it up.

"All right, kid, you came here to get your pretty ass stuffed, and that's what you're about to get."

He pressed his fat cock head against Jordan's asshole and shoved it inside. The thick mushroom disappeared into the compact ring, and Red eased the rest of the length in, filling the boy up, ungluing his guts. Jordan gritted his teeth and willed his ass to relax. Red shoved roughly back and forth. He fucked long and hard, from the tip of his dick to the root, plowing the teenager's ass. He held Jordan's legs hard against his chest while he dicked him with an angry vengeance. The boy was willful and would not be beaten by the older man easily.

Red had stamina, and anger and determination increased his willpower. He fucked hard, adamant that the boy would never forget this encounter. Red came close to orgasm many times, but he always managed to delay his release. He waited until the boy's face was scarlet and wet with tears, until his pride was broken. Red thrust in deep to the hilt and cried in rage and passion. He blew long, quivering waves into Jordan's bowels while beneath him the boy gasped and shuddered as the convulsions of his own orgasm began.

Red removed his cock from Jordan's ass while he was still hard. He pulled off the rubber and poured its contents over the boy's flushed face and into his hair. Jordan licked the seed that splashed over his lips, then he wiped it from his brow and dipped his come-covered fingers into his mouth.

Red called to Derrick. The boy crawled across the floor and knelt before him. He took his master's cock into his mouth and cleaned away the lingering traces of sperm with long, sweeping strokes of his tongue. He murmured thankfully.

Jordan scrambled from the bed and found his discarded clothes on the floor. He began to dress.

"You don't have to go," Red said. "I could do a lot with a boy like you. You'd be well–looked after."

Jordan smiled and shook his head. "No thanks, this isn't really for me. I had a good time, though. Thanks anyway." He finished dressing in the living room. They heard the door softly close as he left.

"Come on then, kid," Red said, turning to Derrick. The young slave was still down on his knees, caressing his master's cock with his obliging tongue. "It's time Daddy taught you how to behave."

Red pushed the boy facedown onto the bed and started working his ass with his fingers.

Goatboy
by Jack Fritscher

On the morning of his 18th birthday, Giles flipped his hot dick onto the Formica top of the kitchen table. The house was empty. He was alone. He was stark naked. His balls hung low against the cool table. He ran one hand up his flat belly. He reached down with his other hand and teased the tip of his big cock, lain like a white sausage on the red Formica.

His soft tube steak rolled like a beached Moby Dick. It was alive. It had a mind of its own. It rolled to the left. Then the right. It pushed its head snub into the Formica, hardened, and marched nose onward, untouched by human hands. It had a mind of its own.

He touched the tip again. A pearl of clear juice wet his finger. He rolled the juice around the head of his meat, which was slithering thick and bulbous across the family dinner table. Blue veins wrapped around under white skin. He felt the blood rushing from all over his strong young body to fill the full width and length of his engorging cock.

It was an experiment.

He placed both hands on the white mounds of his hard butt. He pushed into the table. He wanted to make his cock crawl by itself, unhelped by his hands, across the table.

The experiment was working.

The wet head dribbled its whale's trail of juice, lubing the way for the thick shaft to follow. He was almost fully hard. He pushed his hips into the table. The salt and pepper shakers rocked back and forth. He fucked the table again. His cock took to the pressure and hardened out to its full length.

Within reach, on top of the refrigerator, he had stashed his dad's 16-foot retractable tape measure. It was silver with a yellow circle that read "Stanley Powerlock II." The kind of tape measure you pull out and then push a button to make it retract like sharp lightning.

His teen cock lay big and hard and ripe on the table.

He reached for the tape measure and set its butt against the blond curly hair of his crotch. The case felt cool against the side of his cock.

Carefully he pulled the ruler from its case.

One inch. Two. Three.

His dick pulsed and surged on farther across the table.

Four. Five. Six.

He knew that was as long as his prick record had been on his 12th birthday. He ran his tongue across his lips. He pulled another inch out of the tape. Then another. He touched his chin to his chest, looking down the length of his slender body. His cock jumped when he saw the number 9 appear black on the yellow tape. His balls ached for his hand to cup them. His dick begged for a spit-wet hand to stroke it. Heat flushed his face. He tossed his head up like a wild young stallion. He sighed and bit his lips. He looked down at the table. He looked down at his dick. He looked down at the tape measure.

He had more meat to go.

He felt the way he had during the Olympics: seeing what it meant to go for the gold. He touched the end of the tape and inched it out slowly, and then saw the heavy look of the number 10 riding on the yellow tape moving slowly out from the case. "A perfect 10," he said. And he smiled, pulling the tape just a fraction more, out to the very tip of his rock-hard prick. "A perfect 10 and then some."

He was 10-plus inches long and nearly nine inches around.

He looked down at the table.

He sported a hefty 45 cubic inches of dick.

The sight of his meat made him crazy. He wanted to shout out the news of what he packed away inside his nylon running shorts, inside his red Speedos, and inside his jeans. He wanted his dad to know. He wanted his mom to know.

He took his dick in both his hands and worked them up and down the shaft. He marched around the kitchen. He was a teenage boy in heat. Alone at home. Naked in the afternoon. Crazy with lust at the size of his own meat. Jumping up and down. Making his blood-heavy rod bob up and down and feel so good.

He ran his hands across his tight chest. He rubbed his pert nipples. He flexed his belly and his butt. He gyrated his hips and revolved his big dick in wide circles. He was 18 and crazy and loving it. He had the biggest dick he had ever seen. Bigger than any dick hanging down all wet and soapy in the high school shower room.

He slapped his pud on the table, then harder in his hand. He gritted his teeth and stroked himself up to the edge of shooting his hot load of teen seed all over the kitchen floor.

He fell back against the sink. He turned on the faucet. He filled a glass with water. He drank half of it to slake his thirst, then he plunged his dick deep into the glass.

The water that was left forced its way around his rod and out the neck of the glass. For a moment he thought he had gone too far. His dick, three quarters deep, looked like pressed meat inside the glass tumbler. A slight panic. A tug. He stuck his finger in between his dick and the edge of the glass. He broke the suction. He twisted the glass. He twisted his cock. Pure pleasure. He pulled the glass slowly away from his groin.

He spied a butter dish on the kitchen cabinet. He scooped up three fingers full and shoved the butter into the glass tumbler. He lay back on the cool kitchen floor, jacking off his dick into the glass that held the heat of his meat. He fucked his hips up into the glass. He held the base of his dick with one hand and pounded his big pud into the glass with his other hand.

He was a one-man orgy.

Fuck-crazy.

Come-crazy! His big balls ached. They bounced up against the glass and his hand. They bounced against the cool floor. He breathed deeply, caught his breath, settled back, changed his pace, and slowly, slowly began the slow fuck of his dick, pulling the slippery sucking glass up nearly to the head of his dick, then sliding it back down till the tender head of his meat pushed against the bottom of the glass, pulling the glass up, up, up, then off his dick, teasing his cock head with the smooth rim of the glass, feeling the butter melt, running down the shaft, through his blond pubes, across his balls, and into the crack of his ass.

He was making a mess, and he loved it.

He licked one finger and stuck it up his asshole. He suction-pumped the glass up and down his upstanding cock. He writhed on the floor. His hands smeared the butter across his fresh, young body.

He felt pinned on his back by wrestlers from the senior varsity team. He closed his eyes and imagined their weight pressing down on his hard dick held tight inside a jockstrap inside his wrestling singlet.

He raised himself up from the kitchen floor to a wrestling bridge position: palms of hands and feet on the floor, small of his back arched up, his head hanging down between his arms, his flat belly curved up toward the ceiling, his erect cock pointing straight up into the cool air.

He held the position that Coach Blue had taught him.

He thrust his dick up higher and higher. The 10 inches of his meat vaulted above his pumping, arched body. His dick drove ceilingward.

Small pearls of hot juice squeezed out the tight opening in the big tip and dripped like a teardrop down the mushroom corona of the big head, hanging for a moment on the lip of the crown then sliding fast down the blue-veined tracks of the shaft.

He ached with pleasure, hoisting the 10 inches high above his body. Sweat broke out under the glaze of butter.

He slid slowly to the floor. He panted. His belly heaved. His balls ached. His dick stretched out even above the double grasp of both his hands fisting his meat hard, up and down, smash-masturbating himself to a frenzy.

He entered his final heat.

Greased and sweating, he rose from the floor.

He felt dirty and he loved the feeling. He locked his eyes on some midpoint in the distance like a jock ready to take the high jump. He felt wild and he liked the feeling. It was his birthday and he liked the feeling: 18, packing a real sweet 10 inches.

He could do what the fuck he wanted. No one would know. No one would ever know.

He felt his fresh load ooze toward the head of his throbbing dick. He felt that mean green trigger in the back of his head click.

He walked to the refrigerator. It was clear now. The vision was in his head. It was his birthday. The birthday boy could do anything. And he knew what he would do.

He felt his load building. He slammed his hard cock against the refrigerator. He opened the door. He pulled out the special meat loaf he knew his mom wanted to surprise him with at his birthday dinner.

He knew he could do it. He knew he would do it.

He put the red meat loaf on the floor.

He bit his lip, grinning at the splendid joke, and slid to his knees.

He straddled the meat loaf between his slick young thighs.

He dragged his balls through the ketchup circle on top of the meat.

Then he raised up halfway and with both hands stroked his big 10-incher no more than a dozen strokes before he came, arching his head back, howling like a banshee, shooting his load across the meat loaf, rising up, falling back, then falling forward on his hands and toes, pumping out push-ups, hard-on into the hamburger, until every last spasm of his teenage body drained the seed from his dick, until finally he lay exhausted, spent, drained, and happy across the meat loaf.

He dozed. He slept the dreams of angels. He didn't recall for how long. Finally he woke with a start.

He knew what he must do.

He cleaned the kitchen floor, washed the glass tumbler, and put away his father's tape measure.

He reconstructed the meat loaf, putting it and its extra ingredient back into the refrigerator.

Then he showered, ready to greet his parents when they came home from work with birthday presents in their hands.

The Snow Shoveler
by Aidan Coe

The snow had stopped around noon. The world outside looked clean and white and inviting. I hobbled around inside on my swollen ankle, my latest running injury, and felt sorry for myself.

It was two days after Christmas. The wife and kids were out on our annual post-Christmas shopping trip downtown. After shopping we traditionally had dinner at either our favorite crab house or, if I was feeling particularly prosperous, at one of the grand hotel dining rooms. In deference to my injury, the family had agreed to bring dinner home with treats from Neiman Marcus by 7:30 or 8.

At 3 o'clock I turned on the Christmas lights and lit a fire, then settled in front of it with a book and dozed off. The doorbell startled me awake. I hobbled to the door. "Shovel your walk, sir?" a young guy I didn't recognize asked. "For 15 bucks."

Normally I love to use my snowblower, but with my ankle out of commission I couldn't, so his offer was tempting. But not nearly as tempting as the boy's face: aquiline nose, sensuous lips, arched eyebrows, dark deep-set eyes.

"OK," I managed lamely.

I watched him work. He moved fast, as if the snow were weightless. He was bundled in heavy clothing, but the way he moved made me think there was a body under the wraps as hot as the face. He seemed older than the neighborhood kids who usually came to shovel snow. He was 20 or so. I wondered what his story was.

I stoked the fire and poured myself a drink, then hobbled back to the window to watch him work. Before long he was at the door again.

"Done, sir," he smiled. "Want to check it out?"

The temperature had dropped, and the draft from outside was freezing. "No, thanks. It looks fine," I said. "Why don't you come in and I'll get your money."

He entered the vestibule smelling wet from snow and faintly of sweat, looking glorious. I limped off for some cash, with my heart beating like a jazz drummer on a roll. When I handed him the 20 I was holding my drink, and inspiration hit me. "Cold out there," I said inanely. "Can I offer you a drink?"

He looked surprised. Understandably, I suppose. Ours is a pretty grand house and not often host to snow shovelers. "Yeah, that'd be nice," he said hesitantly. "Thanks. I'd like that a lot, actually. I'm through for the day. It's getting dark already." As if he were convincing himself.

We were standing tantalizingly close in the closet-size vestibule, and I thought I'd faint from lust. "What are you drinking?" I asked.

"Beer's fine," he said.

"You sure you're old enough?" I ribbed him. He laughed. When I turned to leave, he asked me, "What's that you're drinking?"

"Scotch," I said, and before I could stop it the words were out: "A nice 15-year-old single malt." I felt like a fool. "Nearly as old as you."

He laughed. "Scotch. That'd be a treat." His smile was as inviting and as frosty-white as the snow he'd been shoveling.

"I'll get it. Come in and have a seat."

"OK, I'll take my boots off." I didn't discourage him. His boots were snowcapped, and our floors were newly waxed for the holidays. Plus, I like feet, especially men's feet, and I loved his damp aroma. Once his boots were off it was obvious his socks were soaked as well, and he took them off too. At the sight of his bare feet my cock started to swell.

"Let me take your coat," I offered. He handed it to me

and stripped off his bulky sweatshirt as well, leaving his torso draped in a loose, dark-blue T-shirt, threadbare, with sexy little holes in it. It was suggestive—the way it hung on him, sweat-soaked. He looked like a jock with a taut ironman body. I cut out of there before I jumped his bones, then poured him a scotch. Stiff.

When I got back to the living room, he'd surprised me. I'd assumed he'd settle into one of the big, cozy couches flanking the fireplace. Instead he sat on the floor near the fire. He looked like a god, barefoot in a T-shirt and jeans.

"Good scotch," he smiled. "Not that I'm any expert," he laughed. "Nice place you got here. It's like a museum with all this art."

"Thank you," I said, thinking he would make a great addition to the collection. Statuesque. Classical.

"I feel so out of place, all sweaty and grubby."

We talked. He was visiting his older sister, a sibling "who'd made it good." He lived on the family farm in Iowa and worked for his older brother there in season. In winter there wasn't much to do except look for odd jobs. He lived with a waitress who couldn't get off for the holidays. His car had broken down after he'd gotten to his sister's, and he was shoveling snow to earn money for the parts he needed to fix it. Mine had been the fourth walk he'd done, and he had made the money he needed.

I gave him a refill and asked if he wouldn't be more comfortable on one of the couches. "I'm too grungy," he said. "Need a shower."

"That could be arranged," I replied as calmly as I could.

"Really?" He seemed so happy and trusting. "That'd be great. Let's do it."

He followed me upstairs. I stopped at the linen closet and took a stack of towels, then led him to the shower in the guest room. "Sure got a lot of towels," he laughed. "You planning to join me?"

I was speechless and feared I was blushing. I couldn't frame an answer.

"That could be fun," he said quietly.

This was too much. I went to strip off his T-shirt, and his body cradled hungrily in mine. I held him away for a second so my eyes could feast on his muscled chest, and then we locked in an insane, painful kiss that seemed it would never end, until I felt his hips pounding against mine. I stripped off his jeans and sweat-soaked boxers, letting my hands loose on his butt and cock and balls. We were both hard and started kissing hard again. "Shower time," I gasped, wanting to take it slow and easy and prolong my delight in this unexpected treat. We had time. He relaxed his grip on my butt and we climbed into the warm shower.

I soaped him first, exploring every nook and cranny of his incredible body. His was not just another gym body but rather the body of someone who worked hard and played hard. A body responsive to every touch of my hands or tongue and to every intimate exploration. A body that let his pleasure be known through moans and groans.

Then he was on his knees, his mouth sucking my pubes without restraint. It was a new and unbelievable sensation for me, an exquisite pleasure bordering on pain. Then he started licking my shaft and balls, and the texture of his tongue juxtaposed wildly with the warm water running over us. *Holy shit,* I thought, *I'm in the shower with a stranger and haven't negotiated diddly-squat with him...goddamn scotch.* "The condoms are in the bedroom," I gasped, my stiff, throbbing cock slapping his chin.

He looked up at me. "We'll get there." He grinned mischievously, then swallowed my balls totally and sucked them savagely. I hung there in ecstasy for as long as I could.

Finally we quit the shower and toweled each other dry and jumped into bed. We kissed and caressed. He still smelled wet, which excited me. I pulled out some lube. We rubbed each other's bodies with tough hands on tough muscle. I straddled his thighs and joined our hard cocks in my oiled fist and pumped us both to rapture.

I put my condom on first and for the first time entered his mouth and felt his lips embrace all of my cock. I held still for what seemed forever, with my consciousness demolished by his slow, persistent sucking. Then I withdrew and nudged him to turn over. He raised his butt to me, and I explored it with my eyes and hands and mouth before plunging in with my cock. He groaned "Thank you," and that got me all the more excited.

I pumped harder, faster. My hands reached for his cock, and every time I squeezed or pinched it hard he'd thrust his butt upward on my cock. I grabbed his balls, and every time I squeezed or pinched them hard he'd thrust his butt upward on my cock. I reached for his chest, and every time I squeezed or pinched his pecs hard he'd thrust his butt upward on my cock. And every time he thrust upward on my cock, I plunged deep enough into him to explode my mind.

I didn't want it to end. I withdrew and turned him back to me. We kissed, and I nibbled at his body, biting it, his armpits and inner thighs, the backs of his knees, his butt. I sucked his damp, clean-smelling hair. He was laughing and moaning and muttering.

I felt like I was about to burst. I straddled his hard chest, squeezing it with my thigh muscles, and ripped off my condom. He bobbed his head wildly to suck me. I pulled his head up and down on my cock and rammed my hips into his face. He groaned. Sweat poured down his beefy neck and I wet my hands, then reached round for his cock and started tormenting it. I wanted us to come together. He groaned again and his hips pushed upward, forcing me even deeper into him. Then I felt myself swooning into oblivion, losing myself in his mouth, his cock pounding against my thighs. We came.

We lay like zombies for a while. Then I felt him licking my

body. No pattern. Just playful licks. In my belly. Pits. Cheeks. The crack of my ass. The soles of my feet. I was helpless, unable to resist, laughing, unable to stop. Finally I pulled his lips to mine and we kissed—deep, sensuous, languorous. Then we lay still again for a long, long time.

He broke the silence. "My sister is expecting me for dinner."

I chuckled. "And I guess I should compose myself for my family, holiday dinner and all."

He laughed. "I don't think you'll have a problem. Composing yourself and all, I mean. Seems like you're a pretty good composer."

"Thanks," I laughed, and we hugged and lay together silent, motionless, a little longer. "Need another shower?" I asked.

"No, we played safe."

"When are you leaving?" I asked.

"Tomorrow morning," he answered.

I helped him dress. In the vestibule I held him as he put his socks and boots back on, and I helped him on with his sweatshirt and coat.

We kissed again. There wasn't much to say. I watched him walk, shovel in hand, down my clean walk, disappearing into the evening.

Bum-Fuck Missouri
by Mick Fitzgerald

I know hitchhiking is dangerous, but I couldn't help myself. That first summer away from college I had nothing to do, and my best friend Blake asked if I wanted to backpack with him to see his old man, who was all the way in California.

"Sure," I said, "Why not? I ain't got nothing better to do."

Since we attended separate colleges, that was the first time I'd gotten to spend time with Blake in nearly a year. Besides, he was way hot, and that summer I had it bad for him. I was thinking if things happened right, maybe I'd get to see Blake's cock and ass, which was more than what I'd gotten for all our palling around at school, even though it wasn't for me not trying. Blake has never been that swift, so he never caught on.

We got as far as we could by bus before thumbing it. I guess that was around St. Louis. I tried first. I stood there on the shoulder, my thumb out and all and with a sign too, for what felt like hours and hours before I had to stop and take a piss. Then Blake took a try. There he was, in cutoffs and sneakers, with his flannel shirt unbuttoned all the way. He didn't even use his thumb; he just stood there like he was bored. I watched him from the bushes. Man, was I ever hard! Sure enough, in no time this big rig stopped.

"Where you boys headin'?" the driver asked.

"California," Blake said.

"California. I ain't goin' all that way, but I can take you as far as I can."

Blake was sure glad he stopped, but me, I thought this guy was kinda seedy. His name was Cooter. On top of looking like a Cooter (you know: beer belly, scrawny beard, greasy hair), he smelled way bad, like the last time he was near any water was in the womb. That almost made me vomit, and I would have too, right there in the cab, but Cooter had the air on and it blew his shit away from me. To make things more sickening, he played this god-awful country music.

Cooter was a "skazz," but I was kinda glad he was because him being a skazz gave me an excuse to get close to Blake. Shit, I got so close our legs touched, and that got me hard. When I looked down his cutoffs the right way, I saw the top of his Jockey shorts, and that got me even harder. On the sly I started stroking underneath my shirt; I couldn't help myself. And Cooter? Cooter may have been a skazz, but at least he had some taste. He kept looking at Blake, even with traffic, and he kept drooling.

"What you boys gonna do in California? Go surfin'?"

"We're gonna look up my old man," Blake said.

Cooter got interested. " 'Old man?' Is that old man like in 'daddy' or old man like in 'sugar daddy'?"

Blake didn't say nothing, except he whispered in my ear that the first chance we got we'd blow this guy. Like I said, Blake has never been that swift.

We never got the chance. Next thing I knew, Cooter turned off at a gas station and said this was as far as he could take us and still stay on his route.

"I gotta be in Memphis before the end of the day," Cooter said. "Otherwise, I'd take you boys all the way, believe you me." Before driving off, Cooter stuffed a 50 down Blake's shorts.

"Great guy," Blake said.

We were going across the gas station to hitch another ride when the next thing we know, this cop car pulls up, and out comes this cop with cowboy hat, sunglasses, nightstick, and everything.

"You two just hold it right there," he said, and he made us get in the back of his car. He threw our backpacks into the trunk. He said he was taking us to the police station, but when Blake asked if we were being arrested, he wouldn't say. "Let's just say you two are bein' detained."

"How long?" I asked.

"As long as I need," the cop snapped real nasty. "Now, you two just shut your traps! More you talk, the less you'll like it! The less you talk, the more you'll like it!"

He took us to the police station, which was just some old cinder-block shithouse at the town's only intersection. When we got there, he handcuffed Blake and me together, like we were ax murderers or something. He pulled me by the hair, which really hurt. When we got inside, this old fart came from behind a desk.

"What you got there, Lem?"

"I got a six-nine six-nine on an aught-aught-seven-aught," the cop said, real military-like.

"A what?" I asked.

"I said shut your trap! Don't make me have to repeat myself no more! You can see, chief, they do like their talking."

"I hate hearin' that," the chief said, real sorry-like. "And I hate to hear such fine specimens of American youth bein'—now, how old are you, son?"

"We're both 19," Blake said.

"Nineteen," Lem said.

"Nineteen," the chief said. "College boys?"

"Yeah," I said. Then Lem pulled my hair till I said "Yes, sir," then he let me go.

The chief shook his head. "I tell you, Lem. It pains my heart to have such fine, fine specimens of American youth in my jail for a six-nine six-nine on an aught-aught-seven-aught. Just pains it. Don't it you, Lem?"

Lem grinned. No telling what that was for.

"Did money exchange hands?"

Lem put his hands down Blake's shorts and came up with the 50. The chief's eyes bugged out.

"A whole 50! For the two of you! Lem, it pains my heart."

"We gotta check 'em for contraband," Lem said.

"You got a six-nine six-nine on an aught-aught-seven-aught. Looks like we ain't got no choice."

"I want a lawyer! Don't we get to call a lawyer?" I said.

"Now, don't get all hot and bothered, son," the chief said. "You two play your cards right, you'll be out of my station house walkin' in the next hour and there won't be no need for a lawyer. The more talkin' there is, the worse you'll make it for yourselves."

The next thing I knew, the chief and Lem both put on rubber gloves. Then they took us to a bare room in the back with big mirrors all over the walls.

"OK," the chief said. "Who's first?"

"First for what?" I asked.

"I see you like playin' stupid on top of talkin'," the chief said. "OK, let's get your friend first. Strip."

Usually whenever a guy says 'strip' I get hard, but I was so scared shitless, it didn't get up immediately.

Blake took his shirt off first, but because we were still handcuffed together, he couldn't take it off all the way. The best he could do was to take it off one arm and kinda slip it down to the handcuffs. Then he slowly unzipped his cutoffs. Man, did he ever get a bulge! He slipped the cutoffs down his long, smooth legs.

"C'mon," Lem shouted. "This ain't no strip show! We got a whole town to protect. We can't be here all day!"

Blake kinda smiled. My tip was starting to get a little heavy. Blake put his hands under his shorts band and started taking his shorts off. First I saw his hips. Then his smooth ass. Then his hair. Then cock and balls popping out. God, was I ever getting hard! Then in one jerk he shoved his shorts down his legs.

"C'mon now," Lem said. "Over here."

Blake bent over and kicked off his sneakers and tossed them and his cutoffs and his shorts to Lem, who put them in a plastic grocery bag. There Blake was, all bare-assed and buck naked.

"OK, Mister I-want-a-lawyer," the chief said. "Your turn."

I didn't want to do it, to say the least. I mean, there I was with a hard-on in the middle of nowhere, in a jail, in the middle of a strip search, with my best friend, a guy I had the hots for. My clothes were staying on! But then all of a sudden Blake started doing me. He pulled my T-shirt over my arm and head, then he unbuttoned my shorts.

"Looks like we got ourselves a real professional there, chief," Lem said.

Blake didn't even look at them. He was looking right at me, biting his lip—and not even looking down, he unzipped my shorts all the way and pushed them to my feet. I was too far gone to cover my rod. Next thing I knew, he had his hand down my boxers. I felt his cool fingers around my tip and his hand on my balls. God, it was like heaven. I coulda shot right there. Then with one jerk he yanked my boxers to my feet. He bent over and took off both of my shoes and my shorts and boxers too, then scooted them to Lem and the chief.

"Look, chief! Ain't that somethin'? We done got ourselves a blusher!"

"Yessiree, Lem," the chief said as he put my shit in a grocery bag. "What we got there is what they call a real professional." Now, let's leave these boys alone for a while. You and me got work to do with these here things."

Lem and the chief left, and I started shaking. I told Blake it was from standing bare-assed on that bare-assed floor, but Blake knew I was getting hot.

"I wish they'd get some heat in here," I said.

"I got some heat, Tony," Blake said.

Blake looked at me just like he did before (you know: biting his lip), and he put my hand on his cock. Before I knew what was going on, I was yanking it up and down till it got hard, and I was getting real hard too.

"Son, you doin' that thing like what they call a real professional," Blake said, imitating the chief. I just kinda got this shit grin. Then he took my cock and started stroking it. "You know, even though we're best buds, we've never gotten the chance to just fool around. Never thought you'd be into that kinda shit."

"Me neither," I said.

I thought about kissing him. I wanted to kiss him, but I thought that would be going too far. Next thing I knew, he was sticking his tongue out and licking me. I was real sweaty and enjoying it. He went around my eyebrows, over to my ears, then down my neck. He sucked my tits and belly button. Then he was down there licking my hair. I held up my cock because I thought he wanted to suck it.

"I ain't got no rubbers," he said. "Those guys took them. I'd do it if I did."

Then he started sucking my balls and playing with my tip again. With that going on, I couldn't wait. I stood him up and went straight for his cock and balls. I got my tongue all the way around his head, then went straight down the shaft. I put my nose right in his hair and breathed real deep. God! That shit smelled good!

"Do it," Blake said. "Do me, bitch!"

I went down on him. At college I'd go into the library toilet and jack off with guys, but I never gave head before. I went down on Blake and got all of him in my mouth, and his cock tasted real good. Blake was enjoying himself too. I looked up and saw his eyes closed and his mouth open and his body kinda humping back and forth. Then when I did his balls, he really got going. He moaned and yelped.

He couldn't take it too long, because next thing I knew, he pushed me flat on the floor and got on top of me, not right on top but with his balls in my mouth. Then he took my balls in his mouth, and he started humping his cock on my chest. Faster and faster, and I got into the act too. With our free hands we grabbed each other's ass and held on real tight.

Then he came. He shot the biggest-ass wad all over my chest. I came a little later and shot all over his chest. Then he put his head down and licked up his own come. He made me lick up my come too. Afterward our cocks were way red, but it felt real way good.

Things got back to normal before Lem and the chief showed up. They got way red too, and the chief was kinda out of breath.

"Looks like these boys ain't got no contraband on them after all, Lem," the chief said.

"Shame. Looks like we just gonna have to let these boys go on their merry little way, I guess, huh, chief?"

"I guess so."

Lem released us from the handcuffs and gave us our clothes back. We got them back on, and the chief gave us back the 50 and our backpacks. Then he made Lem take us to the nearest bus stop, which was that same gas station where all this got started.

"Bus'll be here any minute," Lem said. "And you boys do come back now, you hear?"

Lem got this know-it-all butthead smirk on his face, but we just kinda laughed at him, 'cause Lem, he just got no clue.

Billy
by S.A. Austin

Billy had transferred to my elementary school when I was in fifth grade. He was tall and thin but not gawky or awkward. He was boyish, with unruly, dirty blond hair and wild gray eyes that darted glances around the place, taking everything in. We played football together, and he was the big, hunky quarterback, and I was his loyal lineman.

I had fantasized about him from the first moment I'd met him on the playground. As we became better friends and his body developed from a boy's to a young man's, the fantasy became more and more satisfying.

Early in our senior season Billy got sick, and I volunteered to drop by and visit him—to take him his homework assignments from school and go over the playbook with him. The first day I went by his folks' place we chatted for a while, and I noticed he was wrapped up in bed under all sorts of covers but was still shivering like mad.

"You want me to turn down the air conditioner?" I asked.

"No," he said. "I think it's somethin' else."

"Cold-sweat thing or somethin'?"

"Kinda. I think it's too much sperm built up inside me."

I tried hard not to act too surprised or to smile too hard. "Really?"

"Yeah, man. You know how it is when you can't jack off and stuff. My system's all screwed up."

"Guess I've never been in that spot. Why don't you just jack off?" I asked as casually as I could. I wanted to ask why he didn't just jack off right now and let me watch, like when we were little kids.

"Because I can't get it up by myself anymore. I like feelin' another person's hand on my pecker when I do that."

183

Oh, shit! I thought. *Here comes the routine about his bitch-ass girlfriend again.*

"So where's your bitch-ass girlfriend when you need her?" I blurted before he could get any reminiscing done.

"She won't help me. She's afraid of catching something."

"Dumb broad."

There was a brief moment of complete silence. I mean *silence.* Enough to fill an hour, but I know it only lasted a few seconds. Enough for me to say the last line, shake my head, and look right into those wild, glaring, gleaming gray eyes, and hear him say, with no smile or hesitation, "You afraid?"

I told myself not to give in too quickly and not to be too clever in resisting either. God forbid he should let me off the hook. Instinct gave me a poker face. I didn't even have to think about being cool that way. It was just a question of doing this without being obvious about the obvious.

"No."

"You gonna help me then?" He sat up with his puppy-boy grin and gave the little head-and-shoulder shake he had perfected long before I ever knew him.

"Christ." I tried to sound a little impatient and put-upon. Meanwhile I was thinking, *Thank God! Everyone knows he gets anything he wants from me. He isn't really giving me an option or a choice; it's an order. We both know that.*

"Please, man. It's just us here, and it's been like three days. I'm goin' nuts."

"All right, all right. I'll do it, but you're in charge of cleaning up."

"Cool!" He pulled the sheets down and propped his head against the backboard of the bed. He had on only white briefs, about a size too small.

His body was still skinny, but it had developed enough that the lines were beginning to show where there would be muscle one day. I could see the center abs line, his chest, and the top of the thigh where it formed the union of groin, hip, and waist.

There was very little hair, and what was there was light-colored and still hidden under the thin white cloth of his briefs. Just a sprig of it rose above the waistband. He was already hard and aimed upward to one side.

I had seen it before and even touched it, but this time was different. I'd never touched it knowing I was going to jack it off.

I reached into his briefs and grabbed his balls and his dick and pulled them out. His package was hot and moist and smooth as silk.

The precome had already begun to dribble out of him, but I leaned over and drooled a great wad of my spit onto the head of his cock. I held it firmly in my hand and made sure I got every drop on it.

It was all I could do to keep from sticking his cock in my mouth and going to town on it right then and there. Not yet, I told myself. Not this time.

I started jacking him off. I squeezed my fist firmly, like milking a cow, and it traveled from the base to the crown and back down.

"Jesus Christ! Where'd you learn that?" he asked as his voice cracked and his hips squirmed.

"I've just always done it this way."

"Wow. That's great. No wonder you never go without jackin' off." His eyes rolled and he relaxed.

It didn't last very long. After a few minutes I felt his hips kick up again, and his breathing changed. I looked at him eye to eye and watched him watching me as he prepared to shoot his load.

His muscles tensed; his hands were clenched in fists; his breathing gave way to a muffled moan of pleasurable pain. His cock pulsed in my hand, and a hot geyser of come shot straight out; a second and a third pulse came just as strong as the first.

He never closed his eyes. He never looked away.

There was come all over my hand and arm and his belly

and chest. He just lay there panting. In spite of my condition that he clean up, I grabbed an old pair of his underwear from the floor and wiped his jism off my hand and arm, and then his body.

"Wow, that was great, man."

"It looked good from here too," I said.

Then we heard the front door open and shut. His mother was back from work.

"I better get goin'," I said, and patted him on the leg as he tried to resettle himself under the covers.

As his mom walked in the room, I stood and turned away and slipped his briefs, the ones I mopped up with, into my pants while I adjusted my raging hard cock. Thank God I always wore my shirttails out.

There was the mandatory round of chitchat with his mom, and then I set out for home.

I was at Billy's early Wednesday. Our games were on Thursday night, so Wednesday we always walked through our game plan on offense and defense and then ran our asses off. The coaches would cut us loose an hour or so early and tell us to get an extra hour or two of sack time.

For years I'd been in the habit of just walking into his house without knocking. When I got to his bedroom he was sound asleep with the covers kicked off.

Light worked its way between the slats in the wooden shutters on his bedroom windows. It shined gashes of warmth on his long legs and flat belly and across his erect penis, pushing against the fabric of his briefs.

I stood silently in the doorway and surveyed what I could of his room. Posters and drawings covered the walls, and his clothes were strewn everywhere.

The room also had an interesting odor to it. It wasn't a harsh blast like a locker room but something subtler, more personal, and sort of intimate. Billy hadn't developed a hard musk scent; it was more of a cinnamon-and-cloves odor. The scent was not completely devoid of sweat but was not overwhelmed by it either.

When I spotted his erection, I thought if I sat and waited long enough I could watch him have a wet dream. That would be cool. But then I wouldn't really get a chance to do anything.

"Hey, Billy. Wake up, lover."

"Hey, man. How long you been there?" he asked as he stretched his limbs and cleared his throat.

"Not long. A couple minutes. You got your assignments done?"

"What's the hurry?" he asked, as he propped himself up, raised his knees, and turned his package to face me.

"None, really. I was just asking to make sure they got done. It's Wednesday, remember?"

"That's right." He smiled and looked relieved somehow.

We chitchatted awhile longer about the playbook, homework, school, and the game coming up. I noticed his swelling wasn't going down any. Billy was never shy about a hard-on, and in the privacy of his own bedroom he was mercilessly obvious.

He finally started to rub himself and fidget a little with his shorts. He watched me watching him and smiled his puppy-boy smile at me.

"You need an extra hand there, Billy?"

"Yeah. At least a hand, if not more," he said, as he yanked his little white briefs off and spread his legs.

"If not more? What's the more you have in mind, young man?" I asked as I moved to the edge of his bed.

He sounded a little hesitant but finally said, "I was thinking, maybe, maybe you might blow me."

Yes! I thought. After all the hours of sniffing and sucking his come and piss from his soaked underwear, I was going to get the real thing!

"I guess. I don't know," I said. "I've never done that sort of thing."

"You don't have to. I mean, I understand if you don't want to."

"No. No, I guess I can try it. You won't get pissed if I'm not any good, will you?"

"You'll be great. I have a feeling about this."

"All right, then. But that's a high expectation to live up to." We smiled and chuckled at each other.

I noticed a brief moment of tension at the beginning, but we got by that, and things went pretty smoothly from that point on.

I wasn't, as I'd told him, a complete novice at sucking cocks. But his would be the first one I'd sucked that I'd fantasized about and dreamed of. The first one I'd wanted and the first one I would do without being forced to.

I approached his cock. It stood long and narrow and rested its head near his belly button. This would be the first time I'd get to make love to him and let him see and feel how much I loved him. How I'd always want him to feel with me.

My thumb and forefinger pinched the base of his cock while my other fingers fondled his sagging ball sac. I teased the head and slit with the tip of my tongue, then ran it up and down the length of his shaft.

His hips shifted from side to side. As I took the shaft farther and farther into my mouth and down my throat, I felt him thrust lightly to and fro.

I did my best to run my tongue all around the serpent in my mouth. I swallowed my saliva mixed with his precome and heard him moan as I did. I felt him tighten and relax his butt.

My arms ran under his legs, my hands controlled his hips, my tongue lashed at his shaft, and my lips pulsated tightly, then loosely, then tightly at the base of his cock.

I could smell his musky butt and balls. His fine, sweaty pubic hair brushed against my upper lip and nose. He tasted like the mixture of cinnamon and cloves that always came to mind, but this time with a dash of salt for vigor.

Finally, I knew he couldn't last any longer. I went to the head of his cock and worked furiously at it. I imagined his shaft must have felt suddenly neglected while its head basked in my attention.

A mass of precome filled my mouth, so much I thought he was peeing. That would have been fine too. Then his hips thrust and his body shuttered. Blasts of hot jism shot into my mouth, and I swallowed and sucked and coaxed as much out of him as I could.

"Oh, God!" he gasped. "Oh, man!"

I smiled at him when things settled down. "Pretty good, huh?"

"Damned good. You're a fuckin' natural, man. How'd you learn that stuff?"

"I don't know. I guess it's like you say, I'm a natural."

"Fuck, man, that was excellent."

"Cool. I'm glad. It wasn't tough, really."

"I'd do something for you, but you've got the game tomorrow and all. You're supposed to save that stuff up for after the game and all, right?"

"I hadn't even thought about it. I mean, you having to return the favor and all. I guess maybe Friday or something, whenever you want to, I guess, if it's cool by you."

"Of course, man. I can't let you go without a thanks, right? I mean it's like a reach-around or something, right? It's only reasonable. Besides, I'm gonna run out of underwear at this rate."

"Yeah, that's cool." His comment about his underwear didn't register until it was too late for me to comment. We heard the front door open and shut again. His mother was home from work. We had spent a lot longer at it than I'd realized.

"I'd better get movin', dude."

"OK. Don't forget these assignments." He pointed to his desk. As he put his briefs back on and slipped under the covers, I picked up the assignments.

He glanced over at me and started to lean forward. It looked like he was going to kiss me good-bye, so I started to lean forward too, but then his mom walked in.

"How are my boys today?" she asked, as lovably chipper as ever.

Nobody Here But Us Cocksuckers
by Tim Chadwick

Church Street Baths, October 7, 1972. I look down at the guy who's sucking my cock. I don't know his name; maybe this bothers me and maybe it doesn't. He's doing a pretty damned good job. If he hadn't been doing such a good job, that would bother me.

His hair is blond, almost white; even in the dark I can see it clearly. I run my fingers through it as I slide my hands behind his head. It's soft like the hair of all my little tow-headed country cousins. Don't get me wrong, it's not like I've had my cousins down on their knees sucking my cock or anything, but this guy's hair is soft like that, like a little kid's.

All I can see of his face as he works his way up and down my cock is his nose and upper lip. The nose is small, and the lips are full and wet. He's slender too, I can see that much, with nice, tight muscles that show through his white T-shirt. Not real bulky muscle like some of the guys I've seen around here, but tight, like he's got no fat on him. I like that. I can feel it—the guy's got a real tight body.

"Oh, Jesus, man!" I moan. Not many guys can take my whole cock down like that. He holds it deep in his throat, pressing his face into my crotch like he wants to suck my whole body into him. Damn, I wish there was more light in this place; I like to watch a good cocksucker work.

The skin on his back is smooth. I feel the motions of his head on my cock as the muscles in his back tense. Damn, this guy really gets into it. "That's it, man, ya, that's it," I say. Suddenly he backs off my dick and looks up at me. Fuck! Look at those eyes: so needy. This kid really wants my meat. And his face: so smooth. He's got a red flush in his cheeks, real white skin, and pale-blue eyes.

He watches me run my finger down his cheek. Why the

191

hell did I do that? He smiles at me and takes my cock back between his wet lips. The kid knows what he wants.

I wonder if he's got his pants down. Can I reach his cock? Wouldn't it be too fucking much if this beautiful kid had a big cock? I can reach his belt. Yeah, it feels like he's got his belt undone. He's not wearing underwear. Damn, his ass is as smooth as his face! And I'll bet it's just as white. Doesn't feel like it's got any hair on it, just a tight little pucker between two smooth mounds. I can feel him moaning on my cock when I rub a finger over his hole. He's opening up to me. His ass is warm and tight on the tip of my finger, then just as tight up past the first knuckle.

I bet this kid will let me have this sweet ass. I bet he'd like having me humping away up inside him. Shit, man! Just thinking about it is pushing me real close, way too close. "Slow down, man," I say. "I don't want to come yet."

He pulls off and looks up at me again. "Stand up," I say. The kid stands and starts to turn around like he's gonna give me his ass, but that's not what I want. I don't usually get into guy's cocks, but I want to find out what this kid's got. I stop him from turning around. "I want to work on your cock for a while."

He looks a little surprised, but he doesn't give me any argument. I squat down so I'm face-to-cock with him. It's just the kind of equipment a guy this good-looking should have—not real big but not real small. A nice thick head half covered by skin. Not many guys his age still have a foreskin and a shaft as smooth as the skin on his ass. When his dick is hard like this, it turns up with no right or left bend, and I can see it pulsing with his heartbeat in quick little bounces.

I run my hands up the back of the kid's legs and pull him to me. The tip of his cock is smeared with precome; it's got a nice salty, sweet flavor. Pushing his skin back with my lips, I lick him clean and then let him slide in. Fits my throat just right, full enough to know I've got a man-size cock in me but not so big I'd choke on it. I like that—just the right size.

His nuts are a good size too, bigger than you'd expect from the size of his cock. I can feel them starting to pull up tight like he's real close to coming. I work my mouth on the shaft of his dick just enough to let him know I like it. I don't want him to come yet, so I pull off and look up at him. "Nice cock, man."

He just smiles at me, kind of nervous-looking and kind of like he wants more but is afraid to tell me what he wants. I wrap my fist around the shaft of his cock and hold it. "Don't want you to shoot off too soon," I say. "I want this to last for a while."

He wets his lips and watches me while taking in everything. I wonder what he's thinking. I've got to be 10, maybe 15 years older than he is. I'm a lot bigger too—taller and maybe 40 or 50 pounds heavier. I'm not fat, but I'm not in the kind of condition this kid's in. I'll bet he's in college—freshman, maybe, or a junior. He doesn't look like he could be much older than that. His belly's tight and smooth. Maybe he's into gymnastics; there's too much definition for him to be a swimmer, and he's not tall enough.

His cock hair is the same white color as the hair on his head, which makes him look like he's got no cock hair at all. His chest is smooth, not a hair on it, and he has small, pink nipples. He shudders when I pinch his nipples. I push his cock to one side and stick my tongue in his navel. He stifles a laugh. He is ticklish, and knowing that almost makes me laugh.

I rub the shaft of his cock over his belly, in the wetness of the spit that I left behind. I go to work on his nuts, taking each into my mouth and gently tugging the sac away from his body. He rests his hands on my shoulders. I slide my lips along the base of his cock, then pull the skin back and take the head of it into my mouth. His hands are on my head now, pulling me gently toward him. I let him pull me all the way down until he's buried in my throat.

I like having this kid's dick in me. I like the stiffness of it, the warmth, the taste, and the trust that you have to give someone to let them suck you off. God, but my nuts are aching. I was worried about the kid shooting off too fast, but having his dick in my mouth is almost too much for me. I back off his cock and watch it pulse with life. I look up at him. He's so fucking flawless, so fucking beautiful, and so fucking horny, and he's giving his perfect cock to me.

Standing up, I reach out and run my fingers along his chin. What a face. He just keeps looking at me with all his need and all his beauty right out there for me to have. With my other hand I pull him closer to me. We are close enough for the ends of our cocks to touch and close enough for me to pull his foreskin over my swollen cock head. I'm cut, and no one ever asked me if I wanted it or not; they just did it. For a couple of seconds I share the kid's skin. I feel the way it surrounds and holds me like a warm mouth, like a tight ass, like nothing else I ever felt.

"You want to fuck?" I ask. He pulls back and starts to turn like he did before. I stop him again: "No, you fuck me." He looks me right in the eye. I can tell he hadn't expected it. I turn around. Hell, maybe he won't want my ass. I feel his hand on my hip, and his fingers press against me as he tries to find the right distance to stand. I spread my legs wide and bend my knees to make up for his being shorter. He adjusts his position behind me. His hand comes farther around my waist, and he pulls himself closer.

I feel him probing around with his dick head like he hasn't done this much. Probably used to being the one who gets fucked. I reach back and find him with my hand. His cock's so hard the skin has pulled back off the head. I can feel that he's spit all over it to make it slicker.

I've only been fucked a few times in my life, but I know how to let a cock enter me without it hurting much.

I let him in. He's taking it nice and slow. Once he's in he doesn't seem to want to pull out. Maybe he's real close and doesn't want to come too fast. His hands are on my hips and they slide around, and he grabs a hold of my cock. One hand's squeezing my balls, real gently. The other is wrapped around my shaft.

Now he's pressed up against me. I feel his entire body from where his cock is buried in me all the way up to where his chest is pressing against my shoulders. The sweat between us feels 10 degrees hotter than body heat; it feels like we're burning.

He keeps himself pulled tight against me and pulls back with his hips. His stiffness slides almost out, slowly, perfectly, slowly, and then back in deep. He bends his knees just enough that I can feel the front of his legs bumping against the back of mine. His cock is sliding out again, a little faster this time. My nuts are tight in his hand. He's jacking my cock in rhythm with his thrusts.

God, this kid is hard. God, this kid is fucking hard. He uses his hip like an old pro as he slams in and out of me. He must be up on his toes to be driving it into me that far. His hand still pumps my cock, but the rhythm isn't the same. He pumps me in little spurts. Hump, hump, hump, and then he jacks my cock real fast. He squeezes my nuts hard as he slams himself way up into me.

I can't hold back. I don't want to hold back anymore. My come rises up from my toes. It slams out of my cock head and washes over my belly. The second blast comes from my shoulders. I can feel my ass clamp on the kid's dick. Pulse after pulse of come pumps out of me, and as it does the kid holds his body tightly against mine. I feel his body jerk against my back as he empties his load deep inside me.

He's still holding onto me, his breathing starting to smooth out. His face brushes against my back and his lips press between my shoulder blades as he pulls his cock out of me. I stand up and turn around. He's got a little grin on his face, a proud little grin. It feels good knowing I put it there. I wonder if he'd let me kiss that sweet little grin. He doesn't turn away. Our lips meet. His breath is warm and smells of come. I wonder for a second whose come it is, then decide I don't care. Nobody is here but us cocksuckers.

Twinkie Birthday Boy
by Bryant Hall

He leaned against the outside of the bar, and I could see he wanted desperately to go into the promised land of Michael's, the gay bar in Tuscaloosa, Ala. But he knew he couldn't get in. The drag diva owner of the bar was smart enough not to let underage kids into her place.

I gave the kid a once-over as I stepped out of the smoky haze inside the bar into the humid August evening. Then I gave him a second look. He was tall and slender, his lashes and curly hair a rich chestnut. A narrow, straight nose and high cheekbones gave an aristocratic cast to his unblemished skin. Full, pink lips (not lipstick—just a natural, healthy pink) and a prominent chin both begged to be kissed. I decided maybe I wasn't ready for bed after all.

"Hi, I'm Mike."

He said his name was Jacob. "Is this your bar?" he asked.

I laughed. "No, Tommy, the owner, named it after his son."

Jacob told me he didn't know Tommy had a son.

"Yeah, he had an unfortunate encounter with a woman a couple years back."

"Happens to a lot of folks," Jacob said.

"So, what brings you out tonight?" I asked. After the hellos, the conversation was starting to drag. But the more I looked at this boy, the more interested I was in talking to him.

"Today's my birthday," he said.

"Oh, congratulations! You're 21, right?"

He smiled. "I wish. Only 18." My dick twitched in my jeans.

"Well, I got ya beat there. When I was 18 we could still drink." Of course, when I was 18 Reagan was president.

"Oh?" he asked. "How old are you?"

"Twenty-seven," I said, honestly. People always tell me I

look younger than I am. Jacob didn't respond to my admission of my age. I took that as a good sign.

"Well, I wish I had something to give you for your birthday," I offered. This kid was cute, and I was thinking with my hormones, as usual.

"Thanks," he said. The conversation was failing again.

"You gonna try to get into the bar?"

"I'd like to, but I lost my fake ID," he said.

"Well, would you like to come home with me?" I've never been subtle. I figured, Nothing ventured, nothing gained. The more I stood talking with this kid, the hotter I was getting. There was a lean, sturdy body under that loose T-shirt and jeans, and I wanted to take a closer look.

"I don't think so," he said. Whoever said twinks would do anything for sex hadn't met this kid. So, I did what any self-respecting twink lover would do who wanted to help a cute boy celebrate his birthday. I begged.

I admit it, embarrassing as it sounds—I pleaded, whined, and cajoled. I sold Jacob on the benefits of coming home with me. We'd have fun. We'd talk. It'd be a nice way to celebrate his birthday.

He didn't say much while we stood on the corner in the heavy heat, watching the cruising cars go by. Occasionally a driver would look at Jacob, then at me; we would look back, but there was never much interest between the street and the sidewalk. The cars moved on, continuing the circle.

Finally, I thought my sales pitch might be making progress. I told Jacob we didn't have to have sex if he didn't want to. If he did, that was fine. He finally agreed.

We walked around the corner to his car and drove over to my apartment, which was only a few blocks away. He said he'd just graduated from high school and was thinking about going to the community college in the fall.

"What do you do for money?" I asked.

"I'm a home health aide," he said. "I want to study nursing.

What do you do?" I told him I was a chef at a hotel downtown. Just introductory conversation, full of details but light on specifics. Before we could say much more we were at my place.

Fortunately, Jacob didn't wrinkle his nose when I got him into my apartment. I'm not much of a housekeeper, and my apartment showed it. Jacob excused himself to go to the bathroom, and I kicked off my shoes and stretched out on the bed.

When Jacob came out of the bathroom he joined me on the bed, and I thought that was pretty nice of him. He kicked off his shoes and lay there. There was no scratching, no fidgeting, and no wiggling toes.

"What do you want to talk about?" I asked.

"I dunno. What do you want to talk about?"

"You. Your birthday. Happy birthday."

"Thanks." I turned onto my side and looked at him. He turned his head to look back at me. The air conditioner hummed.

"You're cute," I said.

"Thanks." I reached out a hand and put it on his tummy. He didn't move or push my hand away. I stroked his tummy through the cotton shirt.

"That feels nice," he said. I leaned forward and pressed my lips against his. He pursed his lips to kiss me back. I kissed him again then drew back, looking into his beautiful green eyes. He held my gaze, and I leaned toward him again. Our mouths met, and this time I pressed my tongue against his lips. His mouth opened like the gate of a treasury—slowly, making me work for the prize I sought.

Tenderly his tongue came to meet mine. Our tongues wrestled playfully, first in his mouth, then in mine, then in the no-man's-land between his lips and mine. I held the tip of his tongue between my lips, sucking on it. I let his tongue go and I started to pull his shirt out of his pants.

"I thought we were going to talk," he said.

"I think we're communicating just fine," I replied, leaning

forward again and working my hand underneath his shirt. He had a nice, firm, smooth tummy, and I stroked his warm flesh eagerly. My efforts were rewarded as he returned my kisses a little more firmly and eagerly. I worked my hand farther under his shirt and stroked from his torso up to his chest. He was sleek and firm, not bulky at all, and the muscles felt smooth and defined.

"Sit up," I said. I pulled his T-shirt off over his head and gazed in admiration at the lean, toned body next to me. Silken-smooth, pale, pink-white flesh swept in a graceful line from the slender collarbone down over the curves of his chest to his tummy, past the discreet, tasteful pit of his navel, and on toward the waistband of his jeans. As counterpoint to his navel, a small red heart tattoo toward his right flank featured his name. JACOB, in neat script letters.

I leaned down and kissed him all over, tasting his clean, sweet flesh. I selected one of his perfect round nipples and sucked on it, pulling on the tender flesh with my teeth and urging it to stand erect.

Jacob's skin smelled fresh and pure. He hadn't yet developed the smell of a man after testosterone has had years to soak into the flesh. My tongue reveled in the satin smoothness of his skin as it trailed across his chest in search of the other sweet nipple.

Throughout my oral attempts to please him, Jacob didn't respond with any real vigor. He moaned a couple times, but he wasn't very expressive about any pleasure he might be receiving. He wasn't going wild as I searched for his pleasure points either, but he wasn't pushing me away.

I moved my hand down his tummy and cupped it over the crotch of his jeans. The full hardness under the denim was a pleasant surprise, because Jacob had been so deadpan in response to my lovemaking. Appearances can be deceiving, but feeling was believing with this boy.

I rubbed the lump his dick made against his jeans, and that

got his motor revving. He spread his legs a little and started rotating and thrusting his pelvis against my hand.

I propped myself on my elbows so that one hand could rub the crotch of his jeans while the other tweaked his young nipples. My apartment was nice and cool, a pleasant relief from the mugginess outside. The cold air made his hairless nipples stand up begging for attention from my lips and tongue.

I kissed my way down Jacob's tummy and reveled in the heady smell of his young flesh. I paused when I reached his crotch and kissed the rough blue denim. Sometimes you have to draw a picture for a twink, and I wanted to be sure this boy knew he was going to get his dick sucked.

I unbuckled Jacob's belt and popped the button of his jeans. I pulled his zipper down and opened the flaps. I felt like one of the discoverers of King Tut's tomb on the verge of uncovering a great treasure.

I eased Jacob's hard penis out through the flap of his Jockeys and discovered there's a reason why "twink" rhymes with "pink." His organ was pink and perfect, satin-smooth, and the knob was in perfect proportion to the shaft. The whole organ was in perfect harmony with Jacob's long, slender body. I breathed a sigh of admiration and held his penis so that it stood straight out from his body.

I took a deep breath and engulfed his entire penis with my mouth, then closed down on his organ when I reached the base. Then I slid my tongue over the entire underside of the shaft. I smiled to myself as his entire body trembled in one great shiver. Not a spasm, but a quiver, as my experienced mouth introduced itself to his young flesh.

Slowly I massaged his organ and delighted his genital flesh as his manhood delighted my lips and tongue and gums. I looked up, and his head was thrown back against the pillows and his arms were limp at his sides. He drew his knees up and gave me better access to his groin. I dove back down on his flesh, and his curly russet pubic hairs tickled the tip of my nose. I looked up again, and he was staring dully at me with his chin on his chest.

I moved down his crotch to his scrotum while licking and nuzzling his smooth pink sac. I tongued his balls, sucking one and then the other, and then drew both into my mouth. *Now I've got you, my pretty,* I thought, as I pulled on Jacob's scrotum with my teeth and he grunted with pleasure.

So far Jacob had been very passive, allowing me to do what I wanted. He didn't show much interest in reciprocating. That was fine; I hadn't been with a teenager since I was one myself. I was enjoying exploring his fine young body.

By now I'd gotten Jacob's jeans and Jockeys off, and I worked my hands under his butt cheeks and lifted his hips off the bed. I tongued down the strip of skin between his scrotum and anus and flicked my tongue over his pink pucker.

He was clean and sweet back there, so I dove into his rump with a vengeance, swabbing his butt clean.

"Do you like that?" I asked.

"Not really," he answered. "I mean, if you want to do that, it's cool." Sucking on his penis had gotten my own uncomfortably hard, so I pulled up off him long enough to strip out of my jeans and drawers.

"You want to suck my dick?" I asked hopefully. He shook his head.

"Can I fuck you?" I asked, my thoughts returning to his delectable boy butt. Another shake of the head.

"Do you want to fuck me?" A pause, then, shyly almost, a quick nod. I smiled at him; he smiled back. I got the latex and lube applied and carefully eased him into myself. Once we'd gotten used to each other, I had him sit up. We then managed to turn over so I was on my back with him above me. This is the best position for the first time with a stranger.

I looked up at him and our eyes locked; he smiled at me as he rotated and thrust his hips. His excitement at finding his manhood in my hot, tight butt made up for his lack of experience as a top. He pumped my butt not vigorously, but steadily and with determination.

Unfortunately, his youth showed through in the end. I was beginning to get into the rhythm of Jacob's humping, his pace picked up for a moment, and he was really riding me. Then, all of a sudden, he stopped. I thought he was resting for the final push to the finish.

"Let me know when you're ready to come," I said.

"I just did."

"Then give us a big kiss," I said, happy that he had been able to get off. He leaned down and pressed his lips firmly against mine for a long smooch. Then he climbed off me and pulled his softening penis out.

We cleaned up, and he got dressed. As he left I told him he had a standing invitation to come over anytime and that he was always welcome. He said he'd try, but that was the only time we got together. Still, I'm glad I was able to help a cute boy celebrate his birthday in a special way.

Working on the Railroad
by Jay Starre

I started working as a lineman on the Kettle Valley line in southern British Columbia in autumn 1978, when I was 27. I was a lineman. For $4 an hour we worked the tracks, replacing worn-out ties, pounding spikes with a sledgehammer. It was as if it was still the early 1900s.

I took to the job right away. I had always been a physical person. I had a farm nearby, and farming is hard work. I was fascinated by how the railroad worked, and I actually liked pounding spikes, reveling in the heavy lift of the hammer, and the slamming down on the spike, and the resounding ring in the quiet of the mountain tracks.

"Look at Rick. He's only been working a week and he can pound spikes already. You are such a lazy little fuck, Tom!" our foreman, Antonio, grouched to one of the guys. I worked in a crew of four: the old foreman, Antonio, who had seen better days on the mostly idle track; and two other young guys—one of them a blond kid who was as lazy as they come, and the other a giant of a man, not quite a moron, but not too bright.

Tom was the young blond who was also the lazy little fuck Antonio was speaking to. It was true: Tom avoided work like it was the plague. But he was pleasant, and cute as hell.

"You sure are muscular, Rick. You get those big arms from milking cows?" Tom teased me from the side of the tracks where he lolled in the autumn sunshine. Antonio and our other crew member, Alf, had headed up the tracks on the motorcar, leaving Tom and I alone to pound spikes. They often left us together; they both despised the lackadaisical Tom and were glad to get away from him. But I didn't mind him at all.

It was an Indian summer that year, hot enough in late

October for me to work shirtless in the afternoon. Tom was chewing on a piece of grass and gazing at me. He often watched me, which I didn't mind either. I would show off, pounding harder, raising my arms above my head, emphasizing my pecs and biceps as I tensed them in action.

"You got no hair on your chest either, like me," Tom grinned. He had peeled off his shirt as well. A total of five minutes of pounding spikes had put him in a lather of sweat and desperate need for rest. I glanced back at him, returning his smile and checking out his naked torso. He was only lightly tanned, and his chest was bare of any trace of hair.

Sprawled along the track with his arm across his chest, he grinned up at me. Hell, he was cute! And something about him was so sexy it nearly drove me mad. He did have some muscles too—we walked miles every day on the tracks, and he had to do some work, shoveling, lifting, etc.—but there was a boyish leanness to his muscles, smooth and inviting. And in those days we wore pretty tight clothes. His jeans wrapped around his tight little ass like glue. He rolled onto his stomach, right in front of me, and spread his legs while I watched.

He pretended to peer into the distance down the tracks while he rolled his butt and stretched out his arms. I was content to get a good eyeful of his lazy but cute ass while I continued working.

I really didn't care if he worked or not. I got my pay, and the truth was, the railroad expected us to work like slaves for low pay, so most everyone dog-fucked it when the foreman was out of sight. Tom was just lazier than most.

I remember that particular afternoon. It had gotten very hot, and Tom had followed me down the tracks as I pounded the odd spike that had come loose or as I replaced missing ones. He actually helped me now and then, but mostly he sprawled across the ties and watched.

"I'm going around the bend to see what's there," I said.

"I'll just rest here. It's break time," Tom smirked.

I hurried off, one thing on my mind: I had gotten hotter and hornier. I intended on finding a quiet spot and jerking my stiff bone until I unloaded. Finding that spot didn't take long, since the tracks were lonely in that mountain valley. One train a day would come by to pick up lumber or grain from an isolated farm or mill. It was miles between habitations. The tracks curved twice, and I knew Tom was safely behind; I figured he was much too lazy to follow. I whipped out my cock, dropped my jeans to the tracks, and spit on my palm. I stood in the sunshine, right out in the open, and whacked my hard meat furiously, thinking of Tom's smooth skin and tight pants and his butt beneath them. The hot sunshine poured over me, sweat dripping from my forehead. I was so horny, I even shoved my hand into my butt crack. I jammed a finger up my own asshole and imagined the hot, pulsing slot was Tom's pucker. I thrust my hips up into the air and swore out loud "Fuck, fuck, fuck!" before I spurted a flying load of come all over the wooden ties.

I came back to find Tom waiting, a grin on his cute face. "What's up there, big guy?" He laughed. There was a strange look in his eyes. I shrugged it off and went back to work.

The good weather did not last, of course. A week later it was pouring rain, the kind of cold rain that precedes snow. We rode up the valley through that rain on the open deck of the motorcar while the wind whipped us and the water soaked us. Tom sat beside me, huddled against my body, using me as a windbreak as we often did with each other in turns. His leg pressed into mine, the heat of it comforting and giving me a raging boner.

"We'll leave you two at the number 8 station house to warm up. Light a fire. We'll be back in two hours," Antonio shouted, as he slowed the car to a screeching halt.

We leaped off the platform eagerly, racing to the shelter of the station house. Antonio had thrown me the key to the pad-lock, and in a matter of moments we were inside the small frame shack, lighting a fire in the old metal wood stove.

"It's fucking cold! And I'm soaked. I'm gonna take off my wet clothes and dry out in front of the stove," Tom announced, as I did all the work of lighting the paper and kindling and getting the fire going in the belly of the stove.

I didn't object as he stripped beside me. The flames took immediately. I was good at laying a fire, and its crackling was a welcome sound in the quiet of the shack. Meanwhile, Tom had shed his clothes down to his baggy flannel underwear and was cozying up to me, trying to absorb the heat of the growing flames.

I was quick to follow his lead, discarding my heavy jeans and coat and flannel work shirt. They were indeed soaked. We pulled up a couple of the old wooden chairs in the small room and laid our clothes over them, shoving them in close to the back of the stove.

I stood beside Tom and sighed with relief. The heat was fantastic; I closed my eyes and absorbed its soothing warmth. There's nothing like a good wood fire when you're wet and cold. "It'll feel better naked, don't you think?" I heard Tom asking.

"Yeah, I'm sure it would. There's no one here but us, get naked if you want," I said—the quaking I was feeling in my gut not quite disguised by my light tone of voice. I opened my eyes to the sight of Tom bending over as he stripped off his long underwear. His pale body was crouched over, his ass toward me. He had slid the one-piece underwear off his arms and chest and was slipping them down over his butt as he crouched to pull them off one leg at a time.

May God have mercy! I was staring at his naked ass. I swear my cock sprang to attention in less time than it took me to gulp in a breath of air. Those plump mounds were pristine-white, alabaster-pale, hairless, and perfect. The crack opened up as he lifted one leg and jumped around as he pulled his underwear over his boot. I was shaking like a leaf, my excitement so powerful I wasn't sure I could control myself. I was on the verge of reaching out and grabbing those plump little butt cheeks when he managed to finish undressing and turned around to face me.

"What about you?" He grinned, his blue eyes sparkling. The heat of the stove was rising up and burning my face, turning it bright-red. Or perhaps it was embarrassment, or, most likely, the heat of passion.

I was staring at his chest and belly. And his cock. It hung there between his thighs, fat and juicy and swelling even as I looked at it. He had no hair on his stomach, but there was a tuft of straw-colored curls at the base of his cock. His ball sac nestled below, full and as hairless as the rest of him.

"Don't be shy. I've seen your hard boner before. When you jacked off down the tracks last week. I watched you."

If I hadn't been beet-red before, I sure as hell was now. My cock was peeking out of the fly of my long johns, attempting an escape and clearly visible to Tom, who stood only a foot or two away. He was smirking, and his own cock was rising to match mine. He took it in his hand and began to stroke it. I was flabbergasted—the little twerp was horny as hell and coming on to me!

Then he reached out and unbuttoned the front of my long johns, sliding a warm hand inside and grabbing my hard cock with it. "Tom!" I croaked, thrusting my hips forward into his hand. I shook my head and laughed.

He was looking at me with that lazy grin of his, one of his hands in my underwear wrapped around my rod and the other pumping his own stiff meat. But I could see him hesitate, the thought that maybe he had gone too far plainly written on his face.

But I wasn't about to lose this opportunity. All trace of reluctance dissipated, if there ever was any to begin with. He had opened the floodgates—now let him look out. I reached out and grabbed his shoulders forcefully, my laughter dying away and my eyes boring into his. "All right, you lazy little fuck, you started it. You got your hand on my hard rod, now you'd better bend over and let me fuck that sweet ass of yours!" I growled.

He did not waver—I'll give that to him. I was 27 to his 19, six inches taller and 40 pounds heavier, mature to his totally irresponsible nature. But when it came to getting his rocks off, he seemed quite capable of taking care of himself. He was the one laughing as he slipped out of my grasp, turned around, and bent over with his hands on his knees. "Fuck me then, you big stud! Fuck my white ass with your hard cock. I can take it!"

I had to shake my head in amazement. He was waving his naked butt around in circles lewdly, the plump mounds flexing and squirming as he spread his thighs wide and waited for me to carry out my threat, or promise. I wasn't reluctant—I was just so excited by the sight of his ass, I was afraid I would come before I could even get it up his butt hole.

I was really shaking, which was strange, because I had fucked before, quite a few times. I even had a sometime boyfriend in a nearby town who would spread his thighs for me now and then. But this was different. Tom was not only cute but had that weird sexiness about him too: soft, young, creamy-pale like some kind of icing on a sweet cake or something. I was wild to fuck his butt.

So it was with trembling legs that I stepped up between his parted thighs. He was looking back at me, his head down but craned around so he could see me. He was still grinning—so far, so good. But what about when I shoved my very fat and drooling cock head into his tight asshole? I wiggled out of my long johns while shoving my stiff cock up into Tom's spread crack at the same time. When my meat touched his silky flesh I almost lost it, and had to grit my teeth to prevent premature ejaculation, not usually a problem for me. But that hot skin was so wondrous—alabaster-smooth, satiny warm. I almost tripped, but then managed to strip completely except for my boots.

"Come on, go ahead and fuck my butt, slam it up me like it's a sledgehammer and your cock is a spike!" Tom chortled, his words as lewd as the grinding of his plump white butt against my crotch.

I grabbed his butt cheeks and shoved my cock into his hot ass crack. The minute the head of my meat slid over his satiny flesh, the warmth of the naked crevice tickling my sensitive knob, I lost it. "Shit, I'm coming!" I groaned, as I convulsed in spasms of orgasmic helplessness. I clutched his butt and unloaded all over his crack.

He was laughing like a hyena, and we both nearly toppled over. I watched my cock squirt goo over his ass and drip down to hang on his crinkled nut sac. He continued to wiggle his butt into my spurting cock.

"Are you gonna fuck me anyway?" Tom managed to choke out through his laughter.

I was huffing and gasping and moaning. But the sight of his sweet ass with my come all over it was as hot as anything that had gone on previously. Still, my cock was flagging, jizz draining it limp.

I got an idea, something I had done a few times and really liked. I dropped to my knees, my hands still on Tom's squirming ass cheeks. I pulled them apart, my face level with his parted buns. There was come there, and I wiped it off with one hand and slid the gooey mess up between Tom's parted thighs. I grabbed his cock from behind and began to rub the sticky semen into his shaft.

"Goddamn, you are perverted!" Tom squealed, his body jerking when my hand gripped his hard bone. He wasn't complaining, though, as I shoved my face right up into his crack and licked his white ass flesh. I ate out his ass, pulling his butt apart with one hand and getting my face right up in there. I could smell his funky butt hole and my own rank come and sweat. It was fantastic. I licked up and down and found the pucker of his hole. I opened my mouth and sucked on the satiny opening.

"You're kissing my butt hole! What a trip, a big stud like you licking my hole, man oh man, yeah, do it, do it!" Tom grunted, his laughter dissolving into guttural pleas.

His ass was soft and hot around my face as I slurped at his asshole. I sucked on it, then jabbed my tongue into the hot pit, amazed at how slick the inner flesh was. It was tight, though, and I had a hard time imagining my cock fitting up the narrow slot. At that moment I was incensed with my own snuffling. Eating ass was something I just loved, although I didn't do it often.

I was down on my knees in the dust of the old station house, naked except for my boots, licking away at Tom's asshole, the heat of the stove radiating through my side, adding to the furnace of my lust. Tom was squirming back into my face, grunting and squealing with the obvious enjoyment of my butt licking.

My cock was no longer limp. It had risen up hard and eager between my legs as I tasted Tom's sweet little butt hole. I could fuck him now, and that was indeed what I planned to do. But for the moment the feel of his hole opening up to my tongue, and his slippery cock between the fingers of my other hand, was exciting enough.

His mewls of pleasure were edifying as well. He called my name out with every jab of my tongue and pump of his hard cock. I thought it was possible I could make him come with my tongue if I wanted. But I desperately wanted to shove my cock up his ass, and I didn't want to risk him coming and then denying me the opportunity.

I rose up and stood between his legs. His head was hanging down, his pale back as smooth and blemishless as his butt. For such a lazy guy he was actually in pretty good shape. His back tapered down to a small waist then swelled back out to those nice plump butt mounds. I had to drill him!

First I reached back between his legs and found his spit-wet asshole with my fingers. I dug into the spongy ring of muscle, teasing it apart with insistent prods and pokes. He grunted and shivered and hung his head between his knees. "Yeah, wow, shove a finger up there, stretch it out!" his muffled voice demanded.

I did. My fingertip slid into the snug pit, snaking into the tight channel as far as I could get it. He was wiggling his butt all over, as if trying to get my finger deeper or escape it. "Do you want my big cock up your tight little asshole?" I asked him, ramming my finger harshly into him.

"Yeah!" he squealed. Then he collapsed onto his hands and knees on the dirty floor. I followed him.

"OK, you got it, Tom. This fucker's going in you!" I said, scooting up between his thighs and shoving my cock back into his crack.

"Do it, go on, fuck me!"

We didn't really know what safe sex was back then. We hadn't heard of AIDS yet and, for some reason, weren't even thinking we could get anything else either. So my cock was bare, no wrapper, as I began to work it right into the center of Tom's elastic little slot. He wanted it as bad as I did. His butt squirmed back into my lap, and he shoved with all his might. Whether he was virgin or not, I didn't know or ask. But his hole was certainly tight. It didn't matter. He gave a mighty shove, and the whole head of my cock popped past the squishy anal rim.

"Jeez!" Tom yelped. But what had he expected? He was the one who had swallowed my cock with his tight butt hole. Even as he shouted, he gave another shove and impaled himself farther on the offending stalk. Another shove and I was halfway inside him. I was gazing down at the juncture of his butt hole and my cock, amazed at how fat and purple my cock looked surrounded by the clenching ring of his pink butt hole. The rim convulsed and spasmed around my cock almost painfully—I wasn't at all sure how it felt for him.

"Fuck me now. It'll make it stop hurting!" Tom gasped.

I thrust with my hips, and it did open him up. I shoved harder, deeper. He wailed and threw his thighs wider, almost right down on his belly now. I fucked him in earnest while he struggled beneath me. His ass writhed around my pounding meat, our bodies colliding without any rhythm. But that seemed to stretch him out, and soon enough, I was sliding in and out without any problem.

"That's better, that feels good. Shove it in me!" Tom said, his butt up in the air and his head craned around to look back at me. He was grinning, the little shit!

"All right, you asked for it!" I answered, grinning back at him. I held onto his butt cheeks and plowed his hole in a steady pounding. He huffed and grunted with every thrust, watching me and smiling all the while.

His hot white body beneath me was so sexy—his plump butt all flushed and pink, the slap of my hips against the soft flesh, and his grinning expression were too much for me. I had to come again. I pulled my cock out and sprayed his sweaty ass cheeks with jizz.

He was laughing. He stumbled up so that he was standing over me on shaky legs. He was gazing down at me, his hard boner in my face. "I gotta come too. Open your mouth!" he ordered. He was jacking off in my face, his hand flying over his fat red pole. He was groaning, his face contorted in passion, staring down at me as he flailed his meat.

I was still quivering from my own orgasm. But I reached out and grabbed him. One hand went around his dangling nut sac and squeezed, the other slid up between his thighs and searched for his butt hole. While he jerked his cock and moaned, I slid two fingers up his stretched and aching asshole.

"Oh, man!" he screamed when I did that. His cock exploded, jism flying in an arc and landing on my forehead and in my hair.

I rammed my finger way up his spasming butt hole while he came, tugging on his nuts and watching his jerking cock. The smell of come was rife in the dusty air.

He fell down to his knees beside me. He was shaking and huffing, but he managed a grin as he melted into my arms. We held each other on the floor like that while we both settled down. I happened to glance up and noticed that through the dusty windows it looked like it was snowing.

"Shit, it's snowing! They'll be coming back!" I exclaimed. We dressed as quickly as we could, and it was a good thing. We heard the motorcar squeal to a halt only moments after we had finished.

We rode the motorcar back to the main station through the falling snow, Tom and I sitting side by side. His leg pressed into mine, and he grinned at me whenever I looked at him. The snow was whipping through my hair, and I suddenly wondered if I had gotten all the come out of it. I had to laugh, and Tom started laughing too when he looked at me. The others thought we were nuts.

When we got back to the station, I waved to Tom and winked before I went to my truck and got in it to go home. I looked back and saw that Antonio was speaking to Tom; I supposed it was to berate him for his lackluster performance as usual.

I was sorely disappointed the next day when I showed up for work and Tom was nowhere to be found.

"I had to lay him off last night," Antonio informed me. "The snow will mean less work now. And you know what a useless shit he is anyway."

I knew Tom lived in a town east of there, but I had never asked exactly where. And later when I tried to look him up in the phone book, there was no one listed under his name. It was a lonely December on the tracks after that. I was laid off as well when it got too cold just before Christmas.

Come spring I showed up for work again. Antonio was there, and Alf. And to my astonishment, so was Tom.

"Hey, glad to see you," Tom said when I greeted him. "I was away back east all winter. I wondered if you'd be back!" I was amazed he had come back, especially since he didn't like the work. And I was amazed Antonio rehired him, since he was such a lousy worker.

That spring was phenomenal. Tom and I took every opportunity to be alone together, which was often. Antonio and Alf still preferred to stick me with Tom, as his laziness hadn't altered.

"If we're gonna waste time getting it on, we'd better get some work done too. You gotta do something," I told Tom after a few weeks. We'd hightail it into the woods almost as soon as the motorcar sped off and left us alone. We'd experiment with sexual positions, how many ways could I spread his butt cheeks, and how many body parts could I shove up his tempting slot. But we still had to pound some spikes.

Alas, Tom proved too lazy after all, and around June he was fired. Even though I had slacked off because I was busy fingering Tom's asshole or wanking my cock in his sweet face, Antonio blamed Tom for our lack of production.

"I gotta go back east and get a job, something easier," Tom had laughed when Antonio fired him. He didn't hold it against the old Italian, even though he had screamed at Tom and cursed him when he finally dismissed him. Tom was too good-natured.

I ached to see him go. Literally. My cock was stiff and throbbing in my jeans when he waved good-bye for the last time. Even though he moved to Ontario, we kept in touch, and a summer never goes by when he doesn't come out west and visit me. His ass is as hot and juicy as ever. I'll never forget my time working for the railroad. Pounding spikes and Tom's sweet twink butt.

Wish They All Could Be California Boys!
by Jack Fritscher

The Southern California sun melted into Scott's lean blond torso. The ocean wind blowing in against the high rocky cliffs cooled the beads of sweat and suntan oil glistening on his inner thighs. He lay alone on the deserted beach. He was nearly naked. His hand groped, rubbed, and stroked the pouch of his bright-red Speedos. He liked the big-bulged feel of his balls and his half-hard cock. His dick was almost as laid back as his head on this morning when he had split from the Rollerblading zoo in Venice Beach, where the skateboarders roared along the strand, dodging the skaters with their headbanger headphones, all of them maneuvering past the hulking bodybuilders hunkering shirtless in their tight shorts and enormous white gym shoes.

Scott had awakened that Los Angeles morning with the alarm, thought twice about it, rolled over naked from his belly to his back on the sheets for a few more winks, and woke up an hour later with the pressure of his hard-on pointing straight toward the ceiling. The sun blazed through the windows of his sleeping loft. On the white-hot wall blazed a full-color poster of the Red Hot Chili Peppers. They were new wave beach boys, younger, blonder, and definitely more muscular than the old Dennis Wilson group of Beach Boys from the '60s. He had beat off to their dynamite video on MTV. He dug their music as much as he liked their shirtless, tanned, athletic look. They were like guys he knew. Shoot! They were like him.

He stretched his naked body. Thought, What the hell! Walked to the phone in the hall, with his morning hard-on bobbing against his belly, dialed the beachfront restaurant where he worked, near Gold's Gym, and called in "well."

"Everybody," he said into the phone, "always calls in sick to get a day off. I'm calling in well. Sort of a mental health day."

His boss, the oldest working lesbian on the California coast, laughed. "You're all my boys," she said. "Enjoy yourself!"

He said, "Thanks."

She said, "Tomorrow I intend to work your buns off."

Alone down on the windswept sand, he didn't doubt that she would. He dozed in and out of a dream. His hand scratched the itch in the crotch of his red Speedos. He wanted his buns worked off OK. His ass puckered for the red hot chili pepper hanging between the legs of the guy strutting through his beach dream: a hunky, hung, big, blond lifeguard prodding him awake with his sand-covered foot, which would lead up his sun-bronzed body to a pair of mirrored sunglasses shielding his handsome face, haloed with a mane of sweat-wet blond hair. The dream made his dick harden.

His daydream doze of eyes cruising him, he would remember later, floated up from some erotic intuition that he was in fact being watched as he lay slathered with Coppertone, on his towel in the sand. He slowly opened his eyes against the glare.

He felt a presence.

His eyes searched along the high rock cliffs. The cove of this beach was deserted. There was no one. But then, suddenly, in the heat-shimmering brightness, there was. On the path along the lip of the cliff, a guy straddled a sleek bicycle. His big basket hung down the ocean side of the bike frame. He fuck-rocked his hips back and forth along the tubular bar between the seat and the handlebars, rubbing his dick hard. His rod tented the crotch of the tight black stretch shorts that bicyclists tug snug around their strong butts and stronger thighs. He was more than staring at Scott. He was cruising him.

Scott groped himself again. He wanted to show the cyclist he was interested. The guy lowered his gloved hand and palmed his nuts in a quick street grope.

It was man-to-man code more ancient than Greece.

The guy kicked his leg over the bike and knocked it up on its stand.

They teased each other in anticipation as the cyclist climbed down the cliff. Scott lay back on his big beach blanket, stroking his hard-on up to full welcome. The cyclist was blond, built, and handsome. He was the kind of young jock a guy would figure for a natural athlete. Scott had dreamed of a lifeguard. This dude, he figured, was close enough.

The cyclist stalked like a panther down the path through the cliff rocks: slow, intense, aggressive. The sea breeze blew cool around the heated whirlwind of his sexy approach. He knelt next to Scott, rubbing his own cock and feeling up the hard hidden rod that was ripe and ready inside Scott's Speedos.

Scott palmed the hard cyclist butt and lay back as the guy straddled across his sun-hot thighs, fingering and tonguing his way up Scott's belly, licking the sweat and sweet oil, biting his nipples, and then landing in a full body press on top of Scott, pressing their mouths together, sliding his tongue deep down Scott's throat. His breath was fresh and sweet.

Their dicks rubbed hard together. Nylon Speedos against nylon bike shorts. The cyclist, pulling his face back from Scott, eclipsed the brilliant sun with his head. "My name's Carl," he whispered. His hand, without more introduction, pulled Scott's dick from his trunks. Scott reached, in turn, for the hard cock he wanted in his own mouth and ass.

They slowly stripped each other's lithe young bodies naked.

Alone together on the sandy beach, they rolled into an easy sixty-nine. Their soft mouths sucked down on their hard dicks. Past lips and tongue, they pulled their juicy cocks down the warm backs of their deep throats. Carl spread his hands and feet to a push-up position over Scott's body and drove his cock down deep into his mouth. He was strong as a high school wrestler. He pumped out the push-ups, fucking Scott's face, driving his thick dick deep down his throat. Scott's own big blond dick rose straight up over the twin eggs of his almost hairless balls. On his every downward swoop Carl dove mouth-first down on Scott's dick, ramming it hard into his own hot wet throat.

They face-fucked like twin pistons.

Carl pressed out the push-ups like a mean machine. His arms and chest and thighs pumped with lean muscle. He was a young athlete whose lower body was built by cycling; he worked his upper body with close to 1,000 push-ups a day. He pumped out a silent cadence, rising on his strong arms and legs almost weightless, pulling his sucking mouth off Scott's dick, pulling his rock-hard dick from Scott's sucking lips. Spit and sweat wet their shafts. On the upstroke, juice dripped from Carl's dick into Scott's face! Long gossamer strands of sex lube stretched down from Carl's mouth to Scott's dick and ran down Scott's balls. Carl slammed down. Scott bucked up. Their event was Olympic.

Carl rode Scott as hard as he ever rode his bike, or any horse back where he had been raised in Montana. They were a match for each other. Young and strong. Blond on blond. Pumping hard body into hard body. Picking up rhythms, one from the other. Both thrusting and sucking with the pounding rhythms of the sea crashing in on the rocks around them in the cove. They sucked long and deep until, finally, winded by the workout, Carl dropped, panting, the full length of his body on top of Scott.

For a sweet while they lay in each other's arms, breathing hard together, their thick cocks pressed between themselves, harder than their breathing. The warm breeze cooled the sweat of their exertion. Scott pushed his hips up against Carl. Carl pushed back, and they began a long, slow belly rub. Their hard meats sliding together from groin to navel in the slick sandwich of their washboard bellies. Their arms wrapped in tight embrace around each other's shoulders, pumping out the deep groans of grinding youth sex.

The blond cocks throbbed together, smoothed through

their mutual sweat, excited through the soft blond down of their youthful groins. Their sensual rhythms rose to impassioned belly bucking.

The blanket beneath them, driven by the force of their belly fuck, twisted and tucked deep into the sand.

They squeezed body to body, chest to chest, nipple to nipple, navel to navel, thigh to thigh, cock to cock.

Their mouths sucked tongue.

Carl rose up to his knees over Scott's body. "I'm gonna come!" His voice was intense. He straddled Scott's shoulders, resting his butt light on his chest. His huge blond dick, thick-veined, stood erect and throbbing over Scott's face, which he held tight between his muscular thighs.

Scott felt the shadow of the enormous rod fall across his sweaty face. Carl took his meat in both his hands and pumped it hard. Its mushroom crown knobbed big above Carl's two-fisted grip. He opened his mouth. Wide.

Bucking like a young marine in the sun, Carl beat his meat, arching his body back, shouting into the sea breeze, shooting the load of his come across Scott's face and hungry tongue. His shining body jerked with the quake of young ejaculation. One last thick bead of white come drooled out the head of his dick. He rammed it down deep into Scott's throat, and, with it buried there, rolled over onto his back into the hot sand, pulling Scott up on top of him without ever taking his dick from Scott's hungry mouth.

Scott swallowed the last thick drop and pulled up off Carl's dick. The heaving blond's meat flopped, still throbbing, back across his body, stretching up past his navel. Scott's own cock was cusped on coming. Exactly as Carl had straddled his face, he climbed across the panting cyclist's chest, tucking Carl's head between his thighs.

"Come on me!" Carl's mouth was hungry. "Shoot your load on me!" He opened his mouth and stretched out his hungry tongue.

Scott dragged his hard cock across Carl's face. With one hand he held Carl's thrashing head steady by his blond hair. With the other he pulled his dick, teasing, stretching it from its head down to its root, exhibiting its full length and thickness. He dragged the weight of his cock repeatedly across Carl's open face. Then he squeezed his meat down, holding it tight around its base to show off the stiff arc of its magnificent jut.

"Shoot your come on me!"

He held Carl's head down by the hair and aimed the long thickness of his cock at the target of the wide-open mouth. He wiped the head of his meat across Carl's tongue. He gritted his teeth. He pumped his meat. He felt the hot come rising from his nuts, flowing like lava up the volcano of his cock. He pulled Carl's head back by the hair and squeezed his cheeks between his thighs. He was grinding the come out of his guts. "Take it!" he said. "Take it!"

Carl's mouth opened wide.

Scott groaned, convulsed, and spewed the eruption of his rocks deep into Carl's mouth. He jammed his cock down Carl's hot and hungry throat, choking him to ecstasy with the length of his fat blond dong.

If anyone had been watching them from the high rocks above, they would have seen them frozen into an almost painterly scene: two boys in a hot blond fuck, poised in the golden sand against the blue ocean and the bluer sky. For a long while they remained locked together, stock-still in the hot sun: Scott kneeling over Carl's face, his dick buried deep in his sucking mouth, both of them panting from exertion.

Finally the breeze cooled them. Scott rolled off Carl's body, and they lay flat on their backs next to each other, silent in the sand, with their still hard dicks glistening in the Southern California sun.

Contributor Biographies

S.A. Austin was born in 1959 in west Texas. He was raised there but attended college in Austin, where he now lives. He spent several years coaching and competing in rowing in the Midwest. He returned to his adopted hometown to write full-time and is putting together a trilogy of books centering on his experiences as a rower and coach. His work also can be found in the anthology *Men for All Seasons,* published by Alyson Books.

Sebastian Caine jealously protects his age and just likes to say he was born in a year with four digits. He admits to being a Taurean, however. He lives in Las Vegas and, unfortunately, has recently broken up with his partner. He is looking for new love and sometimes frequents the scene (albeit lame) in Las Vegas. He's written for several years and has been published a few times, but not in anything quite as exciting as this.

Trevor J. Callahan Jr.'s erotic writing has appeared in *Freshmen, Men, Unzipped, In Touch, Indulge, Beau,* and many other magazines. His work also can be found in the anthologies *Men for All Seasons, Slow Grind, Hard Drive,* and *Bearotica.* He lives and writes in southern New England.

Tim Chadwick is a student at a major California university, working toward a bachelor's degree in English. Because he feels erotic fiction should balance character and plot with as much heat as possible, he considers it far more difficult to write than most other genres.

Dale Chase has been writing erotic fiction for several years. His work has been published in *Men, Freshmen, In Touch,* and *Indulge* magazines as well as the *Friction 2, 3,* and *4* anthologies. One of his stories will be in the upcoming *Bearotica* anthology from Alyson, and another has been acquired by an independent filmmaker and should soon reach the big screen. He lives near San Francisco and is at work on a novel.

Aidan Coe has worked as a professional writer and educator in the United States and abroad. He lives in the Midwest and travels extensively, runs marathons, and skis.

Mick Fitzgerald's stories have appeared in *Inches, Mandate,* and *Playguy.* "Bum-Fuck Missouri" is taken from his erotic novel *Off in America.* A veteran of Desert Storm, he lives in the St. Louis area.

Jack Fritscher wrote *Some Dance to Remember,* the epic novel of the gay renaissance. His fiction from a dozen "twink" magazines is collected in four books: *Corporal in Charge of Captain O'Malley, Stand by Your Man, Rainbow County,* and *Titanic* (the twinkie version of going down on/with the ship). His new novel of the comic ultimate "twinkoid" is *What They Did to the Kid: Confessions of an Altar Boy.* Find out more at www.JackFritscher.com.

Jesse Grant is a writer and editor. He edited the anthology *Men for All Seasons* and was coeditor of volumes 2, 3, and 4 of *Friction: Best Gay Erotic Fiction.* He lives and works in Los Angeles.

Bryant Hall, a graduate of the University of Alabama, is a Midwestern farm boy, who was transplanted to the Deep South, then returned to his Corn Belt roots. While in college, Hall wrote news stories and editorials for the school newspaper. Although not by nature a chicken hawk, Hall says he admires twinks (and all young men) for their uninhibited, exuberant sexuality. This is his first published nonjournalistic piece.

Pierce Lloyd lives in Southern California, where he has too little time and too much fun. His work has appeared in several magazines as well as the anthologies *Friction 3* and *Friction 4*.

Michael Luongo, a freelance writer in Manhattan, writes about gay travel and other issues. His work ranges from academic to gay mainstream and has appeared in Painted Leaf Press's *Latin Lovers, LGNY, Frontiers,* and other gay publications. He is coediting a book on gay travel and has recently completed a novel, *The Voyeur,* about the trials of being a gay sex researcher in Giuliani's New York, loosely based on his own experiences.

C.J. Murray, an artist-writer, lives in southwest Mississippi and is the author of three novels, *The Legend of Story Cazaunoux, The Magic of Isha Swift,* and *Different Dancer.* Murray has two other short stories published with Alyson Books, "The Water Boy" and "Sticky Keyboard." "Zu: Diary of a Gay Vampire" and a collection of erotic short stories, *Sun Perch and Summer Tomatoes,* are in progress.

Jonathan Posey, born in 1981, has been writing since he was 12 years old. His stories have appeared in the *Nifty Erotic Archive,* and he occasionally writes for *Oasis Magazine.* He lives with his turtle and his books in Augusta, Ga.

Keith Pruitt, a massage therapist in Texas, has been writing for 30 years. His short story "Great Scot" appears in the anthology *My First Time, Volume 2,* and he has three other erotic short stories slated for publication in anthologies in the next two years. Pruitt also has dozens of reviews and editorials posted on the Web.

Simon Sheppard is the author of *Hotter Than Hell and Other Stories* (Alyson, 2001) and the coeditor of *Rough Stuff: Tales of Gay Men, Sex, and Power.* His work has appeared in over 50 anthologies, including the *Best American Erotica, Best Gay Erotica,* and the *Friction* series. He's currently hard at work on his next book, *Kinkorama.* He lives in San Francisco, where he's a rather happy Dirty Old Man.

Jay Starre, after leaving the ranch and moving to the big city, became a lifeguard, fitness instructor, and then a full-time writer. He has written fitness articles, poetry, and porn, and enjoyed them all. He has been published in a variety of gay magazines, including *Honcho, Torso, In Touch, Blueboy,* and *International Leatherman.*

Trixi edited the anthology *Faster Pussycats* (forthcoming from Alyson), plays in the band Churchy Bottom (at Geocities.com), and is finishing up her novel *Fish Orchard.* She fondues on the side.

Joel Valley is a 30-something gay man living in Liverpool, England. "Fuckee" is his second published story. He dreams of quitting his nine-to-five job, immigrating to North America, and writing full-time. In the meantime, he works for a small charity firm and lives with his family and an extremely naughty dog named Tara.

Thom Wolf, born in 1973, lives and works in the northeast of England and has been writing erotica since age 18. His work has appeared in *In Touch, Indulge, Men,* and *Overload* as well as *Friction 3.* He likes yoga, music, and sex, and is a rabid Kylie Minogue fan. His first novel, *Words Made Flesh,* was published by Idol in November 2000.

Sean Wolfe lives in Denver with his partner, Gustavo; puppy,

Spanky (a pug); and cat named Comet. He is a former board member of both the Colorado Business Council and the Colorado AIDS Project. He is a regular contributing writer to *Men, Freshmen, Playguy,* and *Inches* magazines, and is currently working on his first nonerotic gay novel. His short stories have appeared in the gay erotic anthologies *Friction 3* and *Friction 4*. Currently he works for Category Six Bookstore, Denver's gay men's bookstore, and spends most of his free time writing.